TAKING SIDES

Frank busied himself for a moment rolling a cigarette. Popping a match into flame with his thumbnail, he said, "I bought a little farm, boys. I'm not bothering a soul by living here. I want to be a good neighbor. But if I'm pushed, I'll push back."

"We're not here to push you, Frank," Dancer said.

"Who sent you to see me?"

"Nobody," Zack said. "We was on our way into town and seen you sittin' out here. In case you done forgot your directions, the Diamond spread is yonder way." He pointed. "This is just one way into town."

Frank's smile came and went very quickly. "So it looks like I'm in the middle of the two spreads."

"Shore looks like it, Frank," Dancer said.

"That might put me in a bad position if push comes to shove."

"It might," Zack agreed. "Was I you, I'd consider sellin' out."

Frank looked at first Zack, then at Dancer. "No deal, boys. I like it right here."

The two hired guns finished their coffee and set the cups on the bench. "You been warned, Frank," Dancer said.

"Indeed I have."

"You takin' sides in this fracas, ain't you?"

"Only if I'm pushed."

"Frank," Dancer said, "I'm tellin' you, if you stay here, you're gonna be in the middle of this thing."

The two gunmen glanced at each other and without another word, turned and walked out of the yard and mounted up, riding away.

    id to Dog, who had been
    r of the house. "I guess I
    nk stood up and hitched
    it."

BOOK YOUR PLACE ON OUR WEBSITE AND MAKE THE READING CONNECTION!

We've created a customized website just for our very special readers, where you can get the inside scoop on everything that's going on with Zebra, Pinnacle and Kensington books.

When you come online, you'll have the exciting opportunity to:

- View covers of upcoming books
- Read sample chapters
- Learn about our future publishing schedule (listed by publication month *and author*)
- Find out when your favorite authors will be visiting a city near you
- Search for and order backlist books from our online catalog
- Check out author bios and background information
- Send e-mail to your favorite authors
- Meet the Kensington staff online
- Join us in weekly chats with authors, readers and other guests
- Get writing guidelines
- AND MUCH MORE!

**Visit our website at
http://www.kensingtonbooks.com**

THE LAST GUNFIGHTER

The Burning

WILLIAM W. JOHNSTONE

PINNACLE BOOKS
Kensington Publishing Corp.
www.kensingtonbooks.com

PINNACLE BOOKS are published by

Kensington Publishing Corp.
850 Third Avenue
New York, NY 10022

All Kensington Titles, Imprints, and Distributed Lines are avail-
able at special quantity discounts for bulk purchases for sales
promotions, premiums, fund-raising, educational or institutional
use. Special book excerpts or customized printings can also be
created to fit specific needs. For details, write or phone the office of the Kensington special sales manager: Kensington
Publishing Corp., 850 Third Avenue, New York, NY 10022,
attn: Special Sales Department, Phone: 1-800-221-2647.

Pinnacle and the P logo Reg. U.S. Pat. & TM Off.

First Pinnacle Books Printing: October 2003

10 9 8 7 6 5 4 3 2

Printed in the United States of America

He lies below, correct in cypress wood.
And entertains the most exclusive worms.

Dorothy Parker

Prologue

Frank poured himself a cup of coffee and put the pot back on the coals at the edge of the campfire. He broke a stale biscuit in half and pitched a piece to Dog, who caught it and wolfed it down with a satisfied look before Frank could put his in his mouth, much less chew it.

After a moment's quiet contemplation of the almost full moon and starlit sky, Frank took a deep drink of his coffee and lay back with his head on his saddle and the campfire behind him. He pulled a dog-eared paperback book from his saddlebag and sipped his coffee while he thumbed through the well-worn pages. He'd picked the book up in the last town he'd passed through, giving only a nickle for it instead of a dime since it was used.

Frank chuckled when he saw the author's name on the cover, just above a drawing of what appeared to be a rather nasty character holding a screaming woman in one arm while he fired a very large pistol with the other. The author's name was listed as Ned Buntline, but Frank had met the man on more than one occasion, and knew his real name to be Edward Z.C. Judson, though in truth he had no idea what either the Z or the C stood for.

Judson had offered Frank what most people would consider an enormous amount of money if he'd tell the writer about some of his many adventures. Of course, Judson had no idea that Frank was already wealthy and that money had little or no importance to him. At their last meeting,

Frank told Judson that not only was he not interested in co-operating with a story of his life, but that he would consider it a personal insult should Judson try to write it on his own.

Frank held the book up so he could get a better look at the woman on the cover. She had long hair, cascading down onto her shoulders from under a hat with a wild-flower sticking up out of it. He wondered briefly if this was to be another tale of Deadwood Dick and Hurricane Nell, or whether this issue would feature Calamity Jane or Buffalo Bill. Frank was acquainted with both Bill Cody and Calamity Jane, and got a real laugh out of the way the pair were portrayed by Judson writing as Ned Buntline.

Buffalo Bill was described as tall and lean, handsome without being pretty, and deadly with a six-shooter. In truth, Bill Cody was just above average in height, ugly as a polecat beneath his large handlebar mustache, and though a pretty fair shot with a long gun, couldn't hit the side of a barn from inside with a pistol.

Frank knew Judson had also taken a great deal of literary license with his description of Calamity Jane, whom he described as petite and pretty and a deadly shootist. While it was true Jane could shoot the balls off a gnat at fifty feet, she was as plain and ugly as homemade soap, though Frank thought her funny and entertaining after she'd had a few drinks of whiskey.

One thing was sure, he thought as he looked at the cover of the dime book. She looked nothing like the woman on the cover, and Jane would shoot the toes off any man who tried to grab hold of her like the bearded gent had in the picture.

Frank drained the last of his coffee, checked to make sure Dog was bedded down next to the fire, and lay back to read a few pages until he fell asleep.

He opened the book to the first page and the title of the first story: "Dangerous Dan Murdock Bites Off More Than He Can Chew."

Hmmm, thought Frank, *Dangerous Dan Murdock is a new character. Maybe this one won't be so bad after all.* He began to read:

Dangerous Dan Murdock drank whiskey after whiskey as he sat at the bar in Wichita, Kansas, one Saturday afternoon. The more he drank, the angrier he became. Dangerous Dan didn't have anything in particular to be angry at; it was just that whiskey always made him a little crazy.

A man sitting down the bar a ways got up off his bar stool and moved toward Dan, a lopsided grin on his face. Dangerous Dan, seeing the man grinning at him like a schoolkid, snarled, pulled his Colt .44, and slashed it across the man's face, knocking him to the floor with blood spurting all over Dangerous Dan's boots.

This infuriated Dangerous Dan even more, and so he commenced to kicking the man in the head, which only made the bleeding worse.

The bartender rushed out from behind the bar, grabbed Dangerous Dan by the shoulders, and pulled him away from the unconscious man on the floor.

"Why in hell did you do that?" the barman asked.

"That fool was laughin' at me," Dangerous Dan answered, scowling as he looked down at the man.

"He wasn't laughing at you," the barman said. "He was just coming down the bar to get one of those pickled eggs in the jar there next to where you were sitting."

"Oh," Dangerous Dan said, though from his grin he wasn't at all sorry.

"You're gonna have to leave the bar," the bartender said, ushering Dangerous Dan toward the batwings.

"That's all right," Dangerous Dan said. "I was gettin' tired of this place anyway."

When he stumbled out onto the boardwalk running along the main street of Wichita, Dangerous Dan bumped into a young lady who was walking by with her arms full of packages.

As the packages tumbled out of her arms and onto the ground, Dangerous Dan noticed the woman was extremely pretty. In fact, he thought her the most beautiful girl he'd ever seen.

"Hey, honey, what's your name?" Dangerous Dan asked, trying his best not to slur his words as he bowed and tipped his hat at the woman.

The young lady gasped and covered her mouth with her hand. Ladies just did not speak to gentlemen until they'd been formally introduced.

When she refused to speak to him or to answer any of his questions, Dangerous Dan got even more angry and he grabbed her by the arm, jerking her around until their faces were just inches apart.

"I asked you what your name was, little lady, an' I expect an answer!" he growled, snarling like a dog after a bone.

The girl's eyes opened wide as her face flushed with fear. "I . . . I'm called Sweet Sue," she stammered.

Dangerous Dan pulled her up against him, his thick black beard almost touching her ruby red lips. "Well, Sweet Sue, how's about a little kiss for old Dan?"

Sweet Sue stared at Dangerous Dan's blackened and stained teeth, and the thought of touching those hideous lips caused her to try and pull away, a loud scream pushing from her dainty mouth.

"Unhand that lady, you blackguard!" a deep, resonant voice called from the street in front of the saloon.

Dangerous Dan couldn't believe his ears. No one dared to talk to him in that tone of voice, not if they wanted to go on breathing.

He whirled around, still holding Sweet Sue up against his thick body. He dropped his hand next to the butt of his .44 and scowled at the stranger who'd just spoken.

The man was tall and lean, with wide shoulders and narrow hips. He was dressed in buckskins and had shiny black boots on that reached up to his knees. He was wear-

ing a brace of pearl-handled Colt Peacemakers and he was scowling right back at Dangerous Dan.

"This ain't none of your business, stranger, so why don't you just mosey on down the road an' you won't get hurt," Dangerous Dan said in his most intimidating growl.

"I told you to let the lady go or I won't be responsible for what I'm forced to do to you," the man said, not looking at all afraid of Dangerous Dan.

"Who are you, mister?" Dangerous Dan asked, wondering if the man knew who he was talking to in such a manner.

"My name's Frank Morgan," the stranger replied. "And if you don't let go of that young lady right this minute, I'm going to have to make you."

Frank's eyes opened wide as he read the name of the hero in the story. *That damned Judson is usin' my name after I told him not to,* he thought, vowing to kick Judson's butt all the way down the main street of whatever town they were in next time he saw the man. Shaking his head, he read on. . . .

Dangerous Dan laughed at the thought of anyone daring to stand up against him. After all, he was the fastest gun in Kansas and everyone knew it.

Dan squared around until he was facing the man named Frank Morgan, and he shifted Sweet Sue from his right arm to his left, so his right would be free to draw his Colt and kill this insolent man.

"Well, then, Mr. Morgan, fill your hand!" Dangerous Dan yelled as he grabbed for his gun.

Seconds later, twin shots rang out and smoke filled the air in front of the saloon. A loud groan could be heard, followed by moaning.

When the smoke cleared, Frank Morgan was leading Sweet Sue off toward her buckboard and Dangerous Dan was down on one knee on the boardwalk, holding his right hand under his left arm.

Frank Morgan had shot the pistol from his hand in a daring exhibition of marksmanship that Wichita had never seen before.

Dangerous Dan screamed out at Morgan's back as he and Sweet Sue walked away, "I won't forget this, Morgan! You and me ain't done yet!"

Frank closed the book and sighed. He wondered briefly if the people back East who read this nonsense really believed the people out West really talked and acted this way. *God, I hope not,* he thought. *It's bad enough that the schoolkids out here read it and are led to believe that the life of a gunfighter is glamorous and exciting.*

He yawned widely and put the book aside as he pulled his blanket up over him, wishing he could somehow get Judson or Erastus Beadle, the other widely read author of the penny dreadfuls, to just once write how it really was to make a living by using your gun. If they did, and if people could be made to believe it, there would be damned few gunfighters in the future, that was for sure.

He rolled on his side and closed his eyes. Dawn was going to come awfully early and he needed to get some shut-eye.

One

Frank first smelled the odor of charred wood, then the smell of burned human flesh. Once that is smelled, the memory of the stink never leaves a person.

Coming from the north, Frank thought, *right over that next little ridge.*

Just to be on the safe side, Frank shucked his rifle from the saddle boot and levered a round into the .44-40. Might be Indians, he thought. Better to err on the side of caution.

He topped the ridge and looked down at the charred ruins of a homestead and several dead livestock. He could not immediately spot any bodies, but the smell told him there were some down there. He also dismissed the thought of Indians. They would have stolen the horses and driven off the cattle for food, not shot the animals and left the carcasses to rot on the ground.

On the ridge, Frank took a long, careful look around him at the carefully tended fields that formed a crude half circle around the ruins of the homestead. He could see nothing moving and more importantly, could sense nothing. Frank rode down to what had been the small front yard of the homestead. He could tell the picket fence had been torn down by several mounted men. He looked down at Dog, his big cur dog, part wolf, part God only knows what else. Dog didn't like the smell, but he was not baring his teeth or growling and the hair on his back was not standing up.

Frank swung down from the saddle, and led his horses over to a watering trough and let them drink a bit, but not too much. Then he walked all around the house, still carrying his rifle. There was no sign of any life. He wasn't expecting to find any.

He looked up at the sound of a wagon rattling up the road. The wagon was followed by a couple of men on horseback. Frank waited in the front yard. He could see a man and a woman on the wagon seat.

The man brought the wagon to a halt in front of the house. The two mounted men sat their saddles and stared at Frank.

"I just rode in from the south," Frank said. "Over that ridge yonder. I smelled the odor of charred wood and death and decided to investigate."

"You say," one of the mounted men said.

"That's right, mister," Frank told him, meeting his eyes. "I say."

"Any sign of life?" asked the man holding the reins of the wagon team. His tone was a lot friendlier.

"I haven't found any yet."

"This was Dick and Abby Norton's place," the man in the wagon said. "They had two boys, Hubert and Charles."

"No sign of them," Frank said. "But I just got here. I've had time to walk once around the ruins."

"Why are you carrying a rifle?" the other mounted man asked.

"Because I didn't know what to expect," Frank said. "And I still don't know about this. Only that it wasn't Indians and it happened hours ago."

"Sometime during the night for sure," the man in the wagon said. "I'm Claude Hornsby and this is my wife, Mavis. The other two are Dan and Hugh."

"Frank."

"Just Frank?" Dan asked.

"It'll do for the time being."

"Let's look for the bodies," Claude said, stepping down from the wagon.

"Maybe they're not dead," Hugh said, dismounting.

"They're dead," Claude replied. "Just like the others."

"Others?" Frank asked.

"It's a long story," Claude told him.

"As if he don't know it," Dan said.

Frank looked at the man and held his temper in check. There definitely was more to this story than he knew. He waited for someone to explain.

"Mr. Frank," Mavis said as her husband helped her down from the wagon seat, "we're farmers in the middle of cattle country."

"And the cattlemen want you out of here," Frank replied. It was not posed as a question.

"Yes, sir."

"I should have guessed it," Frank said. "Same old story. I've seen it before."

"You wear a tied-down pistol," Claude said. "The gunmen the big spreads in this area have hired all wear tied-down guns."

"No one has hired me to do anything," Frank said. "I don't hire my gun."

"But you are a gunman," Claude persisted.

Frank smiled at the way the farmer pronounced it. "I've been called that, yes."

"I don't see anything funny about it," Claude said sourly.

"I assure you, friend," Frank replied. "There isn't." He looked over at Dan. "You know the names of any of these hired guns?"

"Two or three drift in every day, Frank. I've heard the names Paco and Jess mentioned."

Frank whistled softly. "Paco Morales and Jess Stone."

"You know them?"

"I know them. They're bad ones. Top gun handlers. I know they don't like each other."

"Do they like you?" Hugh questioned.

"No," Frank said flatly. "They'd like to kill me."

"Why is that, Mr. Frank?" Mavis asked.

"Oh . . . call it professional jealousy."

"Then you must be famous," Claude said.

"I'm known some here and there," Frank admitted. "Do you want to look for your friends in the rubble? I think it's cool enough."

"You'd help us?" Dan asked.

"Sure. Why not?"

They found the bodies of the man and his wife in the house, in the area that Dan said was once their bedroom. The bodies of the boys were found in the ruins of the barn.

"Someone better ride in and notify the sheriff," Frank said.

That got him some queer looks from the farmers.

"Did I say something out of line?" Frank asked.

"Notifying the sheriff would be a waste of time," Claude said. "He's solid on the side of the big ranchers. Besides, he'd just say the fire was nothing but an accident."

"There is a bullet hole in the woman's head," Frank pointed out.

"That don't make no difference," Hugh said. "He'd say some ammunition in the house exploded and done it."

"I'll go tell the Kalens," Dan said. "Ask them to spread the word. We'll have the buryin' in the mornin'."

"Someone has to tell Paul about this," Mavis said softly.

Frank was standing away from the group, listening.

The men turned to look at the woman. Her husband said, "You're right. And I'm not lookin' forward to that."

The group was silent for a moment. Frank took that time to ask, "Is there a town nearby?"

"There's a no-name town that's pretty much owned by the two big ranchers in this area." He pointed. "They's rooms for let over the saloon. Right down that road 'bout eight miles."

Frank looked at the blanket-covered bodies. "You want some help burying these people?"

"Why would you volunteer?" Hugh asked. "You don't have no stake in none of this."

"No reason. Just being friendly in a time of need."

"We appreciate it, Mr. Frank," Mavis said. "But we can make do. As soon as we get the word out, they'll be folks aplenty. We'll have the buryin' in the morning."

"All right. I'll just wash up a bit, then be on my way. I wish you people the best of luck." He turned to walk over to his pack animal for a bar of strong soap, then hesitated and turned around to face the group. "I heard a saying once that fits this situation."

"What's that, Frank?" Dan asked.

"It's DLTBGYD."

"That don't spell nothing. What's all that mean?" Claude asked.

"Don't Let The Bastards Get You Down."

The men smiled and Mavis blushed. Hugh asked, "What is your last name, Frank?"

"Morgan." Frank got his soap and washed up at the trough while the men stood in shock, speechless.

"Frank Morgan?" Dan finally found his voice.

"Yes," Frank said, drying his hands on an old shirt he'd found on the ground.

"The Frank Morgan?" Claude asked.

"I reckon so," Frank told him. "I don't know but one and that's me." Frank stepped into the saddle and lifted the reins. "You folks take it easy. See you."

He rode off in the direction of the no-name settlement, Dog loping along beside his horse.

As he rode, Frank could understand why there was a fight over the land. The land was lush, the earth rich, suitable for both farming and grazing of cattle.

The road Frank traveled toward town led through a series of beautiful valleys, and there were several more lush valleys behind him, east of the recently burned homestead. The valleys were long and wide, with snowcapped mountains to the north, green rolling hills to the south. In the valleys ran several creeks and a small river. It was a beautiful place, to be sure. Certainly worth fighting over. It was mostly unspoiled by civilization, with no telegraph wires that Frank could spot.

Frank rode into the small settlement at midafternoon. He stabled his horses at the livery and Dog immediately settled into the stall with Stormy, Frank's big Appaloosa. Frank made certain Dog had a bucket of water just inside the stall.

"Does that dog bite?" the man at the livery asked, putting a wary eye on the big cur.

"He's been known to bite," Frank told the man. "But he won't if you leave him alone."

"I'll damn shore do that."

"No café in this town?" Frank asked.

"No. Tell the truth, it ain't much of a town. But they serve food at the saloon. Got rooms there too." He peered at Frank for a moment. "You look familiar. You been through here before?"

"No."

"Lookin' for work, are you?"

"No."

"Too bad. They's plenty of work to be had. I just figured you was lookin' to hire your gun."

"Gun handlers in demand around here, hey?"

"You bet. The GP spread is hirin', as is the Diamond ranch. Top wages, I hear."

"I'm just passing through. Just looking for a bed and a meal."

"You watch yourself in the saloon, mister. They's a lot of randy ol' boys in town."

"Trouble-hunters, hey?"

"You bet."

"I'll be careful. Take care of my horses, will you?"

"Like they was my own. And I'll fight shy of that damn dog too."

Frank walked over to the saloon/hotel and got a room. The clerk didn't even look up after Frank signed his name. The room wasn't much, but the bed looked comfortable enough and the sheets were clean. He washed up as best he could in the hand basin, then walked down into the saloon section of the building. A dozen or so men were idling away their time, most of them seated at tables. Two were standing at the bar. Even though he did not recognize any of them, he could tell all of them were hard cases. They gave Frank a long once-over as he walked to the bar and ordered a beer.

"Just gettin' into town?" the man closest to Frank asked.

"Just got here."

"You pulled in at the right time, for sure. The GP and the Diamond are hirin'. Payin' good wages too."

"Fighting wages?" Frank asked.

"You bet. The best."

"The two spreads fighting each other?"

The gunhand gave Frank a quick curious look, then shook his head. "Naw. Sodbusters are movin' in. Takin' all the good land. Got to get rid of them. You must have ridden in from afar not to know that."

"New Mexico," Frank told him.

The gunhandler whistled softly. "That's afar, all right, for a fact. Say, you want me to put in a good word for you?"

Frank shook his head. "I think I'll pass on this one. But thanks just the same."

"That might be wise of you. They's some bad ol' boys hirin' on."

"Oh?"

"Yeah. Jess Stone and Paco Morales is here. They don't get no badder than them two. Lessen Frank Morgan was to ride in. Now, that would be somethin'."

Frank smiled. "Yeah, that would be something, wouldn't it?" Frank cut his eyes to a man standing at the far end of the long bar. The man was dressed all in black and wearing two guns, slung low and tied down. "Who's that one?" he asked.

The man followed Frank's eyes. "That's Rod Harley," he whispered. "He's near'bouts as bad as them two I mentioned. That feller standin' next to him is Bob Campbell. You heard of him?"

"Yes. He's from down around El Paso."

"That's him, for a fact. I don't know the third man standin' there. All I ever heard him called was Steve."

"Could be Steve Nesbett. Came out of Missouri after shooting a man in the back over a woman."

"Might be, I reckon. Say, you got a name?"

"Frank."

"I'm Dave Moore."

"Pleasure."

Dave took a second look at Frank, and Frank saw his right hand tighten around the handle on his mug of beer. "Frank Morgan?" he whispered.

"Yes."

"Dear God!" Dave whispered. "And you're not buyin' into this fight?"

"No. I'm just passing through."

"Does anyone around here know you're in town?"

"Some farmers. I helped them look for bodies, searching through the ashes of a homestead that was burned out last night."

"I hadn't heard about that. Did you find any bodies?"

"Four. Man and his wife and their two sons."

"Damn!" Dave muttered. "I knew there might be some killin'. But not women and kids."

"Range wars are dirty business, Dave. If both sides would just sit down and talk, maybe each side give a little, they could usually be avoided. But that don't often happen."

"I reckon it don't," Dave said. "And it damn shore ain't gonna happen this time neither."

"After seeing what was left of the Norton place, I tend to agree with you."

"Dick Norton?"

"Yes."

Dave was silent for a few seconds. "I knowed them. They was nice folks. Damn!" he cursed softly.

"Sort of changes things around in your mind, hey?"

"Damn shore does. I just don't hold with killin' women and kids."

"Nobody decent does, Dave."

Dave cut his eyes to Frank. "I never heard it put just like that, Frank."

"There aren't but two kinds of people in this world, Dave. Decent people and indecent people."

"There ain't no in-between?"

"Not in my mind."

"I reckon not," Dave admitted.

"So, are you going to stick around and get hired on?"

Dave shook his head. "I think I'll stick around. But as far as gettin' hired, I got to give that some more thought."

"I thought you would."

"Did you now?"

"Yes. I think deep down you might be a decent person. Say, you had supper?"

"Not yet."

"I'm hungry. You want to join me for a bite? I'm buying."

"Nice of you. Yeah, I'm kinda hungry myself."

Frank finished his beer and stepped away from the bar. As he did, a man stood up from a table and called to him.

"Morgan!"

Frank turned to face the man.

"Thought that was you, Morgan. I been studyin' you since you come in the saloon. Remember me?"

"Can't say as I do," Frank replied.

"George Cummings, Drifter. Now you remember me?"

"Nope," Frank said.

"Down on the strip 'bout ten years back. You pistol-whipped me. Treated me like crap, you did."

"Oh, yeah," Frank said. "I recall now. You were beating that Indian woman. I stopped you."

"She was *my* woman, Drifter. I *owned* her. I had me a right to do anything I wanted with her."

"Slavery officially ended back in '65, George, remember? It was after that conflict called the Civil War."

"That was about niggers, Drifter. Not squaws."

"Is there a point to this conversation, George?"

"Yeah. Point is I'm gonna kill you, Drifter."

"Doubtful, George. Real doubtful."

George pushed a chair out of his way and stepped away from the table. "I owe you a bullet, Drifter. And I'm gonna give it to you right now."

"Then make your play, George," Frank said, his words tinged with ice. "You're keeping me from supper."

Two

A man laughed at that, and George flushed in anger. "I don't like to be made light of, Drifter."

Frank said nothing.

Beside him, Dave eased away a few feet—out of the line of fire, he hoped.

"Did you hear me, Drifter?" George demanded.

"I'm not deaf, George. Are you going to drag that smoke-pole or talk me to death?"

"I want you to sweat a little bit."

"The only thing I'm doing is getting sleepy," Frank told him. "Now I'm both hungry and sleepy."

"Damn you, Drifter!" George swore.

Frank turned his back to the man and signaled for the barkeep to bring him another beer.

"Don't turn your ass to me!" George yelled.

Frank ignored him.

"What's going on in here?" a new voice added, speaking from the batwings.

"Nothin', Jim," a man said quickly.

"The foreman out at the GP," Dave whispered. "Jim Knight. He's a bad one."

Frank nodded his head in understanding.

"What are you all puffed up about, George?" the foreman asked.

"Nothin', Jim," George said. "Nothin' at all."

"That's Frank Morgan standin' at the bar, Jim," another GP hand said.

Jim walked over to Frank and leaned against the bar. "So you're the living legend, huh?"

"I'm Frank Morgan. I wouldn't know about the living legend." Frank took a sip of beer and set the mug on the bar. He turned his head to look at Jim Knight.

He was a bear of a man. About Frank's height. Barrel-chested with plenty of hard-packed muscle under his shirt. Frank figured him to be between forty and forty-five. Somewhere close to Frank's age.

"Something you want?" Frank asked. "Or are you just going to stand there and stare at me?"

The foreman blinked at that. Clearly, he was not accustomed to being spoken to in such a manner. "You got a mouth on you, don't you, Morgan?"

"I asked a question, if that's what you mean."

"Did you come in here lookin' for work, Morgan?"

"My gun is not for hire," Frank told him. "Not now, not ever. Now go away and leave me alone."

"Mister, I think you need a lesson in manners."

"And you think you're the man to teach me?" Frank asked with a slight smile.

"I sure do. Keep pushin' me and you'll find out."

Frank chuckled. "You haven't been pushed yet, Knight. But I can damn sure oblige you if you've a mind for it."

The foreman gazed into Frank's eyes for just a few seconds. He saw something there that made him want to back up. Jim Knight was not a coward, there was not a streak of yellow in him. But he was an experienced man, a man of the West.

"Just passin' through this area, Morgan?" Knight asked in a softer tone of voice.

"Just passing through," Frank replied. "But in the short time I've been here, I haven't liked what I've seen."

"Oh? What is it that you've seen?"

"A farmer and his family burned to death."

"What?" Knight asked. "What family? What are you talkin' about?"

Frank met the man's eyes, and instantly felt he was telling the truth. The foreman of the GP spread didn't know. "The Norton homestead was burned out last night. Man and his wife and two kids were killed."

"No GP hand had anything to do with that. I want the sodbusters off of grazin' land, yeah, but we haven't killed anyone."

"Somebody ordered it."

Knight signaled the barkeep for a drink. A bottle and a glass were placed in front of him. Knight poured a shot glass full of whiskey and stood for a moment, staring down at the amber liquid before downing it neat. He set the glass on the bar and cut his eyes to Frank.

"We had no hand in any killing, Morgan. Not that it makes a damn to me whether you believe me or not."

Frank shrugged. "I'm just passing through, Knight. I'll be gone in the morning. Fight your battles your way and live with your conscience."

The foreman poured another whiskey and slugged it back. He grimaced and said, "My conscience don't bother me at all, Morgan. It's clear as a cold winter's mornin'."

"Glad to hear, Knight. Now then, is there anything else you want to talk to me about?"

"You're hirin' your gun, Morgan. 'Cause that's what you are. Did the Diamond bring you in?"

"Nobody brought me in, Knight. And I told you, my gun is not for hire. Put that out of your mind."

"I don't believe you."

Frank took no umbrage at the foreman's remark. He shrugged his shoulders and said, "I don't give a damn what you believe, Knight. This time. Just don't call me a liar again."

Knight stiffened for a few seconds, then relaxed. "Did you and George have a beef?"

"He did. I didn't."

"He's good with a short gun, Morgan."

Frank looked at the man and softly said, "So am I, Knight. So am I."

The foreman shoved the whiskey bottle away from him and turned to face the crowded saloon. "All GP hands—let's go. Back to the ranch. Right now."

No one argued, and the saloon quickly cleared. Only a few men remained seated at tables.

Frank glanced over at Dave. "Now we can have supper."

Frank stepped out of the saloon/hotel just after dawn, and walked down to the livery with a sack of scraps for Dog. The cook was a person who liked dogs, and he had been more than generous. Frank filled Dog's water bucket and fed the big cur. The liveryman showed up and asked if Frank would like some coffee.

"I sure would."

"Be ready in a few."

While the coffee was making, Frank said, "Sure is pretty country."

"Be a lot prettier if folks would get along," the stable man opined. "I understand the Norton family will be buried this afternoon."

"I hadn't heard."

"Grave diggers workin' as we speak." The man pointed out the window to a hill just outside of town. "Right up yonder."

"I didn't see a church in town."

"The farmers got a lay preacher amongst 'em. Preacher Wright. He'll be handlin' things."

"Is this the first time anyone's been killed over land?" Frank asked.

"No. I'm sorry to say there's been others. Nothin' this bad, though." The liveryman dumped in the coffee, then added some cold water to settle the grounds. "Probably be more," he added.

"Farmers aren't giving up, hey?"

"Nope. And I don't blame them. They filed on this land legal and worked it up. They built homes and by God, they're gonna stay, or die tryin'."

"Sounds like you're on their side."

The man looked at Frank and smiled. "I ain't on anybody's side, Mr. Morgan. Just like you say you are, I'm in the middle."

"Sometimes that's a dangerous position."

"So I been told. Coffee's ready."

Over coffee and cigarettes, the men chatted. "I'm John Platt, Mr. Morgan. Been here for years. I come here with Mark Rogers as a cowhand. He owns the Diamond spread. A couple of years later, Grant Perkins showed up and claimed the rest of the land as his own. He's an arrogant bastard, but then, so is Rogers. They get along."

"Money and power," Frank said. "Same old story."

"Yeah, I reckon. If Rogers and Perkins would just pull in their horns a mite, they'd be land aplenty for all. But on the other side of matters, Paul Adams, the leader of the sodbusters, is no sweetheart himself."

Frank took a swig of coffee before replying. "Oh? How so?"

"Him and his sons control about four thousand acres of prime land, got a couple of cricks and a river runnin' through it. GP spread on one side of the river, Diamond spread on the other. You can figure out the rest."

"I sure can."

"And to make matters worser," the liveryman said, refilling both their mugs, "I seen four wagons filled with sodbusters rattle through here late yesterday. Just at dusk."

"I heard the wagons from my room. I didn't look out to see what they were."

"Farmers with a whole passel of towheaded young'uns."

"More kids to get hurt."

"Shore nuff. And they will git hurt. Count on it. Rogers and Perkins is uncorkin' the bottle now. I may be old, but I still got eyes and ears. I seen more gunslicks ride in last night. Rick Handy was amongst 'em."

"Handy!" That got Frank's attention. "I thought he retired!"

"I reckon he come out of retirement. 'Sides, he's too young for that. You and him's about the same age, I reckon."

"Just about," Frank said. "Last time I saw him was in . . ." He thought for a moment. "Kansas. And it was a land dispute there too."

"You and him had a run-in?"

"No. Nothing like that. At least not yet. I hope we never do."

"But you've seen him work?"

"Oh, yeah. That was years ago, though. In Nebraska." Frank was again thoughtful. "And that was about land too."

"He's fast, ain't he?"

"Very quick," Frank admitted.

"Better than you?" the liveryman pressed.

"I don't know. I hope I never have to find out."

"You pullin' out today, Mr. Morgan?"

Frank paused for a few seconds before replying. "I don't know. I should." He looked at the old man. "You have any idea who Rick is working for?"

John shook his head. "Not yet. Won't take long to find out, though. They'll all be ridin' in today for drinks and cards. Might not be too healthy for you to stick around."

Frank smiled at that. "I'm used to that feeling, John."

"Yeah, I reckon you are. So are you going to stay?"

Frank slowly nodded his head. "Yeah, John. I think I am."

"Then you're sidin' with the farmers?"

"I'm not siding with any faction. Not yet. I think I'll wait and see how hard the ranchers want to play this."

"You know already, Morgan."

Frank took a sip of coffee and nodded his head. "I guess I do, John." He set his mug down on the office desk. "I'm going to get some breakfast. Want to join me?"

"Naw. My old woman fixed me flapjacks and fatback 'bout an hour ago. I'm full. But thanks for the invite. Don't worry 'bout your animals. I'll take good care of them."

Frank walked over to the saloon and took a table near the back. He waved at a man behind the long bar. "The cook got the stove hot?"

"It's hot. Want some breakfast?"

"Yes. And a pot of coffee."

"Coming up."

Frank ate his breakfast—bacon and biscuits and gravy—then leaned back and rolled a smoke. He glanced at the wall clock. Seven o'clock. He looked up at the sounds of boot steps on the boardwalk. Frank waited. The batwings were pushed open and Rick Handy walked in, two tough-looking hard cases with him.

"Now it gets interesting," Frank muttered.

Three

Rick Handy pulled up short when he spotted Frank sitting alone at the back table. His face tightened and his hands balled into fists for just a few seconds. Then he regained control and forced himself to relax.

"Hello, Ricky," Frank said with a smile, knowing how the man hated to be called that.

"The name is Rick, Drifter. Don't call me Ricky."

"Excuse me, Ricky. I didn't realize you were so sensitive about your name."

"I said *don't* call me that."

"Sorry, I forgot. You know how us old folks get, Ricky. We all develop CRC."

"What the hell is CRC?" Rick asked.

"Can't Remember Crap."

"Very funny, Drifter." He cut his eyes as the barkeep began laughing.

"That's a good one, Morgan," the barkeep said. "I gotta remember that one."

"Yeah, you do that," Rick told the man. He looked back at Frank. "I heard you was in this area, Drifter. I also heard you wasn't gonna stay."

"I changed my mind, Ricky."

"So this is the famous Frank Morgan," one of the men with Handy said. "He don't look like much to me."

"Sure as hell don't," the other man said.

Frank ignored the comments and kept his eyes on Handy. "Which spread are you working for?"

"The Diamond, if it's any of your business," Handy replied. "Which it isn't."

"I'm a curious sort, Ricky," Frank said, carefully pouring another cup of coffee with his left hand. His right hand was out of sight, near the butt of his Peacemaker.

"You keep callin' me names I don't like and you're gonna be a *hurt* curious sort."

"Ah, now, Ricky," Frank said, again with a smile. "You wouldn't want to spoil a beautiful morning with gunplay, would you?"

"Let me take him, Ricky," one of the men said.

Frank laughed at the hard case. "What's your name?"

"Dancer. Pete Dancer."

"Don't let your butt overload your mouth, Pete," Frank warned him.

"By God, I ain't afraid of you!" the second man said. "I'm Zack Spence."

"You shut your mouth too, Zack," Frank said. "I was having a conversation with Ricky."

"I'm warnin' you, Morgan!" Handy flared. "I'll . . ." Then it dawned on him what Frank was doing. He took a deep breath, the flush left his face, and he calmed himself. "It won't work, Drifter. But you came close."

"What won't work, Ricky? I was just having a little chat with you."

"You know what you were doin', Drifter. Tryin' to rile me so's I'd make a mistake. Forget it. Come on, boys. Let's have us some coffee and breakfast."

Frank stood on the boardwalk in front of the saloon for a few moments, watching the activity at the general store, located directly across the street. A wagon had pulled up in front, a man and woman on the wagon seat, several kids in the bed. A few minutes passed, then another wagon rattled up, then a third. Claude and Mavis Hornsby and their kids—two boys and a girl—were in the third wagon.

Frank waited and watched, standing in the shadows of the awning. Within the next ten minutes, four more wagons rolled up, followed by five mounted men, all armed, side arms and pistols.

"Paul Adams and his sons," the barkeep said from just inside the batwings. "Sam, Al, Jimmy, and Mark."

"They handle those weapons like they know how to use them," Frank observed.

"They do. Paul Adams come out of the war a Yankee colonel. Lots of medals. His wife died 'bout ten years ago, so I'm told. He come out here 'bout four years ago and filed on some prime land. He was the first sodbuster in this area. Then the others started comin' in. Been trouble ever since. Adams has killed several cowboys, from both spreads."

"I think I'll visit the store and get me some tobacco," Frank said.

The barkeep chuckled. "Good luck, Morgan."

Frank walked across the wide and rutted street. He touched the brim of his hat when Mavis Hornsby cut her eyes to him. "Morning, ma'am."

"Good morning, Mr. Morgan," she said.

"Howdy, Claude," Frank called.

"Morgan," Hornsby said.

"You know that gunslinger, Claude?" Paul Adams called.

"That's the man I told you about, Paul. Frank Morgan."

Frank stepped up on the boardwalk and entered the good-smelling general store. Frank always enjoyed the smell of a general store. Tobacco and bread and pickles in a barrel and candy and leather and dozens of other smells. He walked up to the counterman.

"Three sacks of tobacco and some papers, please."

The clerk put his purchases on the counter and looked at Frank for a few seconds. "You really Frank Morgan?"

"Yes. And you are? . . ."

"Joe Wallace. I own this establishment. Me and my wife, Theda."

"Glad to meet you. I was told the two big spreads in this area owned the town."

"They used to. Dave Hitchens bought the saloon a couple of years ago. I bought this store last year. John Platt bought the livery about the same time. Be more businesses coming in if this land mess ever gets settled. You hiring your gun, Frank Morgan?"

The question was asked just as Paul Adams stepped into the store, followed by his sons and several other men and women.

"My gun isn't for hire, Joe. Not now, not ever. I might step into a fight every now and then, but if, or when, I do, it'll be because I believe in one side or the other. Not for money."

"How very noble of you, Morgan," Paul Adams said, his tone holding a very evident sneer. "A gunfighter with principles. I wasn't aware there was such a thing."

Frank turned to look at the man, his pale eyes turning chilly. "There are probably quite a number of things in this world that you are not aware of. Whoever in the hell you are."

"I'm Paul Adams, Morgan. And you'll watch your arrogant tongue when addressing me."

Frank smiled, the curving of lips devoid of any humor. "I will say what I please, to whoever I please, and whenever I please."

"That's my father you're addressing, sir!" one of Paul's sons said.

"That's your problem," Frank told him. He picked up his tobacco and papers and walked out of the store, pushing past Paul Adams and sons.

"The man is impudent," Paul said.

Frank heard the words and ignored them. He stood on the short elevated boardwalk and rolled a cigarette. It was only from that height that he noticed the caskets in the bed of the wagons. The Norton family, he thought.

"Here comes Preacher Wright," a woman said.

"Let's get up the hill to the buryin' ground," a man said, lifting the reins to his team.

Frank stepped to one side, out of the way, as the crowd left the general store and got into the wagons for the ride up to the community's graveyard.

Paul Adams paused for a moment on the boardwalk to look at Frank. "You are not welcome in this community," he told Frank.

"I can't begin to tell you how upset that makes me," Frank replied.

"Stay off my land," Paul told him.

"With pleasure," Frank said.

Paul Adams and his sons mounted up and led the procession up the hill.

Joe Wallace stepped out of his store to stand beside Frank on the boardwalk. "It's a very trying time for the farmers," he said. "The Norton family were nice people."

"I'm sure they were."

"The farmers have a right to work the land."

"You'll get no argument about that from me."

"I won't?" Wallace asked. There was a note of disbelief in the question.

"Not at all. There is room for everyone in these valleys. But there has to be some give-and-take on both sides for it to work."

The store owner nodded his head in agreement. "That's not going to happen, Mr. Morgan."

"It better happen. Or there'll be more killing."

Conversation ceased as both men looked up the street. Four men were riding into the small settlement. Frank knew one of them.

"Reggie Carlson on the bay," he said.

"Gunfighter?" Joe questioned.

"One of the best."

"You know the others?"

"No. But Reggie wouldn't ride with anyone who couldn't pull his weight in a fight. Do you have any idea how many gunhands the two spreads have hired?"

"Forty or fifty, at least."

"And how many farmers in the valleys?"

"Fifteen or twenty. They come and go, Mr. Morgan."

"Yeah," Frank said drily. "And like the Nortons, some go forever."

Frank sat on a bench in front of the general store and watched the funeral services from afar. Counting the young kids, Frank figured about fifty people were in attendance.

And there were twenty or so hired guns hanging around in the saloon. Frank hoped the farmers and their families would just go on home after the services and not stop at the store for supplies or conversation. Whiskey, guns, and tension make for an explosive situation.

Frank was still sitting on the bench when the first farmer's wagon rolled up and stopped in front of the store; then a second and third rolled up and stopped. Soon there was a long line of wagons.

"Here we go," Frank muttered softly as he rolled another cigarette and waited for the action to start.

The farm families began crowding into the store, and the hired guns began gathering on the boardwalk across the street.

"You people are making a big mistake," Frank said to Claude Hornsby.

"We need supplies," the man replied. "That's the long and the short of it, Mr. Morgan."

Frank did not immediately reply to that. He watched as several hired guns began walking across the street.

Paul Adams and his sons levered rounds into their Winchesters, the sound carrying clearly to the gunslicks. The hired guns stopped in the middle of the street and tensed, their hands hovering close to their guns.

"Don't do anything stupid, Adams," Frank said in a low tone, his words carrying no farther than to Paul Adams. "You've got women and children in the line of fire. Think about that."

Adams cut his eyes to Frank for a moment, then minutely nodded his head. "Put your rifles up, boys," he told his sons. "This is not the time for gunplay."

The sons eased the hammers down on their Winchesters and booted them.

"We came here to get supplies, people," Paul told the farmers. "Let's get what we need and go home."

The moment of tension passed. The gunslicks slowly turned and walked back to the saloon.

Paul dismounted and walked over to where Frank was sitting on the bench. "I really don't know how to figure you, Morgan," he said. "But I thank you for that moment of wisdom on your part."

"I just don't like to see women and kids get hurt, Adams."

The leader of the farmers nodded his head curtly and walked into the store. Frank continued to sit on the bench. He looked across the wide street. Rick Handy stood alone on the boardwalk in front of the saloon, staring at Frank.

"You two know each other?" Claude Hornsby asked, stepping out of the store to stand by the bench.

"We've met a few times."

"I don't think that man likes you very much."

"You could say that."

"You going to stay in this area for a while, Mr. Morgan?"

Frank nodded. "I think I will, Claude."

"Why?" the farmer asked.

"That's a good question. This affair is really none of my business."

"It's a matter of right and wrong, Mr. Morgan."

"And there is right and wrong on both sides. Or perhaps you don't agree with that?"

"There is more right on our side than wrong."

"That's probably true."

Rick Handy stepped off the boardwalk into the wide street.

Frank stood up.

"What's going on here?" Claude asked, looking first at Rick, then at Frank.

"Get all the women and kids out of the way," Frank told him.

"Is there going to be a gunfight?"

"Probably. Do what I tell you, Claude."

The farmer moved swiftly, clearing the area in front of the general store of all foot traffic.

The gunslicks in the saloon suddenly crowded out onto the boardwalk, quickly moving left and right of the batwings, out of the line of fire. Obviously Rick had made his brags in the saloon, after Frank had left, and now the hired guns wanted to see if his words were just that: words, and nothing more.

"I'm damn tired of always hearin' 'bout how fast you are, Morgan!" Rick shouted. "By God, now you get to prove it."

"I'd rather not, Handy," Frank called.

"Are you yeller?"

"You know better than that, Rick."

"Then step out here in the street!"

"All right," Frank told him, stepping down from the boardwalk. "I'm here, Rick. Now what?"

Rick Handy's hand hovered near the butt of his gun. "Make your play, Morgan!" he shouted.

"It's your show, Rick," Frank told him. "It's up to you."

"Now!" Rick yelled, and grabbed for his pistol.

Four

Frank timed his draw and his shot perfectly. His bullet hit Rick's right thumb between the first and second knuckle, breaking the thumb and slamming Rick's pistol out of his hand. Rick screamed in pain and looked down at what was left of his thumb. Not much.

"You ruin't me!" the gunslick yelled. "I'll never be able to hold a short gun again. Why didn't you just kill me?"

"Because I didn't want to kill you, Ricky," Frank called.

"Riders comin' in," someone called.

"It's Mark Rogers," Claude said. "And he's got some of his hired guns with him."

"What the hell's goin' on here?" the owner of the Diamond spread demanded, reining up in the middle of the street.

Frank looked at the men who rode in with the rancher. He knew one of them: Matt Kingston. Matt met Frank's eyes and nodded his head in recognition.

"Are you starting trouble again, Paul?" Rogers asked, turning his attention to the farmer.

"No, he isn't," Frank said, verbally stepping in. "Your hired gun braced me."

"Who the hell are you?" Rogers asked.

"That's Frank Morgan," Matt said softly.

Rogers slowly twisted in the saddle, settling his gaze fully on Frank. "Well, well," he said. "The sodbusters went out and hired themselves a real wolf, hey?"

"Nobody hired me," Frank said. "I was passing through this area and needed supplies and a hot meal. Nothing more than that."

"You say," Roger said doubtingly.

"That's right," Frank said, coming right back at the man. "I damn sure do say." Frank was getting a bit hot under the collar at having his word disputed. "And if you have something else to say about that, get your big fat ass out of that saddle and say it to my face. Don't sit up there like some two-bit potentate, hiding behind your hired guns."

Rogers blinked a couple of times at that. He was not accustomed to people speaking to him in such a manner.

"What the hell's a poo-tentate?" a farmer standing behind Frank whispered.

"Damned if I know," another farmer said. "Sounds like something awful to me."

"You're got a damn smart mouth on you, Morgan," Rogers said.

"Let me take care of him, Mr. Rogers," one of hired guns said.

Matt Kingston laughed aloud at that. "Shut up, Sonny. The West is full of tinhorns like you that Frank Morgan has chewed up and spat out." He looked at Frank. "How you doin,' Drifter?"

"Fair to middlin', Matt. Haven't seen you in quite a while."

"I'm bleedin' and hurtin'," Rick hollered. "Ain't nobody gonna see 'bout me?"

"Nobody gives a damn about you, Rick," Matt said. "Pour some whiskey on what's left of your hand and shut up."

"That ain't no way to talk to a friend," Rick said sullenly.

"Who said we were friends?" Matt replied. He looked at Mark Rogers. "If Frank Morgan says his gun ain't for hire, boss, it ain't for hire."

The rancher nodded his head curtly. "All right." He looked at Frank. "See that you don't tarry in this area, Morgan."

"Rogers," Frank said, "I'll stay around here as long as I damn well choose to stay. And if you don't like it, you can go sit on a cactus."

Again Rogers blinked at Frank's words. A flush began creeping slowly over the man's neck and face. His hired guns tensed in their saddles, their hands dropping near their guns.

"When your boys draw, Rogers," Frank said, "I'll kill you first."

"Hold it, boys," Rogers said quickly. "Just take it easy." He cut his eyes to Frank. "I'll say this, Morgan, and you'd better pay heed to my words. Don't ever cross Diamond range."

Frank stared at the man and said nothing.

"Get your horse, Rick," Rogers told the man. "We'll fix you up back at the ranch."

Frank watched Rogers and his crew ride out of town. Then he stood on the boardwalk and calmly rolled a cigarette.

"I never seen a man shuck a pistol out of leather that fast in all my life," John Platt said from the end of the boardwalk.

The farmers and their families all stood in silent awe, looking at Frank. Claude broke the silence. "And I never heard anyone speak to Mark Rogers like that."

"You made an enemy for sure, Mr. Morgan," Dan Jones said. "And he won't forget neither."

Frank looked back at the man. "Man needs to be taken down a peg or two. Is the owner of the other big spread as bad as Rogers?"

"Worse," Hugh Watson said.

"I thought Rick Handy was slick with a short gun," John Platt said. "But he just barely cleared leather 'fore you shot him, Frank. And you let him hook and draw first." He shook his head. "I swear, I ain't never seen nothin' like that."

"What happens now?" Paul Adams questioned.

Frank tossed the butt of his cigarette into a mud puddle.

"I don't know about the rest of you, but I'm going to get me a cup of coffee."

Frank ambled toward the saloon, which was now almost deserted. He entered the batwings and stopped by the bar to tell the barman he wanted a cup of coffee.

The bartender sneered, until the other man behind the bar sidled over to whisper to him that this was the man who blew Rick Handy's finger plumb off. After that short conversation, the barman smiled sickly and said, "I'll be glad to bring it on over to your table, Mr. Morgan, and will there be anything else I can get you?"

Frank shook his head and moved over to a corner table, where he could sit with his back to a wall and face the front entrance. When he sat down, he noticed a tattered booklet lying on an empty chair against the wall next to his seat. He leaned over and picked it up, smiling when he recognized the same paperback book that he'd started a few days ago but never finished.

After the barman set his coffee on the table along with a bowl of sugar and a small pitcher of fresh cream, Frank opened the book and thumbed through the pages until he came to the place where he'd stopped reading.

Dangerous Dan Murdock was on his knees, hollering at Frank Morgan and Sweet Sue that he would get them for what they'd done to him.

Frank leaned back his head and laughed out loud. The other night, when he'd first read how the fictional Frank Morgan had shot the gun out of the desperado's hand, he'd thought how stupid that was. Everyone who'd ever been in a gunfight knew that in real life you never tried to shoot a man's gun hand; the target was just too small. You always aimed at the biggest, thickest part of your target, the chest. That way, if you happened to be a little high or low or off to one side, with any luck you'd still down the man before he could do the same to you.

Frank shook his head and smirked. Funny how real life

had imitated the fictional one in the book. Here he was, just out of a gunfight in which he'd actually been stupid enough to do exactly what Ned Buntline, or Edward Judson, had his hero doing in the penny dreadful–shooting a gun out of the hand of a man who was doing his level best to kill him. *Course, I had a damn good reason for not killing Handy,* Frank thought wryly. *If I'd blown a hole in him the size of a fist, ten other of his cronies would've drawn and shot me down 'fore I could blink. As it was, my only chance of comin' out of that little fracas alive was to do exactly what I did, shoot Handy but leave him standing.*

He sipped his coffee and read the next few pages of Dangerous Dan's story. . . .

After Frank Morgan and Sweet Sue left, Dangerous Dan Murdock got to his feet and went to the doctor's office down the street. After a brief examination, the doctor declared that miraculously no bones were broken and other than probably having some swelling and bruising over the next few days, Dangerous Dan was none the worse for what had happened to him.

Dangerous Dan returned to the saloon, intending to drown his sorrows in more whiskey, but he noticed that the other patrons were looking at him and smiling, and he was sure they would be laughing behind his back from now on because of what that bastard Morgan had done to him.

He gulped his drink, and slammed the shot glass down on the bar so hard it shattered, before grabbing his hat and stalking out of the saloon, to the sound of muted snickers and laughing behind him.

He flexed his right hand as he walked, noting how stiff and sore it was. He realized it would be days or weeks before it was well enough for him to even think about going up against Frank Morgan again, at least with a short gun.

As he walked past the nicest restaurant in town, he glanced in the window and saw Frank Morgan and Sweet Sue sitting at a table, all cozy-like, having a meal and laughing together. Dangerous Dan was sure they were laughing at him, and it made him furious.

"I'll get that son of a gun," he muttered to himself, and stalked off toward the gunsmith's shop on the next corner.

He stormed through the door, went directly to a shelf on a far wall, and took down a ten-gauge express gun—a double-barreled shotgun with the barrels cut down short so the shot would spread more rapidly. It was a devastating weapon at close range, and didn't take a great deal of skill to hit just about anything within thirty yards.

Dangerous Dan placed the shotgun on the counter and told the proprietor to give him a box of double-aught buckshot. "'Cause I got me a varmint I gotta kill."

"That buckshot's an awfully heavy load for shooting varmints, mister," the proprietor said as he pulled a box off the shelf behind the counter.

"This is a right big varmint," Dangerous Dan answered with a chuckle at his joke.

Uh-oh, Frank Morgan thought as he thumbed the page and took another sip of his coffee, getting drawn into the story in spite of his derision of the author moments before. *I wonder how Judson's gonna get his hero outta this mess. An express gun loaded with 00-buckshot is one of the meanest weapons in the world,* Frank thought, remembering with some roiling of his gut the few times he'd been up against men armed with such weapons.

As soon as he was outside the store, Dangerous Dan broke open the box of shells, put one in each of the twin barrels of the sawed-off shotgun, and filled his pockets with the remaining shells. With a flick of his wrist, he snapped the barrels shut and walked toward the restaurant with the gun cradled in his arms, smiling to himself at the mental image of Frank Morgan shredded and torn apart by the buckshot.

Frank Morgan and Sweet Sue sat in the restaurant, Frank drinking coffee while the young woman drank tea.

"Mr. Morgan, I want to thank you once again for saving me from that ruffian," Sue said, dropping her eyes demurely as Frank stared at her.

"Think nothing of it, Miss Sue," Frank said, thinking he'd never seen eyes so blue or skin so fair. *"Any gentleman worth his salt would've done the same thing."*

The real Frank Morgan rolled his eyes and made a face as he read this dialogue, thinking no self-respecting man of the West would ever talk in such a manner, especially to a woman he'd just met.

Frank shook his head impatiently when the barman ambled over with a pot of coffee in his hand and asked if Frank wanted a refill. He was anxious to get back to the story to see how the fictional Frank Morgan was going to keep from getting his butt blown off by Dangerous Dan and his shotgun.

Sweet Sue looked up at Frank from under long, thick eyelashes and smiled, revealing teeth as white as new snow. "But you were the gentleman who saved me, Mr. Morgan, and I will never forget you for your act of bravery as long as I live."

Frank nodded, and happened to glance out of the window of the restaurant just in time to see Dangerous Dan Murdock leveling a double-barreled shotgun at them from just outside the building.

Without having time to utter a warning, Frank shoved Sweet Sue as hard as he could, and then he dived under the table just as the window exploded into a million glittering fragments and the table disintegrated as the roar of the express gun made his ears ring.

Frank hit the floor rolling and tumbled head over heels until he came up on his knees, his right hand full of iron. He pulled the trigger on his smoke-wagon just as Dangerous Dan finished reloading his shotgun and snapped the barrels shut.

Frank's first bullet hit Dangerous Dan in the middle of

his chest and made him stagger back, but didn't knock the big man off his feet. Dan's eyes opened wide under the shock of the slug in his chest, but he was still strong enough to raise the barrel and take aim at Frank, who was kneeling a mere ten feet away.

Frank knew if Dan fired again, he couldn't miss at this range. He eared back the hammer on his Colt .44 and fired again, aiming higher this time.

A small black hole appeared in the middle of Dangerous Dan's forehead and his skull exploded in a fine red mist as he toppled over backward to land spread-eagled on his back in the middle of the street.

Frank turned quickly to see how Sweet Sue was, and was relieved to see that she was getting to her feet, apparently unharmed by the load of buckshot that had torn their table apart.

"Miss Sue, are you all right?" Frank asked, rushing to help her to her feet.

"Yes . . . I think so, Mr. Morgan," she replied, brushing her dress off with her hands.

"But, sir, did you have to be so rough?" she asked, glaring at him as if he'd done something wrong.

"But, Miss Sue," Frank protested, "Dangerous Dan was going to shoot us through the window."

She glanced outside and saw the bloody body of Dangerous Dan lying on his back.

With a haughty flip of her hair, she said, "That still does not excuse rudeness, sir. Good day to you." She didn't look back as she walked stiffly out of the door and down the street.

Frank tipped his hat back and shook his head. "Well, I'll be hanged," he said, realizing that he would never understand women if he lived to be a hundred years old.

The real Frank Morgan closed the book with a grin. Well, at least Judson had gotten one thing right, he thought as he drank down the last of his cold coffee. *People don't hardly ever appreciate it when you stick your nose in where it don't belong, no matter how much of a favor you do them.*

It was springtime, time for roundups and branding. Cowboys drifted into the area, looking for work. But there would be no roundup or branding this spring, and the only hands being hired were gunhands. The drifting cowboys drifted on, looking for a friendlier climate.

No lawman came to investigate the killing of the Norton family; Frank wasn't sure it had even been reported. Considering the way the farmers felt about the sheriff, he doubted it had been.

The Diamond hands and the GP hands stayed out of the settlement, and Frank stayed close, not at all certain just why he was doing so. He had taken an intense dislike for Mark Rogers, to be sure. But there was more to it than that. Frank just hadn't pegged it down yet in his mind. Injustice? Sure, but there was injustice everywhere, from settlers to the treatment of the Indians.

No, there was more to it than that.

Frank sighed heavily as he sat on a bench outside the general store and smoked. He knew he ought to saddle up and ride on. Knew if he stayed, he was going to get involved in a bad fight.

But he kept delaying his departure.

Frank put his hand out and petted Dog's big head. The cur licked Frank's hand, and then lay down beside him and went to sleep.

Frank watched as a lone rider rode slowly into the settlement. Frank's eyes narrowed as he recognized the man: Steve Harlon. The ranchers were really getting serious now.

Harlon was quick, mean, and deadly. If he had any feeling for human life at all, Frank had never met anyone who had witnessed it. No one knew for sure where Harlon was from. Some said he was from Missouri, others said Kansas. Steve was about Frank's age and height, but not quite as muscular. Frank continued to sit on the bench as Harlon approached, the gunslick reining up when he spotted and recognized Frank. He sat in his saddle for a moment, staring at Frank; then a smile creased his lips.

"Morgan," Steve finally said. "Strange meeting you here."

"I get around some, Steve."

"Indeed you do. I hope we're workin' for the same side."

"I'm not working for either side, Steve. Just passin' through."

"Ah, now, Morgan." The gunslick again smiled. "I know you better than that. You always take the side of the underdog."

At the sound of his name, Dog looked up, his cold brown eyes studying Steve.

"Your dog, Morgan?"

"You might say that."

"Mean-lookin' bastard."

"We get along."

"I 'spect you do." Steve swung down from the saddle and looped the reins around a hitching rail. He stepped up onto the boardwalk, sat down beside Frank, and pulled out the makings, rolling himself a smoke. "No hotel in this dump?" he asked.

"Rooms for let over at the saloon."

"They nice?"

Frank remembered that Steve was very picky about his quarters. "They're clean."

"No fleas or cooties?"

"I haven't scratched once since I got here."

"I insisted on a hotel. I hate bunkhouses."

"I recall that." Frank remembered that Harlon used to take some ribbing about being so fastidious. The ribbing stopped quite abruptly after Steve killed one of his tormentors. No one had ribbed him about that particular quirk of his since that incident.

"Who hired you, Steve?" Frank asked.

"I've had offers from both the GP and the Diamond. I haven't made up my mind as yet."

"It's shaping up to be a real ugly one."

"Aren't they all, Frank?"

"I reckon so."

"I suppose you booked the best room in the hotel?" Steve questioned.

"I think they're all the same."

Steve got up and swung into the saddle. "See you later, Frank. Perhaps we could have a drink together before dinner."

"Maybe so."

Steve nodded his head and rode over to the saloon/hotel. Frank recalled someone once telling him that Steve Harlon had gone to a university someplace; had had plans on becoming a teacher. Frank knew that when he wanted to, Harlon could use very good English.

"You must know that fellow," Joe Wallace said from the open door of his store.

"We've crossed trails a time or two."

"But no trouble between you?"

"Not yet."

"Still haven't made up your mind, hey, Mr. Morgan?"

"I won't until I'm pushed."

"Maybe they won't push you. Ever think of that? Maybe they'll play the waiting game with you."

"Hoping I'll get bored and move on? Maybe so."

"Rumor is you're a rich man, Mr. Morgan. Any truth to that?"

"I'm not going to miss any meals, that's for sure. Why do you ask?"

"Curious, I suppose. Curious as to why a moneyed man would just drift around."

Frank smiled. "I'm a wanderer, Joe. I like to see new places."

"Must be nice," the store owner said, a wistful note in his voice.

Frank did not reply to that. He was watching dust rise up outside of town, the thin cloud getting closer. "A group of riders coming," he observed just as the horsemen came into view.

"Grant Perkins and his hired guns," Joe said after watching the riders for a moment. "You've met Mark Rogers; now you get to meet the owner of the GP."

"I'm sure it will be a pleasure," Frank said.

"Yeah, right," Joe replied, his voice filled with just as much sarcasm, then stepped back into his store.

Five

Grant Perkins didn't even glance Frank's way as he passed by. He reined up across the street in front of the saloon/hotel and stomped inside, his men with him.

"One of Grant's boys must be passed out drunk in one of the rooms," Joe said, stepping out onto the boardwalk. "Probably Victor. He's a mean one."

"How many kids does he have?"

"Three. Victor, Lucy, and Robert. In that order. They're all rotten, especially Vic."

"How about Rogers?"

"Three kids. Mark Junior, Peaches, and Mike."

"Peaches?"

Joe laughed at Frank's expression. "Real pretty girl. 'Bout twenty years old, I'd guess. I don't know what her real name is. All I know is Peaches."

"The kids of the ranchers get along? They socialize?"

"Oh, yes. Truth is, they feel they have no one else to socialize with. That's the way they was raised, I guess."

"No one else on their social level," Frank said. "Sad."

"It was Vic, like I said. There he is."

Frank watched as an obviously drunk Victor Perkins was half carried, half dragged out of the saloon and helped into the saddle. Grant led the procession out of the settlement, heading back to the ranch. He had not given Frank a single glance.

"Vic must be a real quiet drunk," Frank said. "My sleep wasn't interrupted last night."

"He is. He gets liquored up, gets him a whore, and heads for a room. The next morning you can count on his daddy comin' into town to fetch him back home. You have any children, Frank?"

"A son. We don't see much of each other. He lives back East."

"His mother was killed, wasn't she?"

"Yes. Several years ago." Frank stood up and stretched. "I think I'll find me a cup of coffee and then ride out in the country for a spell."

"Good day for it."

Frank rode heading east, being careful to stay on the roads that cut through the valleys. He passed three farmhouses, surrounded by well-tended fields. Some of the farm families waved at him, others did not. After several hours of riding, he turned around and headed west. He reined up at a homestead and sat his horse, watching from the road as the family worked at loading up a wagon with their belongings. Frank walked his horse into the yard and dismounted. The family, a man, woman, and three kids, stopped and stared at him.

"Could I trouble you for a drink of water for my horse, my dog, and me?"

"Help yourself, mister," the man said. "Well's yonder and the water's good."

"Much obliged." His thirst satisfied, Frank walked over to the wagon and leaned against it. "You folks moving?" he asked.

"Yep," the man said. "Pullin' out." He stared at Frank for a moment. "You'd be Frank Morgan?"

"That's right. And I'm not working for the ranchers, if that's what you're thinking."

"Wouldn't make no difference no how. The ranchers won this one. We're leavin'."

"But your crops have just been planted. You going to just pull out and leave them to rot?"

"They ain't worth dyin' over."

Frank looked over what land he could see from the yard. "You have a buyer for your place?"

"Never asked nobody. Got two sections here. My brother owned one. The ranchers killed him last year. Threatened me last month. I'm quittin'.'"

"Nice snug house," Frank observed.

"Sure is. And they's a crick runs through the land. You tasted the water. It's sweet and cold. Deep well."

"How much you want for the land and the house?"

"Are you serious?"

"Sure am."

"What do you figure it's worth, Mr. Morgan? I mean, I was just gonna leave it and take my loss."

"How much do you need to get started somewhere else?"

"More than you'd be willin' to pay for this land, Mr. Morgan."

Frank smiled and named a figure.

The farmer's eyes widened. "Don't josh, Mr. Morgan. I'm up agin hard times with my wife and kids."

"I'm not joking. I have that much with me. Is it a fair figure?"

"You're not jokin'?"

"I'm not."

"That'd get me set up back East somewheres, away from these damn murderin' ranchers."

"Well, not all ranchers are like the ones in this area. But a lot of them can be unreasonable, for a fact."

"You really got that much cash with you?"

"I can pay some of it in cash and the rest in a banknote. I assure you, it's good. I'll give you the names of my attorneys in Denver and San Francisco to contact if you have any trouble. The only thing I ask is you not tell anyone about me buying you out. Anyone in this area, that is."

The farmer turned to his wife. "Mother, fetch me the deeds to this land. We're gonna be set up when we get back East."

After the farm family had rolled out, Frank took a better look at the property he'd just purchased. The house was well built, with a large living area/kitchen combination and two bedrooms. The man had installed a hand pump in the kitchen, and Frank tried it. Cold, sweet water came gushing out. The farmer had donated a bed with a very comfortable feather tick, a table and chairs for the kitchen area, and a rocker for the living area. Frank felt like a king.

He rode back to town and moved out of the hotel. Over at the livery, he rented a buckboard and horse, then went over to the store and bought supplies, including lamps, candles, bedding, and carpenter tools, including a box of nails.

"You settling in somewhere, Frank?" Joe asked.

"Might be, Joe. I might decide to file on some land. Who knows?"

"Are you serious?"

"Sure. You never know what I might do."

"You know anything about farming?" the store owner asked, a dubious expression on his face.

"I've planted a few gardens," Frank replied with a smile. "Do me a favor, Joe?"

"Sure."

"Don't say anything about this?"

"You got it. Want to surprise the Diamond and GP, hey?"

"Something like that."

"It'll be a surprise, all right. I'll keep mum about it, Frank. You have my word on that."

"Good deal. See you, Joe. Give my best to your missus."

Dog hopped up in the bed of the buckboard for the ride back to the country. "Lazy thing," Frank told the big cur.

Dog showed him his teeth.

On the way back to his land, Frank passed several farms and waved at the people working in the gardens or the fields. To a person they stopped their work and stared at the gunfighter driving a buckboard, the bed of the wagon loaded with supplies. Frank smiled at the expression on their faces.

"Going to be interesting when the word gets back to the ranchers," Frank muttered.

He unloaded his supplies and then made himself something to eat and a pot of coffee. After eating his bread and bacon, Frank took a cup of coffee outside. He sat on a bench and drank his coffee and smoked a cigarette, waiting for the first visitor to arrive. It didn't take long.

Claude Hornsby and Dan Jones rode up and dismounted. They stood at the wooden fence around the small front yard, Claude asking, "Mind if we come in, Mr. Morgan?"

"Not at all. Come on in, boys. Fresh pot of coffee on the stove. Cups on the table."

The men fixed their coffee and came back outside. Claude sat on the bench beside Frank. Dan found a small stool and sat down.

"Are you goin' to farm this land, Mr. Morgan?" Claude asked.

"The name is Frank. Not Mister. I knew word would get out about my buying this land. I didn't think it would be this quick."

"People saw you drivin' a buckboard," Dan said. "They put two and two together, that's all. I reckon I should say they hoped that two and two made four."

"I bought this land, yes."

"You goin' to farm it?" Dan asked.

"I'm going to live here. You and Claude want to work the land for the crops?"

"Are you jokin'?' " Claude asked.

"No. You and Dan can split them fifty-fifty. I'm not much of a farmer."

"You bet we will!" Dan said.

"Then it's a deal." Frank stood up and shook hands with the men. "We've got us a partnership, boys."

After the men left, to tell their families about their new neighbor and the deal they had struck, Frank sat on the bench outside his new home and wondered what he'd gotten himself into this time . . . although he knew perfectly well what was facing him: a bloody range war.

He didn't question why he'd done it. Frank was known far and wide as a man who would always take up the fight for an underdog.

He got up from the bench, went into the kitchen, and poured himself another cup of coffee, and then stood looking out the kitchen window at the spread he'd bought. He noticed some of the fencing was leaning and in disrepair, especially the small corral that was next to the barn about a hundred yards from the cabin. The barn itself also looked like it could use some fixing up and maybe even a fresh coat of paint.

Frank shook his head. It was as if once the farmer decided he was going to have to leave, he'd quit caring about his farm and neglected to do the necessary work that went with keeping any place like this in good repair.

Frank glanced at the box of tools he'd laid on the table earlier, and realized he was going to be doing a lot of carpentry in the next few days. The thought made him smile. Frank had always enjoyed working with his hands, especially when the work was outdoors. There was just something about taking a place like this, pretty but somewhat worn down by events, and making it bright and shiny and new again, a feeling of accomplishment that few other endeavors could bring to a man.

Seeing that the coffee was getting low in the pot, Frank

added a handful of coffee and some fresh water from the pump. He threw another couple of pieces of wood into the stove to heat it up, and walked back out onto the porch.

Dog was still lying curled up next to the steps. It was almost as if the animal knew this was to be their new home for a while and was settling in and making himself to home.

Frank smiled and sat on the top step, drinking his coffee and rubbing Dog's hips just in front of his tail, a place that always seemed to make the dog moan with contentment.

Frank's eyes moved over his land, and his heart swelled with the sort of pride owning your own place can give. He wondered, since the feeling was so good and seemed to feel so right, why every time he tried to settle down and make a permanent home someplace, events seemed to conspire to cause him to pack up and move on sooner rather than later.

He snorted through his nose at this thought, being introspective enough to realize it wasn't just events that caused him to move on, but the inner devil within him that seemed to always need new adventures and new places to see in order to be happy.

He remembered a few years back, over in New Mexico, when on an impulse he'd bought a hacienda and a couple of hundred acres of land that ran alongside the only creek in the area that held water year-round. He'd thought at the time he'd had enough roaming around and that it might be time for him to settle down and set a spell.

Things had gone well for almost six months. Frank had bought a few sheep and goats, about the only livestock he could think of that would just about take care of themselves and that could live off the desert-like land of his ranch. He'd even gone to a few socials in town, and had started keeping company, as they say, with a young Mexican widow named Maria. It was nothing serious, and since Maria had been married before, they hadn't needed a chaperone on their many picnics and rides through the countryside.

He was just beginning to believe that he was settled in

for good when once again fate, or the devil within him, reared its ugly head. He went into town one Saturday and rode directly to Maria's house. They had a date to go riding out in the country. Frank had found a natural dam in the creek next to his place where the water backed up and formed a small lake, surrounded by cottonwood trees. It was an ideal place for a swim followed by a picnic in the shade of the trees.

When he knocked on Maria's door, he was surprised when it was opened by Esperanza, Maria's aunt. She was dressed all in black and her face was flushed and tear-stained.

"Esperanza, what's wrong?" Frank asked, his heart hammering painfully in his chest. "Where's Maria?"

In broken English mixed with Spanish, Esperanza told him that Maria was dead, she'd killed herself the night before.

Frank thought his knees were going to buckle before he could get inside and get the rest of the story from Esperanza. It seemed that the previous afternoon, Maria had been walking back from the general store toward her house, which sat on the edge of town, when a group of drunken cowboys grabbed her, dragged her back into an alley, and took turns raping her.

When she went to the sheriff, the men all said that Maria had sold herself to them for money, and so the sheriff had said there was nothing he could do.

Humiliated and ashamed, Maria had gone home and cut her wrists, bleeding to death in the bathtub she'd filled to try and wash away her shame.

Grim-faced and filled with a hatred so intense he thought he might burst, Frank gave Esperanza a handful of money for Maria's funeral and asked her which ranch the men worked on.

Esperanza said she didn't know, and so Frank stalked over to the sheriff's office and banged open the door. The sheriff was leaning back in his chair with his feet up on his desk. His face paled when he saw Frank, for everyone in town knew that he and Maria were courting.

"Who was it, Bill?" Frank asked, knowing the sheriff would know what he was talking about.

"Uh, Frank, listen to me," the sheriff said, getting to his feet and holding out his hands. "There was nothin' I could do. All the men stuck to their story and since there weren't no other witnesses . . ."

"Bullshit, Bill!" Frank almost screamed. "You knew Maria. You knew what kind of woman she was, and you certainly knew she would never do what those men said she did."

"Sure, Frank, I know that. But as a lawman, I got to have evidence before I arrest somebody—it ain't enough to go on my feelings in the matter one way or the other."

Frank nodded. The sheriff had a point. "All right, Bill, that's good enough for me. The law can't do nothing, but I can. Now tell me the names of the men involved."

"Frank—"

"Do it, Bill, and then stay out of this if you want to live to see your next birthday."

When Frank got to the ranch where the men worked, he saw all their horses reined outside the large bunkhouse, it being a Saturday and no one working this afternoon.

Frank pulled his rifle from his saddle boot, unhooked the hammer thong on his Colt, and walked up to the door.

Instead of using the door handle, he just raised his right foot, kicked the door in, and moved quickly through the doorway.

A man next to the first bunk went for his pistol, and was stopped cold when Frank slammed the butt of his rifle into the man's face, shattering his front teeth and knocking him out cold.

The four other men in the bunkhouse froze, their hands out from their sides. "We don't want no trouble, mister," the foreman said. "What is it you want?"

Frank called out five names, and then he asked, "Are you the men that go with those names?"

"Uh, sure, but so what?" the foreman asked. He looked around. "We know who you are, Morgan, but don't none of us here have any business with you."

Frank jacked a shell into the .44/.40 and leveled the barrel at the man. "Do you know the name Maria Hernandez?" he asked, and smiled grimly when the men paled and glanced nervously at one another.

Frank nodded. "I thought you might," he said. "I've come here to kill you for what you did to her."

The foreman shook his head. "Ain't none of us gonna draw on you, Mr. Morgan. We all know how good you are with a gun, an' we wouldn't stand a chance against the likes of you." He smiled grimly. "And I know from your reputation, you ain't about to shoot no man down that don't have a gun in his hand."

Frank shook his head. "Cowards one and all, huh?" He turned, picked up a lantern on a nearby table, and flung it against the wall of the bunkhouse. "Well, you can stay in here and burn like the rats you are, or you can come out this door with you hands full of iron and at least die like men. It's your choice, gentlemen."

He backed out of the door and walked twenty yards away, laying the rifle on the ground next to him, and waited.

As the flames consuming the bunkhouse rose into the sky, the five men finally came running out of the door, firing their pistols wildly in every direction, hoping to hit Frank before he could return fire.

Frank picked up the rifle and calmly, ignoring the angry buzzing as slugs tore by his head and the stinging in his left shoulder as one of the bullets creased him, shot the men down where they stood.

He walked over to the bodies that were sprawled outside the bunkhouse and placed a flower on each of them—flowers that came from Maria's funeral bouquet.

He climbed on his horse, whistled shrilly for Dog to follow him, and rode off to the west without ever going back to the home he'd fashioned on the banks of a creek in New Mexico. He'd been drifting ever since.

Frank stopped his musings as a couple of men rode up to his fence and reined up. Pete Dancer and Zack Spence swung down from the saddle and looked at Frank.

"Howdy, boys," Frank greeted the pair of gunslicks. "Come on in. Coffee's on the stove."

"Friendly of you, Morgan," Zack said, pushing open the gate.

The men stepped into the yard and Dancer nodded at Frank. "Afternoon, Morgan."

"Pete. You passin' through or hirin' on?"

"I work for the Diamond, Frank. Me and Zack both."

"Sorry to hear that."

"Oh? Why's that?"

"I hate to see anyone get tangled up in a nasty range war."

"And you're not tangled up in this one?" Dancer asked.

"Not yet."

"You really believe that, Frank?" Zack asked.

Frank busied himself for a moment rolling a cigarette before replying. Popping a match into flame with his thumbnail, he said, "I bought a little farm, boys. I've got people working the crops on shares. I'm not bothering a soul by living here. I want to be a good neighbor. But if I'm pushed, I'll push back."

"We're not here to push you, Frank," Dancer said.

"Who sent you to see me?"

"Nobody," Zack said. "We was on our way into town and

seen you sittin' out here. In case you done forgot your directions, the Diamond spread is yonder way." He pointed. "This is just one way into town."

Frank's smile came and went very quickly. "So it looks like I'm in the middle of the two spreads."

"Shore looks like it, Frank," Dancer said.

"That might put me in a bad position if push comes to shove."

"It might, Frank," Zack agreed. "Was I you, I'd consider sellin' out. I'd bet that the Diamond or the GP spread would give you a right nice price for this land was you to ask."

"And if you were me, you'd sell out?"

"I'd give it some serious thought. I shore would."

Frank looked at first Zack, then at Dancer. "No deal, boys. I like it right here."

The two hired guns finished their coffee and set the cups on the bench. "You been warned, Frank," Dancer said.

"Indeed I have."

"Thanks for the coffee," Zack said.

"Don't mention it."

"We'll be goin' now," Dancer said. "I reckon we'll see you around now and then."

"Count on it, boys."

"We ain't got nothin' agin you, Frank," Zack told him. "This here war ain't nothin' personal."

"That's nice to know."

"You takin' all this mighty calm, Frank," Dancer told him. " 'Tween the Diamond and the GP, they's about fifty or sixty men ready to fight at the drop of a hat. I'd give that some thought was I you."

"If nobody sent you boys, why are you telling me this?" Frank asked.

" 'Cause you one of us, Frank," Zack replied.

"One of you?" Frank said softly.

"You know what we mean," Dancer said. "You been gunslingin' for a long time."

"But I never hired my gun, Pete." Frank stood up quickly, and both men backed up, their hands instinctively dropping to the butts of their guns. Frank smiled. "You boys are sure jumpy."

The men relaxed, Zack saying, "You know how it is, Frank."

"Do I, Zack?"

"You takin' sides in this fracas, ain't you, Frank?"

"Only if I'm pushed."

"Frank," Dancer said, "I'm tellin' you, if you stay here, you're gonna be in the middle of this thing. The big creek runs right through your property."

"That's nice, Pete. I might decide to go swimmin' from time to time."

Dancer shook his head. "You're actin' the fool, Frank. That ain't like you. Man, you don't want no part of this here war."

"You boys want some more coffee?" Frank asked.

Both gunmen shook their heads. They glanced at each other and without another word, turned and walked out of the yard and mounted up, riding away.

"I have been warned," Frank said to Dog, who had been lying in the shade near the corner of the house. "I guess I have officially taken a side." Frank stood up and hitched up his gun belt. "All right. So be it."

He moved into the house and picked up the tools and nails. *Might as well get some fences fixed up while I got the chance,* he thought. He took the coffee off the stove, figuring he'd had the last of the visitors for the day, and walked out the door toward the corral, intending to start there.

Six

Frank slept well that night and was up before dawn, as was his custom. He washed his face and put water on to boil for coffee. He let Dog out to run the yard and do his business. The predawn was chilly, but the heat from the woodstove in the kitchen would warm the house sufficiently. He lit a couple of lamps in the living area and brightened up the house. The coffee ready, Frank poured a mug and took a chair at the table. He sweetened his coffee and then rolled a cigarette. After a cigarette, Frank got out the skillet, sliced some bacon, and laid out the thick strips to fry. He sliced some bread and laid that aside. He got a jar of jam out of the cupboard and put that on the table. The bacon sizzling in the skillet was making his mouth water. Dog scratched at the door, and Frank let him in.

His breakfast ready, Frank laid a strip of bacon on a thick piece of bread, sopped the bread in the grease, and gave the sandwich to Dog. The big cur took the snack, went to his corner of the living area, and ate his breakfast. He would not bother Frank at the table for food again.

Just after dawn, Frank began a walking tour of his newly purchased land, Dog padding along silently beside him. The land was rich and fertile; Frank could smell the strength of the newly plowed and planted earth. Standing on the bank of the creek, gazing down at the flowing waters, Frank could understand fully why the ranchers wanted to regain control of this land. But he also knew that times were changing all over America. The nation was growing and the people needed food, food that came from the earth as well as food on the hoof.

The farmers and the ranchers were going to have to learn to coexist, but Frank knew that blood was going to be spilled and men were going to die before that happened. But it would happen. It would happen even if federal troops had to be brought in to enforce it. And that had happened before.

Gazing across the creek, Frank watched a few head of cattle grazing peacefully in the distance, on ranch land. Frank wasn't sure whose land. They were too far away for him to read the brands. Frank walked back to the house and saddled Stormy. He did not lock the house. If someone was hungry, they could help themselves to food. That was the way it was in the West.

"You stay here and stay close," he told Dog, swinging into the saddle. "And behave yourself."

Dog trotted back into the small barn and lay down. He lay with his head facing the door to the barn, and woe to anyone who entered who wasn't known by the cur to be a friend.

Frank headed out. He was determined to meet as many of his farmer neighbors as he could this day.

The first house he came to on the road was that of Claude and Mavis Hornsby. They greeted him warmly and invited him in for coffee and conversation.

"Did two gunmen come to see you yesterday?" Claude asked, again mispronouncing the term.

Frank smiled. "Yes. Pete Dancer and Zack Spence. I was warned not to take sides in this range war."

"They used the term *war?*" Mavis asked, worry lines appearing on her face, tanned from days in the sun working beside her husband.

"Yes, Mavis, they did."

"I guess it's all out in the open now," Claude said.

"Go armed at all times," Frank told the settlers. "Short gun and rifle. If you don't have weapons, I'll get them for you."

"You'd do that for us?"

"Of course."

"You're a very complicated man, Mr. Morgan," Mavis opined. "I just don't understand you at all."

Frank smiled that away without comment. "Have you met the new settlers yet?"

"Yes," Claude said. "Four families. They filed on sections west of here. Down at the end of the last valley."

"Good folks?"

"They sure seem to be. They're all from Ohio and Pennsylvania. Came out here to get a fresh start. They're all in their early thirties. With young kids."

Mavis refilled Frank's coffee cup and with a smile, pushed the sugar bowl across the table toward him.

"When we finish our coffee, I'll saddle up and we'll ride together," said Claude. "We'll spend the rest of the day visiting every farm family we can. Those we miss, we'll see tomorrow."

"I appreciate that, Claude. If we're going to win this fight, the first thing we have to do is get organized."

"No point in my packing you a lunch," Mavis said. "You'll be invited to noon by somebody."

Frank smiled, Mavis noticing that the humor did not reach his pale eyes. They remained unemotional. A dangerous man, she thought. A very dangerous man. "Take your pistol," she told her husband. "I'll keep the rifle here with me."

The next house belonged to Dan and Lucille Jones. Frank and Claude were greeted warmly and invited in for coffee and conversation. Lucille had just baked bread and the smell was tantalizing.

"Got fresh-churned butter and some good jam," she told the men.

How could they refuse?

While Lucille slathered butter and jam on her home-made bread, Frank began to tell Dan Jones why he and Claude had ridden out to visit. At Frank's mention of the words "range war," Dan frowned and glanced over at his wife. Lucille's face flushed, but she kept her eyes on the bread she was preparing for her guests.

Frank noticed the look on Dan's face. "I can see that the thought of fighting in a range war bothers you some, Dan."

Dan pursed his lips and looked thoughtful. "It ain't that, Mr. Morgan," he said in a low voice.

"Please," Frank said, holding up his hand. "Call me Frank."

"All right, Frank," Dan said. "Like I said, it ain't that Ma and me are afraid to fight to defend our land in a range war. It's just that we been through all this before."

"Oh?'

Dan paused while Lucille moved to the table and handed Frank and Claude plates with thick slices of warm bread covered with melted butter and fresh strawberry jam and two mugs of steaming coffee.

While the men dug in, Dan told his story.

"Ma and me had this little hardscrabble farm over in Missouri a few years back. It wasn't much, just a few dozen acres, but the land was good and we were happy. We'd started our family and had two kids, a boy named Daniel after me and a little girl name Francis after Lucille's mama."

Frank glanced around the small house as Dan talked, and he noticed there were no signs of children in the place, no toys or small clothes or any other indication of anyone living there other than Dan and Lucille.

"Well," Dan continued, "we had this pond on our place that was fed by an artesian well, so it never went dry, no matter how bad a drought we was having. That's what started all the problems."

Claude nodded. "Other farmers wantin' your water?" he asked.

"No," Dan answered. "The railroad. Seems a group of real important businessmen in the nearest town had talked the railroad into building a line that would go near my place. Trouble is, there weren't no good rivers or streams nearby where they could get water for their steam engines. After lookin' around a bit, they approached Ma and me to sell them the rights to our water and to let them build the tracks through our property."

He glanced at Lucille, and took her hand when he saw her eyes were full of tears at the memories he was dredging up. "Anyway," he continued, "when I told them no, they got these Pinkerton detectives to start harassin' us."

"What'd they do?" Frank asked, though he had a pretty good idea, having seen the Pinkertons at work before.

"Oh, the usual things," Dan answered. "They'd burn our crops, tear down our fences, scatter our few head of cattle." He shook his head. "It got so bad, I was afraid to let Ma go into town by herself."

"Did you finally give up and sell to 'em?" Claude asked.

Dan's eyes brimmed with unshed tears. "Not then. But when I wouldn't give in to 'em, they waited until Ma and me were out at the barn doing our milking one mornin' an' they set the house on fire."

Lucille, unable to stand any more, sobbed, got up from the table, and left the room.

Dan's eyes followed her as he continued his story. "I really don't think they meant to kill us, but our two children were still in the house and must've gotten trapped, 'cause they never made it outta the place 'fore it burned to the ground."

Frank reached across the table and put his hand on

Dan's arm. "I'm sorry, Dan," he said, knowing the death of a man's children was one of the worst things that could happen to someone.

"Well, after we buried 'em, we just packed up an' left. Neither Ma nor me had the heart to stay in the place after that." His eyes raised to look into Frank's and Claude's. "Now, we're set up here, an' there ain't nobody gonna make us run again."

Frank smiled grimly. "That's the spirit."

He and Claude went over the precautions Dan and Lucille would have to take, and then they thanked Lucille for her hospitality and rode on toward the next farm down the road.

"We're not going to be able to eat any lunch," Frank said, riding away after talking with the Jones.

"I'm so full I'm about to pop," Claude said.

"It's not that for me," Frank said. "It's the story Dan told us about the Pinkertons. It plumb ruined my appetite. Whenever I think I've heard just about the worst thing people can do to one another, someone always manages to show me something even more terrible."

"But we'll have to eat something if we're invited," Claude said. "You know that."

"Yes. It would be an insult not to. But coffee only at the next house," Frank said, rubbing his sour stomach.

"Agreed."

And a thick slice of apple pie, as it turned out. Jessica Watson had just baked several pies, fresh and hot out of the oven, and she insisted the men try some.

How could they refuse? To do so would not be neighborly.

After a few minutes of eating pie and talking with Hugh Watson, the men climbed into the saddle—with an effort and a grunt—and rode on to visit the next home.

"This has got to stop," Frank said, stifling a belch. "I'm stuffed."

"Me too," Claude said. "But we might be in trouble."

"Why?"

"Edna Roykin makes the best stew you ever put in your mouth. She adds a lot of spices to it."

"I couldn't eat another bite," Frank said.

But he did manage a small bowl of stew. And another cup of coffee. And, at Edna's insistence, a piece of fresh-baked cake.

"Good God!" Frank said, riding away after chatting with Pat and Edna Roykin. "I think I'm going to die."

"We might be in luck," Claude said.

"About what?"

"Callie Hastings is just about the worst cook in the county. Burl fixes most of the meals."

"That's the best news I've heard all morning."

When they rode up to the Hastings farmhouse, they found Burl Hastings hoeing some weeds in the small vegetable garden at the side of the house. He looked up and grinned at Claude as he sleeved sweat off his forehead and leaned on his hoe, obviously glad for an excuse to stop work for a spell. "Howdy, Claude. How're you doin'?" he called.

"Just fine, Burl. And you?" Claude answered as he and Frank climbed down off their mounts.

"Can't complain, I guess," Hastings said.

"I wonder if we might come in and talk to you about something very important," Claude said.

"Of course. Come on in and set a spell," Hastings said.

As they entered the house, he glanced back over his shoulder. "Can I offer you boys somethin' to eat?" He looked around. "Callie ought'a have dinner 'bout ready soon."

"No," Claude said quickly. "We really can't stay that long, Burl," he added as an excuse not to partake of the in-famous Callie's cooking.

Burl smiled and winked, knowing what Claude meant. "I really can't say as I blame you, son," he said good-naturedly.

Callie Hastings appeared from another room, and Frank

could see why Burl Hastings stayed married to a woman acknowledged as the worst cook in the county—she was beautiful. She had long, flowing hair the color of corn silk, eyes that were as blue as the sky, and the kind of a figure men dream about on lonely nights under the stars.

She was holding a small swatch of material that was obviously a quilt in the making.

"Hello, Claude," she said in a low, husky voice.

"Howdy, Mrs. Hastings," Claude said, quickly taking his hat off and giving a slight bow of his head.

"Callie's a right fine seamstress," Burl said with pride, his eyes aglow with love for his wife.

"Can I offer you gentlemen a cup of coffee, or some cold lemonade?" she asked, putting her quilting aside and moving toward the kitchen.

"No, thank you, ma'am," Frank said, smiling. "We just want to have a few words with you and your husband and then we'll be on our way."

They sat in the main room of the cabin and told Burl and Callie why they'd come and what the couple had to do to protect themselves. Burl asked few questions, and indicated that he would fight with the other farmers if it came to that.

"The Nortons was good folks an' they didn't deserve what happened to 'em," Burl said, his face grim. "And those ranchers need to be taken down a notch or two if you ask me."

On the road again, Frank looked at his watch. It was almost noon. "Let's stop in the shade up here and rest for a time. Like maybe an hour."

"Until the nooning is over?"

"You got it."

"Agreed."

Both men slept for an hour under the shade of a huge

tree. They awakened within moments of each other and exchanged glances.

"I'm still not hungry," Claude said. "I might not eat until this time tomorrow."

"I know the feeling. Let's ride."

Van and Virginia Calen had just finished lunch when Frank and Claude rode up. Van was sitting outside smoking his pipe, and waved the men to a bench.

"You boys are too late for lunch," Van said. "Me and the wife and the kids ate it all up. But we still got coffee that's hot."

Both Frank and Claude sighed with relief, Claude saying, "Coffee would be fine, Van."

Over coffee, Claude explained the situation, Frank adding, "If you folks are going to beat the ranchers, you've got to get organized, and you've got to go armed at all times."

"We're not warriors, Mr. Morgan," Van said. "I hunt, sure. But I've never shot at a man. I don't know that I could."

"Not even if your family was threatened?"

"I don't know, Mr. Morgan. Yes, I reckon I could if that happened." He paused. "Sure I would," he added. "But that ain't never happened."

"Yet," Claude said.

"You have weapons?" Frank asked.

"I got a rifle and a shotgun. I ain't no hand with a pistol."

"Stock up on ammunition," Frank told him. "And make certain your wife knows how to use the weapons. That's important. There'll be many times that you're away from the house. If you don't have the money on hand to buy extra ammunition, I'll help you."

"We're tellin' everyone this, Van," Claude said. "It's war now."

"Is this land worth it, Claude?" Van's wife, Virginia, asked, stepping out of the house to stand by her husband. "Is a piece of ground worth killing people over?"

"The ranchers sure think so, Virginia," Claude answered. "Look what they done to the Norton family."

The farmer's wife slowly nodded her head and walked back inside the house. She returned with a coffeepot. "I made fresh." She filled their cups and went back into the house.

"You met the new people yet?" Claude asked Van.

"Yes. Nice folks. They got a bunch of kids too."

"You tell them about the situation here?"

"I laid it out for them. They said they was here to stay. They filed on the land legal-like and it was theirs. They intend to build homes and stay. I think they meant it."

"We'll go see them now," Claude said to Frank. "We got time."

"Let's do it."

As they climbed on their horses, Frank added to Claude, "Let's just pray that the new people we're gonna visit haven't had time to bake any cakes or pies or bread yet."

Claude laughed. "Yeah. I'm gonna have to go on a diet after this little trip is over."

Seven

The new settlers were still living in their wagons while they worked on building their homes. When they had all gathered around and Frank was introduced, they were, to a person, clearly in awe at meeting the famous gunfighter.

"You're on our side?" Frank was asked.

"Looks that way," Frank replied, eyeing all the small children that were busy playing all over the place. He counted nine kids, all of them under ten or twelve years of age.

"We have weapons," another man explained. "But we never thought we'd have to fight in order to farm the land."

"Welcome to cattle country," Frank said bluntly.

"You sound like you agree with the ranchers," a woman said.

Frank glanced at the woman. About thirty, he guessed, very attractive. "Ma'am, let me tell you something. When the ranchers came into this area, they had to fight Indians and rustlers. They suffered through drought and blizzards and the occasional flood. But they buried their dead and stuck it out. They tamed this land. No, I'm not on their side. But I can see some things from their point of view. There's land here aplenty for all of you. And the ranchers have no *legal* right to keep you out. But they're going to try to run you out. Bet on that."

"Or kill us," Claude added.

"Yes," Frank agreed. "Or kill you."

"Would you look over our weapons, Mr. Morgan?" another young settler asked.

"I'd be happy to."

Since the settlers lived so close together, it didn't take long for them to produce two rifles, three shotguns, and four pistols.

"This is it?" Frank asked.

"We're farmers, Mr. Morgan," another young man said. "We came here to work the land."

Before Frank could reply, a woman said, "Four riders coming. Riding in from the west."

"They had to come through the pass then," Claude said, looking up the road. " 'Cause the road ends about two miles west of here."

Frank waited until the quartet drew closer. "Gunslicks," he said.

"You know them?" Claude asked.

"I know one of them. That's Ray Hinkle on the black."

"I never heard of him," Claude said.

"He's a back-shooter," Frank explained. "Shoots from hiding. And he's a crack shot. The other three must be real trash to be riding with him. Very few people will have anything to do with Ray."

"Where does he live?"

"No one knows for sure. I haven't seen him in several years. I thought maybe someone had done the world a service and shot him."

The four men reined up in the road and stared at the men, women, and children. Ray stared at Frank for a moment, then said, "Morgan. What are you doin' here?"

"I live here, Hinkle."

"Morgan!" one of the riders blurted out. "Frank Morgan?"

"You takin' up farmin' now, Morgan?" Hinkle asked, a sarcastic tone to the question.

"Maybe."

"They's money on your head, Morgan," another of the quartet said.

"So I hear," Frank replied, rolling a cigarette. "Somebody back East wants me dead. You want to try to collect it?"

"I might."

Hinkle and the two other men quickly backed their horses away from the mouthy gunman.

"We're out of this, Morgan," one of the men with Hinkle said. "We been hired on at the Diamond. We wasn't hired to fight you."

"What's your name?" Frank asked the man who thought he might like to collect the bounty money.

"Harris. Funny thing, Morgan. I heard it was your own son that wanted you dead."

"You can hear all sorts of things, Harris."

"You must have been a real sorry-assed father to your boy, Morgan. For him to hate you that much."

Frank said nothing. He had already been in communication with Conrad, his son back East, through his attorneys. The young man had heard of the money being offered for Frank's death, but claimed that he personally had nothing to do with it. Private detectives were working to try to find the man, or men, who had put up the money.

Frank had never believed that Conrad had been involved in any way.

Harris slowly swung down from the saddle, never taking his eyes off Frank and being careful to keep the horse between them.

Harris has been over the hill and across the river, Frank thought. *He's damn sure no pilgrim.*

Harris stepped away from the horse to face Frank, his right hand hovering close to the butt of his pistol.

Claude and the newly arrived settlers moved swiftly out of the way.

"Don't be a fool, Harris," Frank told him. "Even if you got lucky and killed me, you'd never collect the money."

"Why's that?"

"It's against the law to put a bounty on a man's head. Besides, you don't know who put up the money, or even if it's real." Frank knew what was coming next, and he wasn't disappointed.

"That don't make no never mind to me, Morgan. I'll be the man who killed Frank Morgan. I'll be able to name my price after that."

"Don't be a fool, Harris," one of the men he rode in with said. "Back off, man."

"Shut up, Carter," Harris said without taking his eyes off of Frank. "I can take him."

Frank waited.

"You better listen to Carter, Harris," the remaining gunslick said. "We're come a long ways for you to die 'fore you collect your first paycheck."

"Shut up, Brown," Harris told him. "I done told you all I can take Morgan. And I will."

"This is crazy," one of the young settlers said. "You men stop this. Why are you fighting?"

"Ask Harris," Frank said.

"'Cause we is who we is," Harris said.

"Well . . . that makes no sense at all to me," the farmer replied.

"It don't have to," Harris said. "It makes sense to me. Now shut your mouth up."

"Be quiet, Mosby," Claude told the young farmer. "Stay out of this."

"Draw, Morgan!" Harris said.

"It's your play," Frank told the man. "If you're in such a hurry to die, you start it."

"You a damn coward!" Harris yelled.

Frank said nothing.

"I'm tellin' you to drag iron, Morgan!" Harris said, the sweat suddenly popping out on his face.

"After you, Harris," Frank said softly.

"You nothin' but a yeller dog!" Harris said.

Frank smiled.

"I want to take the children away from here," a woman spoke. "I don't want them to see this."

"Then get your damn brats clear," Harris said. "Go on, do it."

The woman herded the kids away, behind a wagon, the children protesting all the way.

"I want to watch," one young boy said.

"No. Be quiet," the woman admonished him.

"Now then, Morgan," Harris said. "You better hook that hog leg. I'm fixin' to kill you."

"I told you, Harris, it's your play. I won't pull on you."

"Damn you, Morgan!" The sweat was really popping out on Harris's face.

Frank stood very still, very calm. His eyes never left Harris. Nothing else mattered. Frank did not hear dogs barking or birds singing. His heart thudded slow and steady in his chest. He waited.

"I'll kill you, Morgan!" Harris yelled, and grabbed for his gun.

Frank's draw was cat-quick and his shot was deadly accurate. The .45-caliber slug hit Harris in the chest. Harris's boots flew out from under him and he landed flat on his back, dead.

"Jesus God!" a farmer behind and to one side of Frank whispered. "I never even seen the draw."

"Harris never even got his pistol clear of leather," another farmer said.

"I wanna see!" a boy hollered from behind the wagon.

"Hush!" a woman told him.

"Is that man dead?" a farmer's wife asked.

"Dead as a rock," her husband replied.

"Lord have mercy," the woman said.

Frank walked over to where Harris lay on the ground and

looked down at him. Then, without a word, he holstered his Peacemaker and walked back to the group of farm families.

"We'll bury him, Frank," Hinkle said. "And he was wrong. He had no call to challenge you."

Frank nodded, and watched as Harris's body was laid across his saddle and tied down.

"We'll be goin' now, Frank," Hinkle said. "I hope we don't run into you durin' this little dispute over land."

"I hope so too, Hinkle," Frank said.

Frank waited a few minutes, giving Hinkle, Carter, and Brown time to get gone, then turned to Claude. "We best be getting back. It's a long ride to your place."

"That's a beautiful horse, Mr. Morgan," a girl of about ten said, looking at Stormy. "What kind of horse is that? I ain't never seen one like it."

"It's an Appaloosa, honey. The Nez Percé Indians raise them."

"He's beautiful."

Frank looked at the group of farm families. "You folks be watchful and go armed. When you go into town for supplies, go in a group. I'll check back with you in a few days."

"Thank you, Mr. Morgan," a woman said. "And we're glad you're on our side."

"Yes, I guess I've crossed the line now," Frank replied. He stepped into the saddle and lifted the reins. "See y'all."

Back at his house, Frank stabled, rubbed down, and fed Stormy. Then he fed Dog. That done, he sat down on the bench by the front door and relaxed. He wasn't hungry and gave no thought to supper. He felt no emotion about the killing of the hired gun Harris. Harris had bought into the game and lost. No one forced him to do so.

Frank was very sorry the women and kids had to be there. But that was something entirely beyond his control.

With a sigh, he stood up and went into the house, Dog padding along with him. He stoked up the kitchen stove and put on water for coffee. He lit the lamps in the living area, for dusk was fast approaching. The coffee made, Frank sugared his and took the steaming cup outside, once more sitting on the bench, Dog on the ground beside him.

Frank drank his coffee as the night began to slowly settle around him. Several riders passed by, slowing to a walk as they approached Frank's place, but not stopping. Frank sat on the bench and watched the dark shapes of the horses and riders until they were out of sight. Then he fixed another cup of coffee and rolled himself a smoke.

A lone horseman came up the road, coming from the direction of the settlement. The horseman reined up in front of the house.

"Frank?" a familiar voice called.

"Right here," Frank said. "Who am I talking to?"

"Dave Moore. We met in the saloon, remember?"

"I remember. What's on your mind?"

"I'm pullin' out, Frank. I ain't gonna have no part in killin' women and kids."

"Is it getting down to the wire, Dave?"

"Real soon."

"You know anything about farming, Dave?"

"Sure. Hell, I was raised on a farm. Why do you ask?"

A smile formed on Frank's lips. "Tell you what. Why don't you spend the night here? You can bunk in the barn. Lots of hay in the loft. Hell, you don't want to be ridin' at night. Nearest town is miles away. Be dawn 'fore you got there. We can talk some and I'll tell you what I got on my mind. I think you'll go for it."

Eight

Dave was laughing so hard, Frank thought he might bust the buttons on his shirt. The gunhand finally wiped his eyes and nodded his head in agreement with Frank's suggestion.

"Hell, why not, Frank? I don't like neither one of those damn snooty ranchers. I might actually like farmin'. Yeah, by God! Gettin' back to the land sounds good to me."

"I had a hunch it would, Dave."

"You got a piece of property in mind?"

"Two sections just up the road. Family pulled out last year, Claude told me. No one's filed on it."

"Has it got a house on it?"

"Yes. But it's not completed yet. Needs a little work to get it ready."

"I can do that. My daddy was a fine carpenter."

"And Claude told me the man left some equipment behind too."

"Sounds better and better, Frank. Come the mornin', we'll ride over and take a look. If it's anything at all like you was told, I'll take me a ride over to the county seat and file on it."

"Sounds good to me. Now then, how about some coffee?"

"I could do with a taste." Dave chuckled. "Imagine me a *farmer!*"

* * *

"He did *what?*" Grant Perkins yelled at Jim Knight, his foreman.

Jim repeated what he'd heard in the saloon.

Grant began cussing, and didn't stop until he was out of breath.

"You through now?" Jim asked calmly.

"Yes, goddamnit, I'm through."

"Good. Grant, why get so upset about one man filing on farmland?"

"Because he came into this area to work for us."

"So did Harris, but he got stupid and tried to take Frank Morgan. So what?"

"I didn't like Dave Moore first time I laid eyes on him," Perkins muttered. "Jim, get my horse saddled, will you? I'm goin' to ride over and have me a talk with Rogers. It's time for us to make a move."

"Seems like a move has already been made, Grant. The Norton family is dead, ain't they?"

"I didn't have a damn thing to do with that, Jim. But by God, I'm glad it was done."

"Killing women and kids, Grant?" Jim asked softly.

"If it has to be that way, yes. This land belongs to me and Mark Rogers. All of it."

Jim's eyes narrowed momentarily and he nodded his head. "I'll get your horse saddled, Grant."

Frank and Claude met with the rest of the farm families homesteading in the long series of rich fertile valleys. Claude deliberately left Paul Adams for the last one on the list.

"I wondered when you were going to get around to me, Claude," Paul said. "Have a seat over there in the shade." He called to one of his boys. "Bring us a pot of coffee."

"Right away, Pa."

The men sat on cane-bottomed chairs in the side yard,

under the shade of a towering old tree. Paul looked at Frank. "So you're going to play at being a farmer now, right, Morgan?"

"I filed on some land, yes, *Adams*."

The rich farmer gave Frank a sharp look at the use of his last name. Then he slowly smiled. "You plan to really farm it, Frank?"

"I've arranged for Claude and Dan Jones to farm it on shares. I'm going to help Dave Moore plant his crop. Starting tomorrow."

Adams sighed. "So the gunman is really going to farm."

"He was raised on a farm, in the Midwest, I think. The land is in his blood."

"But will he stick with it, or will the pull of adventure be too strong?"

"Only time will tell."

"I suppose so."

"We're getting the farmers organized, Paul," Claude said.

"So I hear. It seems that Frank Morgan has done in one day what I was unable to do over the course of several years." He looked at Frank. "You must be a real wonder-worker, Mr. Morgan." It was said with no small amount of sarcasm.

"No," Frank said, getting very weary of Paul Adams's attitude of superiority. "I just suggest things that the farmers should do. Not order them to do it."

"I was an officer in the Union army in the War Between the States, Mr. Morgan. I have found that people need someone to take charge."

"I was an officer in the Confederate army during the War of Northern Aggression, Mr. Adams," Frank came right back. "My men did what they were ordered to do because they respected me."

"Are you saying I have no respect?" Paul demanded, his face getting red from anger.

"Not at all. What I'm saying is there is a right way and a wrong way to do things."

"Now, gentlemen," Claude said.

"Claude's right," Frank said. "Let's just leave it at you don't like me and I don't like you, Adams. But for the good of all, we'll work together."

"I can do that," Paul said gruffly.

"Good," Frank replied. Then he smiled. "Yonder comes your boy with the coffee. We'll have a toast to working together and staying alive."

A very small smile crossed Paul's lips. "I'll sure drink to that."

Long after Grant Perkins had left the ranch house, Mark Rogers sat in the study alone, drinking coffee and brooding over the situation. He occasionally scowled at the thought of Frank Morgan buying farmland and taking sides with the sodbusters. Then that damned hired gun, Dave Moore, had to go filing on land.

"The country's going to hell," Rogers said. "The next thing you know there'll be a damn church and then a schoolhouse for all the squatters' brats."

"What are you mumbling about, Mark?" his new foreman, Pat Sully, asked, stepping into the office. Rogers had fired his old foreman after the man refused to burn down any more homes of farmers.

"Pour us a drink, Pat," Mark said, "and have a seat. We've got some war plans to make."

"'Bout damn time," the foreman said, pouring the whiskey. "Things is gettin' out of hand with them sodbusters."

"Frank Morgan is the man who's gettin' them all together. I want him dead."

"We got some boys on the payroll who'll be more'n happy to oblige you."

"I want the squatters to see that Frank Morgan is not bulletproof. I want him shot down like a mangy coyote . . . in front of the squatters. Who is the best gunhand on the payroll?"

"Oh . . . Paco Morales, Pete Dancer, Steve Harlon. Take your pick."

"Harlon still bunkin' in town?"

"Yes. He don't like associatin' with normal people. He insists on a bath every day. Strange man."

"That's gonna make him sick one of these days. All that soap ain't good for a body. No . . . not Harlon. I hear tell him and Morgan is sort of friends."

"I'd call on Paco then. Oh, by the way. The news in town is that when Moore rode into the country seat to file on his land, Frank had him file on a couple of acres to build a church house and a school."

Mark threw his empty shot glass across the room into the cold fireplace. "Son of a bitch!" he shouted. "I knowed that was comin'."

"It's gonna be built just outside of town, west side. Joe Wallace done ordered all the materials."

"Call Paco in. He's got a job to do."

The beginning of the end of the dynasty of the GP and the Diamond ranches came in the form of Reverend Richard Carmondy and his sister, Lydia. Richard was the new preacher and Lydia was the settlement's new schoolteacher.

"I wonder how the central church committee back East heard of this place," Pat Roykin said.

Frank was standing with a group of farmers in the general store when Roykin spoke.

Frank said nothing, only smiled briefly. Without the farmers' knowledge, he had sent a number of wires out from the county seat.

"However they learned, it's a godsend," Dick Wilson said. "Now we have a real church and schoolhouse."

"And the central committee back East is paying their salary for a couple of years," Dan Jones said. "This town is on the move, folks. Don't you agree, Mr. Morgan?"

"Wouldn't surprise me a bit if several businesses didn't start up soon," Frank replied.

"Really?" Callie Hastings said. "Oh, that would be wonderful. I wonder what sort of businesses."

Frank shrugged at that. "I wouldn't know. I reckon we'll just have to wait and see."

"Earl Martin, the blacksmith from over at the county seat, is coming in to set up a place," Joe Wallace said. "Least that's what I heard."

"I know Earl," Tom Johnson said. "His wife, Mary, sings and plays the piano at the Methodist church. She's really good too."

"And we're gettin' a weekly stage run too," John Platt said. "They're gonna use my livery for team changes."

"We're goin' to be a real town!" Bob Frazier said.

"Who's that riding up?" Wilson questioned, gazing toward the edge of town.

Frank knew at first glance. "Paco Morales."

"Wonder what he wants," Claude said.

"Me," Frank said.

Nine

Paco reined up in front of the saloon and slowly dismounted. He turned to face Frank, standing on the boardwalk in front of the general store. Paco smiled. "Frank," he said politely.

"Paco," Frank said, returning the greeting.

"Is it a good day, Frank?"

"Seems to be."

"For dying?"

"Are you planing on dying this day, Paco?"

Paco laughed. "Oh, no, Frank. Not me. You."

Frank smiled at him. "I have no plans to die this day."

"Plans can change."

"Did Mark Rogers pick you to brace me, Paco?"

"You might say that."

"Did he pay you yet?"

"Why would you ask that?"

"Because I want you to have enough money in your pockets to bury you."

Paco got a good laugh out of that. "You've very amusing, Frank. I always enjoyed your sense of humor."

"Ride out of here, Paco. Ride out and live a long life."

"Ah, Frank. You know I can't do that."

"Why?"

"I took the man's money." He frowned. "No matter what people say about me, I am not a thief."

"I never said you were."

"But you want me to become one."

"Throw Rogers's money on the ground, Paco. That way your honor is secure."

"Then I would be a liar."

"I don't see it that way."

Paco shrugged his shoulders. "It really makes no difference to me how you see it, Frank."

"Claude," Frank said, without taking his eyes off of Paco, "get everyone out of the way."

Upon hearing those words, Paco walked to the center of the wide street. "All this could be avoided, Frank."

"Oh?"

"Yes. You get on your horse and ride out of this area."

"Can't do that, Paco."

"Won't do it," Paco corrected.

"This is my home, Paco. I live here."

"You live nowhere on a permanent basis, Frank. That's why you are known as The Drifter."

"Maybe I've changed, Paco. People do change, you know."

Paco laughed at that. "Not you, Frank. You are like that man in the fairy tale. That Robin Hood person."

"That's quite a compliment."

"It was not meant to be such. Enough talk, Frank. It is time for you and me to settle this."

A small crowd had gathered, the crowd making up the entire population of the settlement.

"It's your play, Paco."

"It's your life, Frank."

"Works both ways," Frank reminded the man.

"I suppose that is true. Really, though, it is a pity."

"Dying usually is."

"Oh, not that," Paco said. "What I meant is that the legend of The Drifter ends here."

"Perhaps not, Paco. Have you given that any thought?"

"Men like you and me, Frank, we cannot entertain such thoughts. We have to believe our time will never end."

"When I am too old to live by the gun, Paco, I will hang mine up. Ride out of here. Go back home and live a long life. Mark Rogers is not worth dying for."

"I could say the same for your little piece of land."

"Then I suppose we have nothing else to talk about, Paco."

"It would seem so."

"You wanted this showdown, Paco. It's your play."

Out of the corner of his eye, Frank was aware of a buggy stopping just at the edge of the short street. A man and a woman.

"Reverend Carmondy and his sister, Lydia," Frank heard someone in the crowd say.

"They sure picked a hell of a time to ride into town," another farmer replied.

"It's been interesting having your acquaintance, Frank," Paco said. "I will certainly attend your funeral services to show my respect."

Frank said nothing. His cold pale eyes bored into the gunfighter's black eyes. The men were about forty feet apart, Frank standing on the edge of the boardwalk, Paco in the street.

The buggy rolled closer.

Claude stepped off the boardwalk and walked into the street, halting the buggy. "Don't come any closer, Reverend," Frank heard the farmer say. "There's about to be some gunplay."

"Some cowboys crazed by strong drink, I'm sure," Lydia said. "How dreadful."

"No, ma'am," Claude said. "That's the Mexican gunfighter, Paco Morales, in the street, facin' Frank Morgan yonder on the boardwalk."

"That man is really Frank Morgan?" Reverend Carmondy asked.

"Yes, sir," Claude replied.

"Heavens!" Lydia said, fanning herself with a little hanky.

"This is terribly barbaric," Reverend Carmondy said. "Can't you stop this, sir?"

"No, sir, I can't," Claude told him.

"Paco, honey," a soiled dove called from an open window on the second floor of the saloon/hotel.

"Not now, Alice," Paco said. "I'll be with you in just a few minutes."

"Hurry, Paco," Alice called.

"She's going to have a long wait, Paco," Frank said. "Unless she plans to crawl into the pine box with you."

Paco smiled. "You are being foolish."

"I'm tired of this, Paco. Make your play."

The smile faded from the Mexican's face. Frank could sense that Paco was ready to hook and draw. Steve Harlon had stepped out of the hotel to stand on the boardwalk, far out of the line of fire. He stood watching with a look of interest on his face. And well he should be interested, for the odds were very good that he too would soon face Frank Morgan.

"Somebody should stop those men," Reverend Carmondy said.

"I wouldn't get in their way for no amount of money," Hugh Watson said.

"Oh, I simply can't continue to watch this!" Lydia said. But she made no attempt to avert her eyes.

"Are you going to stand there in the road like a potted plant, Paco?" Frank taunted the man. "Or make your play?"

"You must be in a hurry to die," Paco replied.

Frank smiled, for he detected a slight note of nervousness in the man's voice.

Frank waited on the boardwalk.

Paco's hand suddenly twitched and Frank pulled iron. As fast as a rattler's strike Frank pulled, cocked, and fired his Peacemaker—faster than the human eye could follow.

The muzzle of Paco's Colt had just cleared leather when he felt a hard blow in his chest. Paco's boots flew out from under him and he found himself on his back, in the middle of the street, looking up into a clear blue western sky.

"Sweet Mother of Jesus," someone in the crowd whispered.

"No," Paco said. "This cannot be. No man can match my speed. No one can best me."

"I must go to that man," Reverend Carmondy shouted, clucking at his horse. "He needs spiritual comfort in his hour of need."

"What he needs is a damn good doctor," the soiled dove hanging out of the second-story window shouted.

"You watch your mouth!" Lydia shouted at the woman.

The soiled dove told Lydia where to stick her comment.

"I beg your pardon!" Lydia shouted as her brother was getting out of the buggy.

The painted lady of the evening repeated her suggestion, adding, "And do it sideways, sister."

"Well . . ." Lydia huffed. "I never!"

"Well, in that case you ought to try it, lady," the soiled dove called. "Hell, you might like it."

Frank stepped off the boardwalk and walked over to where Paco lay. Reverend Carmondy was saying a short prayer over the dying Mexican. He looked up at Frank.

"You should be ashamed of yourself!" the preacher said.

"Why?" Frank asked.

"You've critically wounded this man!"

"No, I haven't," Frank said. "Take another look at him. He isn't wounded. He's *dead!*"

The body of the Mexican gunhand was hauled off to the local undertaker's, where it would be displayed on the boardwalk in an upright coffin for a couple of days until it made its final trip to the nearby cemetery. The crowd had resumed their talking and shopping at the general store. Frank was sitting at a table in the saloon, having a drink.

Steve Harlon walked in and up to Frank's table. Frank waved him to a chair and Steve sat down.

"You're pretty good, Drifter," Steve said. "But I think I can take you."

Frank smiled at that. "Want a drink, Steve?"

"The barkeep knows what I want. He's making a fresh pot of coffee. My comment doesn't worry you, Frank?"

"About you taking me? No. Not at all."

"You're very sure of yourself, aren't you?"

"I suppose so."

A pot of coffee and two cups were placed on the table, and the bartender quickly backed away, leaving the two men alone.

"Paco was sure of himself too," Steve said.

"Paco didn't make a study of his opponents."

"And you have done that?"

"Oh, yes."

"You're studied me?"

"Indeed I have."

"And you think you're better?"

"I know I am."

"You are a very arrogant man, Drifter. Either that or you're playing mind games with me."

"Up to you to decide which, Steve."

Steve poured a cup of coffee. A look of irritation passed over his face when he discovered there was no sugar bowl. He softly cursed.

Frank waved at the barkeep, making a spooning and stirring gesture. The barkeep nodded his head.

"Settle down, Steve. Sweetener's on the way."

"I like sugar in my coffee when I can get it," Steve said. "It's simply one of life's little pleasures."

A group of farmers entered the saloon and lined up at the bar, ordering drinks. Steve glanced over at them.

"Sodbusters," he said. "Willing to die for a few acres of land. I don't understand them."

"The backbone of this nation, Steve," Frank told him.

"So I've heard. Why don't they stay east of the Mississippi River and let the cattlemen have the land west of the river?"

"There's land aplenty for everybody out here, Steve. It's just a matter of working together and managing it."

"Sodbusters are a bother, Frank. I don't like them. I don't like the fences they're always stringing."

"You'd better get used to it. The farmers are here to stay in the West."

Steve turned his hard eyes to Frank. The two fast guns locked glances. "Not in this area, Frank."

"Yes, Steve. In this area."

"I'm sorry to hear that, Frank. That makes us enemies."

"Doesn't have to," Frank countered. "You could always ride on out of here."

Steve picked up his coffee cup and pushed back his chair. "You can keep the pot here, Frank. I know how you like your coffee. I'll just get me a place at another table."

"Don't you like my company, Steve?"

"You're beginning to stink like pig shit, Frank. I just never did like that smell."

Frank did not take offense. Instead, he startled Steve by laughing out loud.

"Something funny about pig shit, Frank?"

"You eat bacon, Steve?"

"You go to hell, Drifter!" Steve said. He turned his back to Frank and stalked off to a table across the room.

Frank watched him walk away. He knew Steve was not looking for gunplay this day. It was not yet time for that. But it would come. Soon enough.

Ten

"When you've finished your coffee, I want you to meet someone, Frank," Claude said, walking over to Frank's table.

"The preacher and his sister?" Frank said.

"How did you know that?"

"They're the only two people in town that I *haven't* met," Frank replied with a smile.

"Oh. Sure. That's right. They're really nice people."

"I don't believe they have much use for me, Claude. Maybe we'd better put off this meeting."

"They just got into this area a few months ago. They're from back East, you know."

"Boston probably."

"I think that's right, Frank. You're a good guesser."

"You really want me to meet them now, Claude?"

"Why not?"

"They just saw me kill a man. I doubt if they've ever seen anything like that. Not if they're from overcivilized Boston."

"Overcivilized?"

Frank waved a big callused hand. "Forget I said that, Claude. All right, I'll meet them. Let me have another cup of coffee and a smoke, okay?"

"Sure. I'll have a cup with you, if you don't mind."

Frank signaled the barkeep for another cup.

"You think Mark Rogers sent that gunman into town to kill you?" Claude asked.

"Sure. Probably wanted him to kill me in front of you folks. Send a message."

Claude smiled. "That's what I told Reverend Carmondy and his sister. I guessed right on that one."

"You're a pretty good guesser yourself. Drink your coffee and let's go meet the Boston folks."

"I was informed that you really are the very famous pistol shooter, Mr. Morgan," Reverend Carmondy said, after reluctantly shaking Frank's hand.

"I suppose that's true, Preacher."

"And I was also just informed that the man you dispatched to his Maker was in the employ of a local rancher who is determined to drive the farmers off their land."

"That is true," Frank replied.

"I have never before witnessed such a dreadful spectacle," Lydia said. "Such things simply aren't done in a civilized part of the country." Again she fanned herself with the little hanky.

"Well . . . give us time, ma'am," Frank told her, eyeing the lady. Lydia was a truly beautiful woman. Light brown hair, great figure, heart-shaped face, dark green eyes. "We're still in the growing stages out here. However, you'd better brace yourself, for you're sure to see more killing before this issue between the ranchers and the farmers is settled."

"Perhaps I could speak to the ranchers," Reverend Carmondy suggested.

"Personally, I think you'd be wasting your time," Frank said. "But . . . it's a free country."

"I shall go with you, brother," Lydia said.

John Platt joined the small group. "The girls over to the saloon want to know if Reverend Carmondy would say a word or two at Paco's buryin'. They took up a collection to pay you for your services."

"There will be no charge for it," Carmondy replied. "Certainly I will conduct the services."

"I'll tell the girls," John said.

"Will the, ah, girls be there?" Lydia asked.

"With all their feathers, frills, and paint," John replied with a grin. "They might even sing a song in Paco's memory."

"Oh," Lydia said. "He was a close friend of theirs?"

"He was a damn good customer is what he was."

"Oh, my," Lydia replied.

"That's what the girls used to holler about five minutes after Paco got to their room. But they hollered it with a lot more enthusiasm."

"I see," Lydia said, her face flushing a bright scarlet.

"I doubt it, ma'am," John told her with a chuckle. "I really doubt it. See you good folks later."

Paco Morales was buried without fanfare the next day. No one from either the GP or the Diamond ranches was in attendance. Reverend Carmondy, his sister, Lydia, the grave digger, and four whores attended the services.

"What the hell am I supposed to do with Paco's horse and gear?" John Platt asked Frank later that afternoon.

"If no one shows up to claim them, and I doubt if anyone will, they're yours," Frank told him.

"Fine animal," John said. "And the saddle is inlaid with silver. Hell with it. Let's go have a drink."

"That might not be a good idea," Frank said. "I saw Victor Perkins ride into town and go into the saloon about half an hour ago."

"Oh, he's no bother. He'll drink a bottle of whiskey, then go upstairs with one of the women."

"I don't want to have to put lead into a drunk."

"You won't. Vic is no gunhand. He fancies himself a lover, not a fighter."

Vic was propped up at the bar, drinking alone, when John and Frank walked into the saloon. Vic glanced at them, nodded his head in greeting, then turned his attention back to the booze.

Frank noticed immediately that the young man was not wearing a gun.

John had followed Frank's eyes. "He seldom packs iron," the liveryman said. "Can't hit the side of a large barn when he does. He's a big disappointment to his dad. His sister, Lucy, now, that's another story. She's a hellion. And a crack shot. Folks tend to fight shy of her. She's got a bad temper and a foul mouth."

"I've known a few like her."

The men took seats as far from the bar as they could. John ordered a beer and Frank requested coffee.

"I seen all the lumber roll into town this morning," John said. "We'll have us a school and a church house 'fore long."

"You a churchgoin' man, John?"

"Not so's you'd notice. You?"

Frank shook his head. "No. But I certainly believe in a higher power, and I suspect I'm going to be judged harshly when my time comes. I think perhaps church is too late for me."

"Preachers would argue that with you, Frank. But I know what you're sayin'. For you to take off your guns now would be the same as signin' your own death warrant. You wouldn't last a week."

That statement flung Frank back into bitter memories. He slowly nodded his head. "I've tried to explain that to a couple of women over the years."

"And they didn't buy it, did they?"

"No, they didn't."

"Bless their hearts, women see things different from a man."

"Come on, now, Vic, baby," a woman called from the landing on the second floor.

"In a few minutes, Sally," Vic said without turning from the bar.

"Now, baby," Sally insisted. "You know you don't do me no good after you've had too much to drink."

Vic tossed back what was left in his glass. "You're right. I'm comin' up."

John and Frank sat in silence and watched the young man stagger across the floor and make his way up the stairs.

"He's drunk already," John said. "He wasn't always that way. I 'member him as a young'un. He was a good boy. I don't know what happened to him. But he sure changed."

"Heads up, Frank," the barkeep called. "Trouble coming in."

Frank looked at the batwings just as they were pushed open. Rod Harley stepped into the saloon. The man, dressed all in black, stared at Frank for a few seconds, then walked over to the bar, deliberately putting his back to Frank and John.

"Beer," he told the barkeep.

"There goin' to be trouble here?" John whispered the question.

"Probably. I guess the ranchers are pulling out all the stops now. Paco's not yet cold in the ground and they're sending in another gun to try and nail me."

"Couple of sodbusters walkin' across the street, headin' this way. They picked a hell of a time to get thirsty. You know that feller all dressed in black, Frank?"

"I've heard of him. Rod Harley."

"He quick on the shoot?"

"So I'm told."

Burl Hastings and Van Calen walked into the saloon and up to the long bar. Rod Harley glanced at the pair and grimaced in distaste.

"Smells like hog crap in here," the gunman said.

The farmers tensed, but other than that made no sign they had heard anything.

"Don't you pig farmers ever take a bath?" Rod asked, turning to look directly at the pair.

"We're not looking for trouble," Van said.

Rod laughed at that. "No, of course not. You hide behind Frank Morgan and think he's going to protect you."

"That's a damn lie," Burl said, his face reddening.

"You callin' me a liar, sodbuster?" Rod asked.

"I'm saying that we haven't hired anyone to protect us," Burl replied. "We can fight our own battles."

"Then why don't you get a gun and face me?" Rod asked with a sneer.

"Because they're not gunslicks," John said.

Rod cut his eyes, looking at the liveryman. "Who asked you to stick your lip into this, old-timer?"

"I don't need no one's permission to speak," John said.

"You packin' iron, old-timer?" Rod questioned.

"No, he isn't," Frank said, standing up. "But I am."

Rod smiled at that. "Took you long enough to make up your mind, Drifter."

"Here I am, Rod. Now what the hell are you going to do about it?"

Rod turned to fully face Frank. "Kill you," he said simply. "You got it to do. You ready?"

"Yeah." Rod snaked his .45 from leather.

Eleven

Frank's shot hit Rod in the belly and drove him back against the bar. Rod triggered off a round that hit the coffeepot on the table and sent hot liquid all over John. Frank put another round into the man dressed all in black, but still Rod refused to go down. Rod fired again, the slug knocking a hole in the ceiling.

"Good God!" a woman yelled from the second floor. "What the hell's goin' on down there?"

Rod cussed Frank and cocked and fired again, his bullet going wild and up into the ceiling once again.

"Goddamnit!" a woman screamed. "It was just gettin' good."

Frank put a third slug into Rod, and this time the gunman sank to his knees, his pistol dropping from a numb hand to clatter on the floor. Rod clawed for his second six-gun and managed to drag it out of leather. But he couldn't find the strength to cock it.

"Give it up, Rod," Frank urged.

"Hell with you, Drifter," Rod gasped. "I'm gonna kill you." He tried to lift his pistol, but could not. Blood leaked from Rod's mouth and he dropped his pistol to the floor.

Frank walked the short distance to the man and kicked both pistols away. He looked down at Rod. The man was leaking blood out of the bullet holes in his belly and chest and blood was dripping from his mouth.

"Damn you to hell, Drifter!" Rod gasped.

"It was all your play, Rod," Frank told him.

Rod closed his eyes and shivered in pain. "Hurts."

"Who sent you, Rod?"

"Perkins. They's more guns comin', Drifter. One of them will get you. You can't live . . . through this."

"You got kin, Rod?"

"No. No one who gives a damn, that is."

"I'll see you get planted proper."

"Have that preacher say a few nice words over me, Drifter."

"All right."

"I'll see you in hell, Drifter."

Frank watched in silence as Rod Harley closed his eyes for the last time.

The man gasped once, and died.

"Wahoo!" Sally yelled from the second floor. "Now you got it, baby. Stay with it. Ride 'em, cowboy!"

Reverend Carmondy conducted the services for Rod Harley, with only Frank, Lydia, and the grave diggers in attendance.

"Very quaint custom here in the Wild West," Reverend Carmondy remarked. "You kill a man, then attend his services."

"I guess I owe that much to Rod," Frank replied.

"It might have been you in the ground this day," Lydia said.

"The only way that would happen is if my pistol misfired."

"You're very sure of yourself, aren't you, Mr. Morgan?" she asked coldly.

"I have to be, Miss Lydia. I've got too many men gunning for me."

The three of them walked toward the edge of the graveyard. Lydia gestured toward four fresh graves. "Did you dispatch those people too, Mr. Morgan?"

"No, ma'am. Those are the graves of the Norton family. Father, mother, and sons. Dick, Abby, Hubert, and Charles. They were killed by the ranchers."

"Oh," she said in a small voice. "I didn't know."

"Now you do."

"Yes. So I do. But when will it stop?"

"When both sides agree to sit down and talk and reach some kind of agreement."

"That doesn't seem to be such an insurmountable problem."

"You don't know how much the ranchers hate the farmers."

"I'm beginning to," she replied.

"It wouldn't surprise me a bit if they burned down the church, once it's built."

"You can't be serious!" Richard blurted. "Burn down a house of God? I never heard of such an atrocious act."

"We'll see," Frank said. He gathered up the reins and swung into the saddle. "You folks have a nice day."

Grant Perkins and Mark Rogers met in a line shack in the mountains. It was cold that high up, and a fire was set in the potbellied stove. Coffee was boiling.

"Now what?" Grant asked.

"We keep sending men against Frank Morgan," Mark replied.

"I got a better idea. Let's burn out the farmers."

Mark walked over to the stove, poured two cups of the strong brew, and sat back down at the beat-up old table. "Whatever. We have to do something. The sodbusters started building that damn church and schoolhouse today."

"We'll burn it first. Soon as they get the frame up, we'll burn it down."

"I want that damn Frank Morgan dead, though."

"As soon as we torch the church. He'll go on a rampage. Then we can ambush him."

Mark nodded his head. "That sounds good to me. Yeah. Ambush the son of a bitch. And I've got just the man for it."

"Who?"

"Ray Hinkle. He's supposed to be the best."

"Sounds good to me."

"What do you think about Frank Morgan?" Lydia was asked by Lucille Jones. The Carmondys were staying with the Joneses while the church/schoolhouse and their quarters were being built.

"I find him . . . well, rather attractive, in a rough-looking sort of way." Lydia looked around quickly to see if her brother had heard her reply. He had not.

Lucille smiled. "So do I, Lydia. He's also rather mysterious, don't you think?"

"Oh, yes. Where is his home?"

"Oh, he bought some land just outside of town."

"No, I mean his *real* home."

Lucille shook her head. "I don't know. I don't think he has one. But I've heard that he's a rich man."

"Rich? A wandering gunman is rich?"

"Yes. You know he's called The Drifter?"

"It fits him. A horse, a dog, and a gun. That's all he appears to have. And he's rich?"

"Yes, he is," Dan said, stepping into the kitchen of the home through the back door.

"Coffee, honey?" Lucille asked.

"Please." Dan smiled at his wife. "Any of that cake left?"

"I'll get you a piece."

"What is Mr. Carmondy doing?" Lydia asked.

"Sitting outside, reading the Bible." Dan sat down at the table.

"If Frank Morgan is a rich man," Lucille said, "why does he wander about the country?"

"I don't know," Dan replied, sugaring his coffee. "He's a strange man. Complex, I guess some would call him."

"That's a good description of him," Lydia agreed. "Yes. Complicated fits him well."

"All hell's about to break loose in this country," Frank said to Dog. He was sitting on a bench outside his house, enjoying the cool of the late afternoon, Dog on the ground by his side. "And we're right in the middle of it." Frank put a hand down on Dog's head, and the big cur stirred under his touch.

"The farmers think it's been rough so far," Frank continued. "But they ain't seen nothing yet. It's about to get nasty, I'm thinking."

Dog looked up at Frank.

"So, ol' boy, I want you to be extra careful. Don't leave this area." He smiled. "I just wish to hell you understood what I was saying." Frank looked into Dog's dark eyes. "Sometimes I think you really do. And I hope this is one of those times. 'Cause if one of those gunslicks hurts you . . . well, that would really rile me good."

Frank looked up as half a dozen mounted men rode past his place. The horses wore the Diamond brand. None of the men looked in Frank's direction.

"I hope no farmers are in town," Frank said as the Diamond crew rode past. He made a mental note to tell the farmers not to go into town alone and to always go armed. He'd told them that before, but a reminder wouldn't hurt.

"Real cowboys are getting scarce in this area," Frank muttered. "Either that, or the working hands are staying close to the bunkhouse."

Frank went into the house and fixed supper, including a big pot of coffee. Then he fed Dog. After he'd eaten, he took his cup of coffee outside, to once more sit on the bench in the cool of the night.

He didn't dwell much more on what the immediate future held in store. He felt he knew. The Diamond and GP spreads were going to pull out all the stops and the future looked bloody.

"And I'll be right in the middle of it," Frank said to the gathering darkness.

The silent darkness closed around him.

"So be it," Frank said.

He finished his coffee and went to bed.

Twelve

"Got two new businesses comin' in," John Platt said as Frank swung down from the saddle at the livery. Frank had not been to town for several days.

"Oh?"

"You bet. Got a ladies' shop comin' in. One of them that's spelt with two p's and an e on the end. A shop-pay, I think they call it. Really high-class. The other one is a leather and gun shop. Them carpenters workin' over yonder is from the county seat. The businesses will be ready in a couple of weeks. Frank, did you have anything to do with this?"

"No, I didn't, John. But the valleys are getting populated and that sort of news gets out."

"I bet you Perkins and Rogers is both fit to be tied 'bout this."

Frank had to smile at that. He felt John was right: The GP and Diamond owners were probably livid with rage.

"Don't you 'spect, Frank?" John pressed.

"I'm sure you're right."

"The new preacher and the schoolmarm is over to the general store visitin' with Joe and Theda. That Lydia Carmondy is a good-lookin' woman. She's ripe for pickin', I'd say."

"She's very attractive, for sure."

John grinned at Frank. "I figured you noticed."

"Be kind of hard not to notice."

"I'd say so. For a schoolmarm, she's a looker for shore."

John sobered, losing his grin. "Probably got a temper like a rattler, though. Woman that pretty's got to have some mean faults."

"I wouldn't know, John. Any Diamond or GP hands causing any trouble in the valleys?"

"Not a peep outta none of 'em. And that kinda worries me. I wonder what Rogers and Perkins is up to."

"Maybe nothing."

"Don't be believin' that, Frank. You can bet they're plottin' and a-schemin' somethin'."

"Probably." Frank cut his eyes to a lone rider just reaching the far edge of town. "And there he is."

John followed Frank's eyes. "Who is that?"

"Bobby Doolin."

"You've got to be kiddin! I heard he retired ten years ago and bought a ranch down in Mexico."

"He did. His gun isn't for hire; hasn't been in years."

"Then what the hell's he doin' here?"

"He's been looking for me for years. Takes five or six months off every year just to try to find me."

"I gather he don't like you much."

"You might say that."

"What the hell did you ever do to him?"

"I killed his brother."

"That might be enough to rile some people. I never heard nothin' 'bout his brother. Didn't know he had one."

"Jeff was a two-bit thief. Fancied himself a gunhand. He braced me down in Kansas ten years ago. 'Bout this time of year. I tried to talk him out of it, but he wouldn't listen. He pulled on me. He died hard. Took three, four days. Shortly after that, Bobby started tracking me. Now he's found me."

"Doolin was said to be fast."

"He is."

Doolin reined up in front of the livery and dismounted.

He looked at Frank and smiled. The smile was reminiscent of a snake's grin. "Hello, Morgan," Bobby said.

"Doolin," Frank replied.

"You're a hard man to find, Morgan."

"I stay on the move."

"I been lookin' for you for a long time."

"Now you've found me."

"I sure have. You didn't have no call to kill my brother. None at all."

"Your kid brother braced me, Doolin. Forced my hand. I didn't have any choice in the matter."

"You don't now neither."

Frank smiled grimly. "You know, that's what that little piss-ant brother of yours said just before he tried to draw on me an' got killed 'cause of his big mouth." Frank hesitated just a second, and then he added, "Guess lettin' your mouth override your ass runs in the family."

Richard and Lydia Carmondy stepped out of the general store with Joe Wallace. Joe pointed toward the livery, and the three of them stepped off the short boardwalk and began walking toward the stable.

"The preacher and his sister wanted a wheel on their buggy repaired," John said. "I fixed a loose rim. It's over yonder on the east side of the barn."

"Relax, old man," Bobby told John. "There ain't gonna be no trouble right off. I want me a bath and a hot meal first." Again he smiled at Frank. "Then I'll deal with you, Drifter. Where's the bathhouse?" he asked John.

"What passes for one is behind the hotel, which is on the second floor of the saloon. Ask the clerk."

"I'll do that. You take good care of my horse, old man."

"I take good care of all horses," John said. "No matter who they belong to."

"That's very funny. Just see to my horse, old timer." Bobby turned away and walked toward the saloon/hotel.

"Who is that man, Frank?" Joe asked.

"A retired gunfighter who came out of retirement."

"Working for the ranchers?"

"No. He's looking for me."

"A friend of yours?" Richard inquired.

"Not hardly. He came here to kill me."

"Good heavens!" Lydia said, fanning herself with a hanky.

Frank watched her, hoping the lady had brought an ample supply of little hankies, for she sure gave them a workout.

"An old grievance?" Joe asked.

"It happened many years ago, down in Kansas."

"It must have been something terrible for a man to carry a grudge for many years," Lydia said. She was giving her hanky a rest.

"I shot his brother," Frank told her.

The hanky went back into action. "My word! Was his brother a desperado?"

"He was a loud-mouth piece of crap."

The hanky became a blur as Lydia fanned herself. "You certainly do have a unique way with words, Mr. Morgan," Lydia said, her familiar blush reappearing on her face.

"I apologize if I offended you."

"Them carpenters is comin' right along," John said, hoping to lighten the conversation.

"Yes," Joe replied. "We're going to be a regular town very soon."

"Lot of riders coming," Frank said. "From the east and the west."

"Diamond and GP men," John said, shading his eyes with a hand. He looked at Frank. "I don't like this, Frank."

"What does this mean?" Lydia asked. "Why are all those men coming into town?"

"We'll soon know," Frank told her.

"Your buggy is repaired if you're ready to pull out,"

John told Reverend Carmondy. "And I'd shore suggest you and your sister do that. It's about to get real touchy here."

"No," Richard said. "I want to speak with the ranchers."

"I'll go with you," Lydia said. "A voice of peace must be heard." She looked at Frank. "Guns will not settle this matter. Violence begets violence."

"Well said, sister," her brother said.

"Suit yourselves," Frank replied.

The GP and Diamond riders, about twenty in all, swung in and reined up in front of the saloon.

"Rogers and Perkins and their foremen," John said, eyeing the men. "And a whole passel of gunhands."

"It's a show of force," Frank said. "I'm guessing they're hoping this will scare off some farmers."

"How childish," Lydia said.

"Them ain't children, missy," John told her. "Those guns they're packin' are real."

"Who is that young man standing next to Rogers?" Frank asked.

"That's his son, Mark Junior," John replied. "He fancies himself a hand with a gun."

"And he's wearing one too."

Frank and the liveryman watched as Richard and Lydia walked across the street and up to the ranchers and their hired guns. They conversation became very heated in only a few minutes.

"Somethin's gonna pop over yonder," John warned.

"It won't be a gun. The preacher's unarmed."

"Uh-huh," John said dubiously.

"I hope," Frank added.

Mark Rogers suddenly slapped the preacher, knocking the man to the dirt.

"Oh, hell!" John said.

"You beast!" Lydia screamed, kneeling down beside her brother.

Even from where he stood across the street, Frank could see that Richard had a bloody mouth.

"Shut up, you psalm-singing bitch!" Mark Junior shouted at Lydia.

"That does it," Frank said, and began his walk across the street.

Behind him, unknown to Frank, John reached for a Winchester and levered in a round.

"Morgan's comin'," a gunslick called out.

Across the street, Joe Wallace had picked up a rifle and levered a round into the chamber. His wife, Theda, did the same, stepping to the wide front doors of the business to stand by her husband.

Inside the saloon, the barkeep picked up a sawed-off double-barreled shotgun, checked the loads, and walked to the batwings.

"Stay out of this, Morgan," a Diamond gunhand warned as Frank approached. "This ain't your affair."

"The hell it isn't," Frank replied. "Are you all right, Richard?" he asked the preacher, who was getting to his feet, holding a bloody handkerchief to his busted mouth.

"I'll live," Richard said.

"You buy into this and you're dead, Morgan!" Rogers called. "You're outnumbered twenty to one."

"And so will you be," John Platt called from in front of his livery as he drew a bead on Rogers with his Winchester. "I'll put lead in you, Mark. I swear I will."

A look of surprise crossed the rancher's face. "You'd shoot me, John? After all we went through, you'd shoot *me?*"

"And I'll blow your head off, Grant," the barkeep said from the batwings. "I'll get you and several more before it's all over."

"And we'll get three or four more before the gun smoke is gone," Joe Wallace called from the front doors of the general store. "Bet on it."

The ranchers and their hired guns all took long looks around them. The three rifles were bad enough, but the double-barreled Greener less than twenty feet away would do terrible damage. And they all knew Frank Morgan would not go down easy. He'd kill three or four before he was down.

"Now just settle down, people," Grant Perkins said. "Don't let those fingers get itchy on the triggers."

Frank pointed at Mark Rogers. "You! Step out here and face me."

"I'm no fast gun, Morgan," the rancher said.

"Fists, Rogers. Just you and me."

Rogers smiled. "You're a fool, Morgan. I'll beat you to death." Mark stepped out of the crowd and let his gun belt fall.

Frank unbuckled his gun belt and looped it on a hitch rail. "You got it to do, big mouth," he told the rancher. He stepped closer and busted the man in the mouth with a hard right fist.

Thirteen

Rogers's head snapped back and he was staggered by the force of Frank's punch. He sleeved his face and saw the blood from his ruined nose soak into his shirt. Roaring like an enraged grizzly, Rogers shook his head and charged Frank. Frank sidestepped and hammered Rogers's kidneys with hard blows as he passed, making the big man grunt with pain and fury. Rogers spun around quicker than Frank was expecting and popped Frank on the jaw with a big fist swung from the hips. Frank shook his head and backed up. The man could punch.

"Kill him, Pa!" Mark Junior hollered.

Rogers bore in, both fists swinging, blood streaming from his face. Frank ducked and bobbed and weaved; he knew more than a little about boxing. The moving about seemed to infuriate the rancher, especially after a few of his wild punches hit nothing but air.

"Stand still and fight, damn you!" Rogers yelled, breathing hard through his mouth.

"Come get me, you big ape!" Frank taunted the man, dancing on his toes from side to side, grinning around a swollen lip.

Rogers snarled something incomprehensible and rushed Frank. Frank gave the man a left and right to the jaw that stunned the bigger man. Rogers backed up, dazed, and just for a few seconds dropped his guard.

Frank stepped up to the mark and hammered the

rancher. A right to the mouth, a left to the side of his head, a right to the belly, a left to the face. Rogers stumbled backward, grunting with each blow, blood pouring from his mouth and nose. The man was a barroom brawler, but he knew nothing of boxing.

Frank tripped the big man and punched him twice with short, sharp blows to the face as he went down. When Rogers just lay there, moaning and writhing in the dirt, Frank stepped back. "Get up and fight, you bastard," Frank told him. "Or would you rather fight women and little children like the cowardly bully you are?"

On the boardwalk, Bobby Doolin stood and smoked a cigar, watching the fight with interest. He knew from years of studying Frank Morgan that Morgan was an excellent fighter who seldom lost a bare-knuckle fight.

Rogers slowly got to his feet and stared at Frank from under cut and bleeding brows, his eyes almost swollen shut. He took a deep breath and charged Frank, hoping to get him in a bear hug and crush the life from him.

Frank nimbly sidestepped and kicked the big man on the side of his knee with the point of his boot. The knee made a sound like a tree limb snapping in half and Rogers went down, hollering in pain.

"Aw, hell, Pa!" Mark Junior said. "You can do better than this. Get up and whup his ass."

If the rancher even heard his son's words, he did not acknowledge them. He rose to his feet, swaying unsteadily, and lifted his fists slowly up in front of his face.

Frank had already started a punch from just about knee-high. The blow caught Rogers on the side of the jaw. Rogers's head exploded in a burst of light and pain as the blow connected. He fell back. Only the hitch rail saved him from hitting the dirt. The man clung desperately to the rail, his legs splayed out crookedly in front of him.

Frank stepped closer and went to work on the man's belly, pounding the man with lefts and rights. Rogers gasped with each blow and began to sink slowly to the ground. Frank stepped back, wound up a right fist, and blasted the rancher on the side of the jaw. Mark Rogers went down like a stone. This time he did not get up.

The rancher stayed on his hands and knees for a few seconds, watching the blood pour from his face to stain the dirt under him a bright red, and then he collapsed face-first into the bloody dirt.

"Aw, Pa," Mark Junior said. "Get your face outta the horse crap. That ain't dignified."

"Get him up and put some water on him," the Diamond foreman ordered. He looked at Frank. "This ain't over, Morgan. Not by a long shot."

"Anytime, anywhere," Frank panted in response.

Mark Rogers was dragged over to a horse trough and dunked in, face-first.

"Oh, my!" Lydia exclaimed breathlessly, giving her little hanky a workout. "That was . . . quite exhilarating."

"What the hell did she say?" a hired gun whispered to his partner.

"Damned if I know," his partner replied. "Sounds plumb nasty to me."

Mark Rogers pulled his head out of the trough. He coughed and sputtered for a moment, then tried to stand up. He could not. His wobbly legs simply would not support him. He sat down hard, clinging to the side of the horse trough.

"I'll kill you, Morgan," the rancher said through busted, bleeding, and swollen lips.

Frank ignored him and buckled on his gun belt. He looked up into the cold eyes of Bobby Doolin. Doolin smiled at him, then abruptly turned away and walked back into the saloon.

Frank glanced at the preacher. "Go over to the store and get you something to put on that busted mouth. Go on, Lydia. You go with him." Frank pushed through the crowd of gunslicks and entered the saloon, walking up to the bar. The bartender had put away his Greener.

"Give me a beer," Frank told him.

"Hell of a good fight, Frank," the barkeep said, pulling Frank's beer. "Rogers had it comin' to him."

"It isn't going to change anyone's mind."

"Probably not. But it was damn sure worth seein'."

Frank took a long swing of the cool beer. Tasted good. "Thanks for your backup," he told the barkeep.

"Don't mention it."

"You made some enemies today, for sure."

The bartender shrugged his shoulders. "They'll get over it." He smiled. "If they want a drink, that is. Nearest other waterin' hole is a two-day ride away."

Frank smiled, then grimaced at the pain in his swollen lip where Rogers had hit him. "In that case, I think they'll get over it quickly."

"You're pretty good with your fists, Morgan," Bobby Doolin said from the shadows of a rear table. "Remind me not to tangle with you bare knuckles."

Frank slowly turned around. "Fists or guns, Doolin, either way, you'll lose."

"You're a very confident man, Morgan."

Frank grinned at Doolin. "Some have even called me arrogant, Bobby, but I prefer to think of it as knowing the limitations of my enemies." He turned his back to the gunman and picked up his beer—with his left hand. He let his right hand hang down next to his hip.

"Your right hand sore and getting stiff, Frank?" Bobby questioned.

"My right hand is fine."

"That's good, Frank. I wouldn't want you to have to try and beat me with a bum hand."

"Worry about yourself, Bobby," Frank told him, watching the gunman's image in the big mirror behind the bar.

Bobby smiled. "Relax, Frank. I won't brace you today.

When I do, I want it to be on the up-and-up. Not like when you killed my little brother."

"That was as fair a fight as it could be, Doolin."

"He didn't have a chance, Morgan," Bobby said, his words tinged with bitterness. "My brother was no gunhand."

"Then he shouldn't have braced me."

"He had his pride."

Frank sighed and reached into his vest pocket for the makings. He rolled a cigarette and popped a match into flame.

"You understand pride, don't you, Frank?" Doolin pressed the issue.

Frank did not reply. He drank his beer and smoked.

"Answer me, Morgan," Doolin said, standing up.

Frank turned to face the man. He'd had enough of his jawing. "Don't talk to me about pride, Doolin. Your brother didn't have nothin' to be proud of. He was an asshole, just like you, an' it was that that got him killed. He thought 'cause his big brother was good with a gun, then he should be too, but he wasn't." Frank paused and stared into Doolin's eyes. "If you're ready to meet your Maker an' be judged, we can call out the band and dance right now," he growled.

Doolin tensed and then smiled, his body relaxing. "Naw, Frank. Not now. Later." He stepped away from the table and walked to the stairs without looking back. On the landing, he paused and looked at Frank. "When I kill you, Morgan, I want it to be out in the open. With lots of people watching. I want as many people as possible to see you fall." Doolin walked up the stairs to his room.

"That man's sure got a angry bee in his bonnet," the barkeep said.

"An old grudge is eating at him like a sickness," Frank replied. "He refuses to see but one side of the issue."

"You're gonna have to kill that man, Frank."

"I know." Frank spoke the words softly. "Or he's going to kill me."

"He's that good?"

"He's quick as a snake. Only the real good ones are still around. Most of the others have been long in the ground." Frank smiled grimly. "You don't get to be Doolin's age without knowing how, and when, to use a six-killer."

"How about the ones the ranchers have hired?"

"A few are pretty good, and you can bet the ranchers paid plenty to get them here. The rest are big talk and little else."

"And you're caught right in the middle between the whole bunch."

Frank smiled and finished his beer. "Sure looks that way, doesn't it?"

As he rode Stormy toward his new farm, Frank thought about the day he'd killed the younger Doolin more than ten years before. Frank had been in Kansas City for about a week, staying at the Dorchester Hotel. One night, while he was soaking in a hot bathtub in the communal bathroom, Frank saw a hand reach in through the door and take his hat off the peg it was hanging on. Frank jumped out of the tub and rushed to the door, only to find his hat lying crumpled in the hallway, minus the expensive and distinctive hatband it'd had on it. The band was made of solid silver conchos sewn onto a rawhide strip that encircled the hat.

Three days later, while eating in the hotel dining room, Frank saw a young man enter with three of his friends. The man was dressed all in black, with a black leather vest and black hat that had Frank's hatband on it.

Frank let the men get seated and give their order, and then he approached the table.

"Howdy," Frank said amiably when he stood next to the man wearing his hatband.

The man glanced up at Frank, and then made a show of ignoring him and spoke to his friends across the table.

Frank tapped the man on the shoulder. "Excuse me, but that's my hatband you're wearing and I'd like it back."

"What?" the man exclaimed, staring up at Frank as if he were crazy.

"You heard me," Frank repeated in a low, hard voice. "Now, the only question is, are you going to give it to me or am I going to have to take it off your dead body?"

The man jumped to his feet and squared off, his hand moving toward the pistol on his right hip. "I bought this hatband myself off a Mexican over a month ago," he said angrily.

"You're a liar," Frank said calmly, "and I can prove it."

One of the other men at the table stood up. "Now just hold on, mister," the man said.

Frank sighed. "Take the band off," he said, "and look at the back of one of the conchos. My name, Frank Morgan, is engraved on the silver, as well as the name of the man who made it for me in New Mexico last year, Felipe Hernandez."

"You . . . you're Frank Morgan?" the man asked, moving backward a step.

"Yep, and that's my hatband."

"Maybe you oughta just give him the band, Jeff," the man said, sweat breaking out on his brow at the mention of Frank's name.

"Hell, no," Jeff Doolin said. "I done told you this ain't his band, it's mine, bought fair and square."

Frank shrugged. "Then all you have to do, mister, is let me see the back of the conchos. If my name isn't there, I'll apologize and pay for your and your friends' meals."

"Nobody calls Jeff Doolin a liar," the young man said, his fingers twitching next to the butt of his gun.

"If you go for that gun, all they'll be callin' you is dead, Mr. Doolin," Frank said calmly. "Now, either hand me that hatband or hook and draw."

Doolin snatched at his pistol, and Frank's slug took him in the upper right shoulder before he could clear leather.

The young man spun around and hit the floor, moaning in pain, holding his right shoulder with his left hand.

When Frank saw that none of Doolin's friends were going to join in the fracas, he bent over and took the hatband off the wounded man's hat. He handed it over to the man who'd spoken earlier. "You see the names Frank Morgan and Felipe Hernandez on the back of one of the conchos?" he asked.

The man examined the band and then he nodded quickly. "Sure do, Mr. Morgan."

"Thank you, gentlemen. Now, you'd better get a doctor to take a look at the young Mr. Doolin there 'fore he bleeds to death."

As it turned out, Jeff Doolin didn't bleed to death. Instead he got an infection in his wound and it took him almost a week to die . . . a slow, painful, agonizing death.

Frank left Kansas City the day Jeff Doolin was buried and two days before his older brother, gunfighter Bobby Doolin, arrived and found out what had happened.

The incident almost made Frank hang up his guns, for he'd done his dead-level best to spare the life of the young thief. Stealing a hatband was not exactly a crime a man should be killed for, Frank had reasoned, and for a time he was despondent over the results of the showdown in the hotel.

But life went on and Frank continued to drift, moving from one lonesome town to another. It was two years later that he heard Bobby Doolin was looking for him, seeking revenge for him killing his younger brother.

As he rode, Frank thought about this and other events in his past. Maybe it was time for him to finally settle down. Hell, the farm he'd just bought seemed as good a place as any, and better than most.

He chuckled to himself as an image of Lydia's pretty face flashed into his mind, and he thought of how nice it would be to have someone like her in his life, someone to come home to after a long day tilling the fields or taking care of livestock.

Now he laughed out loud. He could just see the famous gunman Frank Morgan walking behind a plow-mule or herding stubborn cows into the barn for early morning milking.

No, right now he had other things on his mind, like saving the lives of farmers who were too inexperienced to save themselves, or their wives and children, from the greed and avarice of the ranchers.

When he finally arrived at his farm, he put Stormy in the barn, whistled for Dog, and was relieved when the cur staggered out of a pile of hay in the corner of the barn, yawning and stretching. Frank laughed and rubbed Dog's ears. "I swear, you lazy hound, you'd sleep through the barn burnin' down if I let you."

Dog followed him as he went to the house to fix them both something to eat.

Over a meal of biscuits so stale he had to dunk them in his coffee to chew them and a half dozen scrambled hens' eggs, Frank read another story in his paperback book. This one concerned a young man who traveled around the country engaging in bare-knuckle fights until finally meeting up with a farmer's daughter who convinced him to marry her and settle down on a farm next to her daddy's.

Frank smiled at the romantic picture the story painted about bare-knuckle fighting and the men who made their living doing it. He remembered a few years back when he was braced in a saloon by a man who thought he was tough. The man threatened to beat Frank to death, so Frank gave him the chance, whipping the man soundly and suffering only a split ear himself.

After the fight, a broad-shouldered man with close-cropped hair and an Irish accent came over to Frank's table. Without saying a word, he bent over and applied a bit of plaster to Frank's ear, causing the bleeding to stop immediately.

"Thanks, mister," Frank said. "Can I buy you a drink?"

"Now what kind of a question is that to ask an Irishman, boyo?" the man replied with a wide grin, and sat down. He stuck out a hand the size of a ham and said, "My name's John L. Sullivan, and I'm pleased to meet you."

Frank's mouth dropped open. "John L. Sullivan the prizefighter?" he asked incredulously.

John slapped his chest. "One and the same, me fine friend."

"But don't you usually fight back East, in Boston and New York?"

John leaned forward and whispered, "Yeah, but I'm out here on a publicity tour. My manager has me going into all these towns and offering to fight anyone, gloves or bare knuckles, for five hundred dollars."

He leaned back as the barman put a glass of whiskey on the table. John took the man's arm and said, "Now don't be hasty, my man. Just leave the bottle an' we'll settle up with ye when we're done."

As they talked and became friends, John told Frank he was a very gifted amateur fighter, but he had some basic flaws in his setup, and that's why the man had been able to hit his head and split his ear.

After another few whiskeys, John offered to take Frank out back and give him some lessons in the manly art of self-defense. Frank readily agreed, and for the next two hours the two big men sparred out behind the saloon, John showing Frank how to keep his left hand high to protect his head and face while keeping his right fist at his side, ready to unload a haymaker when the opportunity arose.

Frank ended up buying John and his manager dinner at the finest hotel in the town, and watching the next morning when John beat the crap out of two big, strapping farm boys who outweighed him by fifty pounds.

As he climbed on the stage, John winked at Frank, who was standing nearby. "Remember, ol' son, keep that left hand high," he called.

Frank looked down at Dog, who was chewing on a biscuit as hard as one of his bones. "Yeah, boy, John L. is some kinda fighter."

The church/schoolhouse was finished in record time. The carpenters began work on a small house for Richard and Lydia Carmondy. Another team of workmen came into the settlement and began working on the two buildings that would house the new businesses. The sights and sounds of progress were very evident in the settlement.

"And we still ain't got a name for this place," John Platt said. "But I tell you what we need more than a name."

"What?" Tom Johnson asked, waiting in the livery while his wife, Colleen, shopped at the general store.

"A café," John replied.

"You know," Tom said after a few seconds' hesitation, "that's what Charlie Jordan did back East."

"Who's Charlie Jordan?"

"One of the new bunch of farmers that come in last month. He isn't happy working the land. That's what his wife, Becky, told my wife. Charlie had him a little café back East."

"You don't say?"

"Sure enough. Him and Becky both cooked, and I can tell you flat out that he's a better cook than farmer."

A week after that conversation, the building that would house the brand-new Sunburst Café was started. No one knew who put up the money for the café, and when Frank Morgan was asked about it, he would only smile.

* * *

"We've got to stop it now, or give it up forever," Grant Perkins told Mark Rogers.

Mark said nothing in reply.

"Did you hear me?" Grant persisted.

Mark looked up at his longtime friend. The bruises on his face from the beating he'd taken during his fight with Frank had faded, but were still visible, like shadows on his skin. Physically, he was fine. Mentally, the rancher was slowly slipping toward the edge of a breakdown. The big man had never lost a fistfight in his adult life. And losing to Frank had taken a tremendous toll on him, especially since it happened with not only his son watching, but half the town. "Yeah, I heard you."

"Well?"

"Do whatever you feel is necessary. You can use the men I hired. I done told my foreman you're the boss."

"What the hell's wrong with you, Mark?"

"Nothing."

"That's crap! Look, if you're all upset about losing that fight with Morgan, don't be. One of the gunhands on my payroll told me that Frank learned to box from a professional fighter named Sullivan. It's gonna take a professional to beat him."

Mark nodded his head without enthusiasm. "I guess so."

"You interested in what I have in mind?"

"No. Just do it."

"And I can use your men?"

"I done said you could."

Grant stood up and put on his hat. "You need some rest, Mark. Maybe you ought to go to the city and get yourself a woman. Get laid. Get drunk."

"That's a good idea. I'll think about that."

Grant moved toward the door of the line shack. He paused and looked back at his friend. "I'm going to rip the lid off this thing, Mark. Blood is going to flow."

"Good luck."

Fourteen

Frank stood in the doorway of his house and rolled a cigarette. Just as he ducked his head and thumbnailed a match into flame, a bullet tore a chunk of wood out of the frame. Frank jumped back into the house, and Dog headed for safety behind a sofa that had been delivered just the day before.

Frank told Dog to stay put and grabbed up his rifle, exiting the small house out the back door, circling around and working his way behind the barn. Frank would be surprised if the man who was shooting at him was anyone other than Ray Hinkle. Ray was known as an ambusher. Ray also did not like Frank. The man had made that known more than once.

Frank waited silently. He would not make a move or throw a shot until he had a target. He'd learned a long time ago that patience was at least as important in a gun battle as shooting straight was.

The shot had come, Frank guessed, from a small grove of trees just across the road from his house, the only logical place if the shooter wanted to remain hidden. On either side of the stand of timber there were acres of open land with little or no cover for anyone to hide behind.

Frank waited.

* * *

Miles away from Frank's place, one of Paul Adams's sons, Jimmy, lay badly wounded in a ditch, several miles from his home spread. He had been shot in the back from ambush earlier in the day and lay unconscious. The only thing that had prevented him from bleeding to death was the mud he lay in. It had formed a natural bandage of sorts over the wound. His father and brothers were frantically looking for the young man.

Also miles away from Frank's place, farmer Bob Frazier watched in horror as his wife, Nellie, was stripped naked and assaulted by masked men. Bob had been knocked unconscious, and when he woke up he had been tied to a post.

"Stop it!" Bob shouted to the men. "Have you no decency? My Nellie is a good woman."

The men laughed at his pleas as one by one, they took turns raping the woman.

Bob could do nothing except try not to look at the scene through the tears that formed in his eyes. His mental agony ended abruptly when one of the hired guns shot him in the head. Nellie Frazier was left nearly unconscious, naked, and savagely beaten on the ground, just a few feet from her dead husband.

Nellie lay there, her mind fuzzy from the agonizing pain of her wounds, and watched through eyes swollen nearly shut as the man who shot her husband holstered his pistol.

He looked down and saw her watching him, and he must've had at least a shred of decency buried deep in him somewhere, for he blushed under her accusatory gaze. Kneeling, he growled, "What're you looking at?" into her face, and rolled her over onto her face so she couldn't see him anymore.

She lay there, trying not to suffocate in the soft dirt as

she heard hoofbeats of the departing desperados. Her mind went to her children and she thought, *Thank God the kids are off visiting and weren't here to see this.*

She must've passed out, for it was sometime later that she came slowly awake and realized she was going to have to get up or she would surely die here and she didn't want anyone to find her looking like this. With teeth gritted against the pain, she dragged herself over to the post where her dead husband was tied, and pulled herself to her feet using his ropes as handholds.

She bent over and kissed her fingertips and put them against his cold ones, and then she staggered into their farmhouse. Too weak for a full bath, she used a washcloth to clean the worst of the filth and blood from her body, and managed to pull on a dress to cover her nakedness.

With every muscle in her body aching and burning with pain, she took a quilt from her bed and walked outside to lay it over her husband's body, stopping momentarily to utter a short prayer and to tell him she would see him soon.

Moving slowly, she went into the barn and let the livestock out to graze, not feeling up to milking the cow. The kids would have to do that later, she told herself.

It took all of her strength to throw a saddle on their horse and to climb up in the stirrups. Pulling on the reins, she got the mount headed toward the neighbors' house, where the kids were visiting, and kicked the horse into a slow canter.

The jarring made her feel dizzy, and she almost fainted before she could get the animal stopped. She leaned over the saddle horn and vomited dark red blood onto the ground. Realizing she was more hurt than she thought, she turned the horse back around, and finally managed to get off it and into the house, where she collapsed onto her bed just before fainting once again.

* * *

Frank's patience finally paid off. After almost an hour of no movement in the copse of trees across from his house, he saw a small bush move slightly. Squinting his eyes, he could see a leg sticking out from behind a large oak tree. The man waiting there must've cramped up and had to straighten out his leg, Frank thought. He pulled up his gun and took careful aim. After a moment, he took the shot. He heard the ambusher cry out in pain. Frank clambered to his feet, and he was off and running across the road, circling the stand of timber and coming up behind the wounded man. As Frank suspected, it was Ray Hinkle. He was trying to crawl to his horse, dragging his bleeding leg behind him and moaning in pain and frustration at being shot.

"Give it up, Ray," Frank called from behind the wounded man.

Hinkle stopped his crawling, and cursed Frank as he rolled over onto his back and stared at his enemy with eyes filled with hatred and envy.

"That make you feel better, Ray?" Frank asked.

"I almost had you, Morgan. If you hadn't ducked your head to light that damn cigarette, I'd have put a lead pill right between your eyes and blowed your damned head off."

"Well, Ray, continuing with 'what if,' if your aunt had been born with balls she'd have been your uncle."

Hinkle looked at Frank and frowned. "Huh?"

"Never mind, Ray. Who hired you to ambush me? Was it Grant or Rogers?"

"Go to hell, Morgan."

Frank bent down, shucked Hinkle's pistol out of leather, and picked up his rifle off the ground from where the ambusher had dropped it when Frank shot him. "Nice rifle, Ray."

"It's served me well," Hinkle growled through teeth gritted in pain, wondering what Morgan was getting at.

"Meaning you've killed a lot of people with it."

Hinkle did not reply.

"That leg's bleeding bad, Ray. Tell me who hired you and I'll tend to it."

Ray cussed Frank again, using different words this time, but the meaning was still clear.

"Have fun crawling into town," Frank said, swinging the rifle over his shoulder and turning to walk away.

"Huh? What do you mean?" Hinkle asked as he took a bandanna from around his neck and placed it against the hole in his leg, trying to slow the bleeding down.

Frank stopped and turned back around to face him. "I mean I'm going to take your horse."

"You can't do that, Morgan," Hinkle whined, his voice full of fear at the thought of not having a horse to get to town on.

"Watch me."

"I'll die out here!"

"Probably. It's a long way into town and the way that leg of yours is leaking, I figure you'll run out of blood 'fore you make it a mile."

"Grant Perkins. He's the big he-wolf now," Hinkle groaned, pushing harder on the bandanna as blood began to flow around it.

"What do you mean?"

"He's the boss. Somethin's happened to Rogers. He don't act right, so I've been told."

"Rogers is out of this?"

"I reckon so. He told Grant to run things. That's the way I heard it anyways."

Frank stared at Hinkle for a long moment. "I ought to kill you right here and now, Ray."

"But you won't, Morgan," Hinkle said with a grimace and a slight shake of his head. "That ain't the way you do things."

"You're sure about that?"

"I'm sure, Morgan. Tell you what: You back off and get me get on my horse, and I'm gone."

"You expect me to believe that?"

"I ain't no liar, Morgan. If I say I'll do something, I'll do it."

"It's gotten back to me that several times over the years you've said you were going to kill me."

"Yeah, well . . . them was just words."

Frank had noticed that Ray Hinkle had let go of the bandanna with his right hand and was slowly inching it toward his belly. *He's got a little derringer behind his belt buckle,* Frank thought. *Go ahead, Ray, make your play. We'll settle this once and for all right here and now.*

"You hear me, Morgan? Them was only words. A man's gotta make his brags ever now and then."

"I hear you, Ray." The hammer on Ray's rifle had been in full cock position when Frank picked it up. Frank tightened his grip on the rifle and moved the muzzle slightly on his shoulder. Hinkle did not notice the movement.

"How about it, Morgan? You let me go and I'm out of this country for good."

"Sure, Ray. I'm game for that."

"You mean that, Morgan?"

"I said it, didn't I?"

"I'm gonna get up to my knees now, Morgan."

"Go ahead."

Hinkle got to his knees and made a grab for his belly gun. Frank let him make his move until the little derringer was in plain sight and Hinkle was earing back the hammer. Then Frank jerked the rifle off his shoulder and shot the man without bothering to take aim.

The bullet entered Hinkle's body just under his right arm, close to the armpit. It blew out the left side, smashing Ray's left arm as it exited. Ray Hinkle gasped once, coughed up a mouthful of blood, and then collapsed, dead on the ground. Frank smiled grimly at the thought that

Hinkle was killed by a bullet from his own gun, one that the back-shooter had admitted had been used to kill many others.

Frank got Ray's horse and tied the man belly-down across the saddle. He put Hinkle's rifle in the boot, then led the animal out of the timber and across the road. He saddled up Stormy, told Dog to stay in the barn, and headed for the GP range.

At the main gate, Frank untied the rope holding Ray in the saddle and let Ray's body fall to the ground. He ground-reined Ray's horse, and then laid Hinkle's rifle across the dead man's body. Frank stepped back into the saddle and headed for town.

"All hell's fixin' to break loose, Frank," John Platt told him as Frank swung down from the saddle at the livery.

"What happened?"

"Bob Frazier's been killed and his wife raped. Bob was tied to a fence post and forced to watch it 'fore they killed him."

"Damn! Who did it?"

"Don't know for shore. But that ain't all. John Adams's boy, Jimmy, was bushwhacked out on John's land. Left for dead. John himself dug the bullet out and the boy's restin'. He might make it."

"The lid's coming off, John." Frank told the liveryman about Ray Hinkle and how he'd admitted that Grant Perkins had hired him to back-shoot Frank out at his farm.

"Damn," John said, shaking his head. "You're right, Frank, things is heatin' up somethin' fierce 'round here." He paused and glanced over Frank's shoulder. "And speakin' of heatin' up, here comes a couple of gunhands riding into town now."

Frank looked. "That's George Cummings on the bay. I don't know the other one."

"I do. He's been around for a time. Name's Nick Barrow. Fancies himself a fast gun."

"Never heard of him."

"He ain't never faced no real gunhand. He's kilt a couple of farmers, back some months ago. I reckon he's got the blood lust runnin' hot and hard in him."

"I hate to hear that."

The two gunhands reined up in front of the saloon and started to enter, but they both spotted Frank and paused on the boardwalk as they made some comment about it. They stared at him for a moment, and then shared a laugh as they walked through the batwings.

"They know you're here," John said.

"Yeah. But first they have to get some courage out of a bottle and talk it up in front of the people in the saloon 'bout how they're gonna take the famous Frank Morgan down."

"And then?"

Frank grinned in eager anticipation. "Then I reckon there'll be a showdown between us."

Fifteen

Frank sat in the small livery office, drinking coffee and talking with John. He felt certain that a showdown with Cummings and Barrow was only a few drinks of whiskey away. As they talked, he realized how alive he felt. It was always thus for him just before, during, and even after a gun battle. He always figured it was the possibility of imminent death that caused the feelings, not at all unpleasant, of being more energized and more in touch with everything and everyone around him.

He'd tried to tell a woman about these feelings once, a woman with whom he was having one of his infrequent romances. When he found he couldn't make her understand these feelings, he realized he could never make her understand him either and the romance had died a natural death, unmourned by either of them.

"You could just ride on out of here," the liveryman said, interrupting Frank's thoughts of old loves and new conflicts.

"I could," Frank agreed. "But that would only delay things, and might possibly get some unsuspecting homesteader, in town for supplies, killed."

"That's true. But they's two of them waitin' to gun you down, Frank."

"I've faced two before."

"I reckon you have."

"Hinkle told me that Rogers told Grant to run things,

that something is the matter with Rogers. Have you heard anything about that?"

"No, not lately. But I know that Mark can sometimes act funny."

"Funny?"

"He loses his grip on things. Don't act right. Like some-thin' is loose in his head."

"You've seen this personally?"

"I shore have. Several times when I was workin' for him. It ain't no pretty sight neither."

"The fight may have triggered . . . whatever is wrong with him," Frank opined.

"Might have. But don't go blamin' yourself. He's had this ailment for many years." John glanced out the open window. "Cummings and Barrow just stepped out of the saloon, both of them hitchin' at their gun belts. Oh, my," John added.

"What is it?"

"Preacher Carmondy and his sister a-sashayin' up the street. Looks like they're headed for the café."

"They always manage to be in the wrong place at the right time," Frank said, thinking for some unknown reason about how the sun made Lydia's hair shine like fresh-oiled saddle leather and how full and red her lips were, as if they'd just been kissed and were swollen with desire. . . . He shook his head and looked around, blushing, as if John could read his silly thoughts.

"They ain't been in their new house a week. Why didn't they stay put awhile longer? Maybe have another cup of coffee?" John complained.

Frank smiled at the liveryman and stood up, adjusting his gun belt and loosening his rawhide hammer thong. "Maybe Lydia can't cook?"

"Now that there is a possible, by God. But as fine a lookin' woman as she is, what man would care?"

Frank laughed and silently agreed with John. He turned

toward the door. He didn't have to check his Peacemaker. He knew it was loaded up full, six and six. "No point in putting this off, I reckon."

"I guess not," John replied. His eyes were sad, filled with the knowledge that this might be the last time he and Frank would talk.

Frank walked out of the office and out of the livery. Unseen by Frank, John Platt picked up his Winchester and levered a round into the chamber. If by some strange twist of fate Frank took lead from one of those yahoos, John would finish the fight, by God.

Richard and Lydia had just stepped up onto the new addition to the boardwalk, and were a few steps away from the café when both of them spotted Frank. They looked toward the saloon and saw Cummings and Barrow, and sensed instantly there was about to be trouble.

"Into the café, sister," Richard said, taking Lydia's arm. "Gunmen are about to ply their devil's trade."

"But there are two of them against Fran . . . ah . . . Mr. Morgan!"

"Morgan is a cold-blooded killer, sister, dear. Save your sympathies for someone worthy of them."

"But he has a decent streak in him, Richard. I know it . . . I can sense it. Why else would he stay and pick up the farmers' fight?"

"I'm sure I don't know. Into the café, dear."

"Now, by God, you'll get what's comin' to you, Morgan!" George Cummings hollered. "Me and Nick's gonna see to that."

Frank said nothing as he continued walking, closing the gap between them.

George and Nick did not spread out as more experienced gun handlers would have done. They stayed close together, almost touching.

Lydia removed her brother's hand from her arm. "I'll sit at the table by the window, Richard. I want to see this."

"It's barbaric, Lydia!"

"I still want to see it. Get us some coffee, please."

With a sigh of exasperation, Richard seated his sister by the window and walked to the counter.

"Trouble outside?" Charlie Jordan asked, wiping his hands on his long apron and craning his neck to try and peer out of the front window.

"Frank Morgan appears to be marching toward another shoot-out," Richard said with disgust in his voice. "With two ne'er-do-wells in front of the saloon."

"Heavens!" Becky said, coming out of the kitchen to stand by the front door, wiping her hands nervously on the apron tied around her front. "So much violence."

"Yes, isn't it just awful?" Lydia said, digging in her purse for another handkerchief.

"You stop right there, Morgan!" Nick yelled when Frank was about fifty feet away from the pair.

"Yeah, that's far enough, Morgan," Cummings said.

Frank stopped and stared at the men confronting him. He had a half smile on his face and his hands hung at his sides. It was apparent he felt not the slightest twinge of fear or apprehension.

"It ends right here and now, Morgan," Nick said. "You ain't good enough to get both of us."

"So which one lives and which one dies?" Frank asked calmly. "The choice is up to you boys."

"We live and you die," Cummings said.

"Yeah," Nick said with a smirk. "That sounds good to me."

"How about we all live?" Frank asked.

"Huh?" Cummings said.

"You boys turn around and walk away and I'll do the same."

"Can't do that, Morgan," Nick replied.

"Why?"

" 'Cause we done made our brags, that's why."

Most everyone in the little village, including the work-men from out of town, had gathered on both sides of the street to watch and listen.

"Brags are wishes," Frank said. "Nobody with any sense will hold you to them. Living is more important, don't you agree?"

"Enough of this talk," Cummings said. "Time for you to make your play, Morgan. So do it."

"Not me, boys. This is your time in the sun. You wanted this action, you start it."

"By God, we can do that!" Nick said.

"All right," Frank said. "I'm waiting."

"You think we won't?" Nick shouted.

Frank said nothing. He waited, still with a smile on his face.

The sun was high in the sky and the day had turned out hot. Sweat was forming on the faces of Cummings and Barrow.

"You ready, Morgan?" Cummings asked.

"I've been ready," Frank replied.

"Now!" Nick yelled, and grabbed for his six-gun.

Frank's draw was as smooth as silk and honey. Nick never even cleared leather before the bullet from Frank's Peacemaker struck him a hammer blow in the chest, cre-ating a small, black hole in his denim shirt just over his heart. Nick's boots flew out from under him and he landed on his back in the dirt. "Oh, Mama!" the would-be gun-slick hollered, his hands going to his chest as if he could somehow hold in the blood that was pumping out in a large stain on his shirt. He drummed his feet on the ground as he screamed, creating a small cloud of dust around him.

George Cummings held out both hands, chest-high, his face a mask of terror at the ease and speed with which Morgan had shot his friend. "Don't shoot, Morgan!" he shouted. "I yield. Don't shoot."

"Unbuckle your gun belt," Frank ordered, the barrel of

the Peacemaker trained on George's head. "Let it fall to the street."

"I'll do it," Cummings said, fumbling with the buckle. "I'm doin' it. Just don't shoot, Morgan." Cummings's rig fell to the street.

"Kick it away from you," Frank ordered.

Cummings kicked the gun belt away. The man's face was pale and slick with sweat, and his eyes were so wide that the whites of his eyes showed all around the pupils.

"Oh, my God!" Nick yelled in a high-pitched whine. "I'm hurtin' somethin' awful. Oh, Lord, somebody hep me," he pleaded, whipping his head back and forth as if looking for divine help.

Behind him, Frank could hear the sounds of pounding hooves. But he did not turn around to look.

"It's Paul Adams and his sons, Frank," John Platt called from the livery doorway, where he stood with his Winchester cradled in his arms.

"Damn you, Morgan," Nick said, "I think you kilt me." And he stiffened in the dirt. Those were the last words he would ever speak.

Frank lowered his pistol and turned to face Paul Adams, but he kept watch on George Cummings out of the corner of his eye.

"My son lies near death, Morgan," Adams said, sitting his horse, looking down at Frank. "Shot in the back by some damn cowardly ambusher."

"Probably Ray Hinkle," Frank told the farmer. "He tried to kill me earlier today. I left his body at the main gate to the GP spread."

"Good," Paul said. "I applaud you for that. But Grant Perkins and Mark Rogers are still alive."

"And you plan on tackling them alone . . . just you and your remaining sons?"

"I do."

"You'll be riding into a death trap, Paul," Frank said.

"They've got ten guns to your every one, an' they're manned by men who are used to killing others, not farmers like you are."

"Be that as it may. Perhaps we will be successful in ridding this world of two very evil men."

"Doubtful," Frank told the man. "You'll never even get close to either main house before you're all gunned down."

"You have a better plan, Morgan?"

"No. But I don't intend to throw my life away needlessly without any chance of success. Think about this, Paul: You'll be sacrificing your sons if you go through with your plan."

The farmer's face hardened for a few seconds, then softened somewhat. "You might be correct. I will admit I have allowed emotion to take control of common sense."

"Now you're thinking," Frank said. "Go on back home and stay with your son. He'll need you by his side."

Paul was silent for a moment. Finally he turned eyes filled with hatred on Frank. "You hear what happened to Bob and Nellie Frazier?"

Frank nodded slowly, his face sympathetic.

"Mrs. Frazier needs medical care," Paul continued. "She is in a deep state of shock, I believe the doctors call it. She tried to ride for help, but she was too badly injured and collapsed in the effort. Several of the farmers' wives are with her. No one, including myself, knows what to do for her. Do you?"

Frank shook his head. "No, I'm sorry. I don't. Rest is the best thing, I would guess."

Paul nodded his head and picked up the reins. "Thank you, Morgan. I s'pect you're right about the futility of us trying to attack Rogers and Perkins all by ourselves. We'll wait awhile and see what happens." He spurred his mount, and he and his sons were gone in a cloud of dust.

Frank cut his eyes to Cummings. The man had not moved. "Get on your horse and ride out of here, George.

Don't tarry. If I see you again, you'll be buried in this valley. There won't be no warning nor any second chances. If I ever set eyes on you again I'll shoot you dead. Understand?"

"I'm gone, Morgan."

"Move!"

George moved. Very swiftly. The last time anyone saw him he was riding south, leaning over his saddle horn and whipping his horse as hard as he could while he looked back over his shoulder as if the devil were after him.

Sixteen

Richard and Lydia Carmondy stood on the boardwalk and watched as the body of Nick Barrow was dragged away. Lydia's hanky was fluttering like a flag in the wind as she fanned her flushed face. Frank walked over and stepped up on the boardwalk just as Charlie Jordan stepped out of the café.

"Is the coffee hot?" Frank asked him.

"Hot and the best you can get in the territory," the café owner said proudly.

"Well, I'll sure have me a cup then," Frank said, smiling at the man. "Maybe two or three."

Richard and Lydia followed Frank into the café. After Frank was seated, he noticed them standing before his table. The reverend's face was set and stern-looking, and his lips were puckered as if he'd been sucking on a lemon. Frank sighed and motioned for them to sit down at his table. He figured he was in for some moralizing from a man who knew next to nothing about human nature.

"Who was that man you so handily dispatched?" Richard asked, his tone suggesting he thought Frank had done the town a disservice.

"A man who fancied himself slick with a pistol."

"Obviously he wasn't nearly slick enough," the preacher said drily.

"In this game, not nearly is just as bad as not at all,"

Frank replied just as drily. He looked up as Charlie placed cups of coffee on the table. "How about some pie?"

"My God, man!" Richard blurted out. "You just killed a man. How can you think about food?"

"I was hungry before the shooting and I'm still hungry," Frank told him. "As satisfying as killing pond scum that need it is, it don't do nothing for an empty stomach."

"Incredible," the preacher muttered, shaking his head and looking heavenward as if the Good Lord would appreciate his distaste at talking with such a man as Frank Morgan.

"You looked so brave standing out there all alone," Lydia said, a slight blush coloring her cheeks as she batted her long, thick eyelashes. "I was afraid for you."

"Well, ah, thank you," Frank replied. "Actually, to be honest, that was the second time I faced a gun today."

"Oh?" Out came the little hanky once again.

Frank wondered if she bought them by the dozen as he explained about Ray Hinkle as briefly as he could.

"You think this Hinkle person is the one who shot Paul Adams's son Jimmy?" she asked as the hanky waved back and forth.

"Yes, I do. But he won't be shooting anybody else. He's taking himself a dirt nap right now."

Richard looked pained as he rolled his eyes. "What a quaint little expression."

"How do you like your new house?" Frank asked, abruptly changing the subject.

"It's very nice," Lydia replied. "I know we're going to love this area . . . as soon as present matters are settled."

"It'll be settled before the end of summer," Frank told her.

"How can you be so sure?" Richard asked.

"Tempers can't continue to run as high as they have been without boiling over," Frank assured him. "When they finally reach the boiling point, the end will be in sight."

"They haven't reached that point yet?" Richard asked.

"Not quite."

John Platt walked into the café, and Frank waved the liveryman over to the table. John called for Charlie to bring him coffee, and sat down next to Lydia. She moved over slightly away from him and raised the hanky to her nose as the familiar odor of horse manure followed John to the table.

"One of the workmen just told me that we're gettin' a doctor," John said, a note of pride in his voice.

"Oh, that's wonderful!" Lydia said from behind the hanky.

"They're startin' on his office in the mornin'," John informed the group. "The doctor is due to arrive in a few days. He's a young feller, just out of medical school somewheres back East."

"Boston, I'm sure," Richard said.

"Oh, no doubt," his sister agreed.

John sugared his coffee and said, "What we need next is a paper, and someone to run it."

"Oh, wouldn't that be marvelous?" Lydia said. "Richard could do a regular column on the Bible."

"Yeah, that would shore be interestin' readin'," John said with a quick wink at Frank that the Carmondys couldn't see.

"Are you a Christian, Mr. Platt?" Richard asked, as if he suspected he might be sharing coffee with a heathen.

"I reckon. I was baptized as a young feller back home. But I been backslidin' for a good many years."

"I shall expect to see you at services this Sunday," Richard said, sticking out his chest and lowering the timbre of his voice as if it were a command from God himself. "Fellowship is a wonderful thing."

"Right," John said with about as much enthusiasm as a man facing the thirteen steps to the gallows. "That's what my old woman keeps tellin' me . . . 'bout ten times a day."

"Mrs. Platt is a good Christian woman," Richard said. "My sister and I are so looking forward to having dinner at your home this evening."

John choked on a mouthful of coffee, coughed a couple of times, then nodded his head. "Supper? Tonight?"

"Yes. Have you forgotten?" Lydia asked.

"Musta slipped my mind," John muttered.

Conversation stopped as the door opened and Bobby Doolin stepped into the café. The gunfighter walked to a corner table and took a seat. "Coffee and a piece of pie," he called to Charlie.

"Coming right up."

Doolin looked over at Frank and smiled. "You lucked out again, Morgan. That fellow you gunned down was no gunhand."

Frank laid both big, callused hands on the table. "Doolin, I'm getting really tired of your mouth," he said in a low, hard voice, his eyes burning holes in Doolin's face.

Bobby laughed. "You know what you can do about that, Morgan."

"Oh, my," Lydia said. The hanky commenced to waving to and fro once more.

"You want me to do it now, Doolin?" Frank put the question to him and half rose from his chair.

Doolin's smile faded and his face turned as hard and cold as a granite tombstone. "You want it now, Morgan?"

"That's up to you," Morgan said, getting fully to his feet.

Doolin's insolent grin returned. "I'll finish my coffee and pie first," he said as lightly as if he were declining an offer to go fishing with a friend.

"If this lady wasn't sitting here, I'd tell you where you could put that coffee and pie, Doolin."

Lydia's hanky began working at high speed, and her face flushed scarlet while her chest heaved with heavy breaths.

Doolin frowned. "Don't be vulgar around women, Morgan. That's not like you at all." Like many Western men, Doolin held a good woman in high regard, and would never consider being crass in front of one.

Frank glanced at Lydia. "If I offended you, Miss Lydia,

I'm truly sorry, and I assure you it won't happen again," he said, taking his seat once more with a look at Doolin that would have frightened a lesser man to death.

"Thank you, Frank," she responded. The hanky slowed considerably.

"I don't want to cause no trouble in front of a lady," Doolin said, sugaring his coffee, his lips curling in a smirk.

"That's fine with me," Frank said.

"But you and me, Morgan, we'll settle this thing between us real soon. Count on that."

"Whenever you want it." Frank finished his coffee and pie in silence. After a few minutes, he pushed back his chair and picked up his hat. "Nice seeing you folks," he said to Richard and Lydia.

"We'll see you in church this Sunday?" Richard asked, a scornful note to his words as if he already knew the answer to the question.

"Doubtful," Frank replied, trying to keep the sarcasm out of his tone. "But my thoughts will be with you."

"See you, Frank," John said over the rim of his cup.

Outside on the boardwalk, Frank stood alone for a moment. The sounds of hammering and sawing filled the air. A new town was soon to be. But Frank had no doubt that its birth would be heralded in more blood. He just hoped it wouldn't be his own.

"Far as I'm concerned," Mark Rogers said, "we can burn the whole damn town down to the ground."

"That'd be like my mama used to say, Mark," Grant replied. "Cuttin' off your nose to spite your face."

"Whatever," the rancher said sourly. Then he started humming. His eyes took on an odd sort of glaze.

"Mark?" Grant questioned, leaning closer to the man. "Mark, can you hear me?"

"I doubt it," Mark Junior said from the doorway to the study.

Grant turned to look at the young man. "Are you sober, Mark?" he asked.

"Sober as a judge. How's Victor?"

Grant cussed at the mention of his oldest son.

"Sorry to hear that."

"What's wrong with your dad, Mark?"

"Well, with Daddy, it used to be he'd feel these spells comin' on and he'd hide in his bedroom, pretendin' he had a bad headache. But we all knew it was another spell."

"I recall those headaches. I never knew it was a spell like this."

"This is a bad one. I never seen one last this long. I'm wonderin' if he's gonna come out of it."

"Of course he will!"

"I don't think so, Grant. They've never lasted this long before."

"What's wrong with the old fart now?" Peaches Rogers asked from the doorway.

Grant grimaced at the young woman's words. He looked at her. A very pretty young lady with a mouth like a garbage barrel, and if the gossip around town was correct, the morals of an alley cat in heat. "Show some respect for your father," he told her.

"Go to hell," Peaches replied, walking over to her father. The senior Rogers was sitting in a chair, his mouth open. A bit of drool leaked from one corner of his mouth, and his eyes had the long stare of death in them. "You're disgusting," she said to him. "You ought to be put in an asylum."

"Shut up, Peaches," Mark Junior told his sister. "Make yourself useful. Gather up Daddy's guns and store them away. Out of his reach."

"Well, that's a good idea," she agreed. "You're not entirely stupid, brother, no matter what everyone says about you." She glanced at Grant. "Lucy tells me that home-steader's kid is gonna make it."

"When did you see my daughter?"

"She left a few minutes before you got here."

"I told her to stay home!"

"She don't pay no more attention to you than I do to that drooling bag of crap there," Peaches replied, jerking a thumb toward her father. She turned to her brother. "Looks like you're in charge now, brother. What are you gonna do about the squatters?"

"Burn them out."

"I'll believe that when I see it."

"You sure that's the way you want to go?" Grant asked the younger man.

"That's what Daddy was talkin' 'bout doin' 'fore he went off his bean."

"Then we'd better talk."

"Suits me. Peaches, you take care of Daddy."

"Yeah, sure. I'll look after the old fart, make sure he don't mess himself or nothing."

The two men walked out of the study into the front yard. Grant said, "Your sister needs her mouth washed out with soap."

"She definitely needs her butt kicked," Mark agreed. "Now then, I been thinkin' 'bout the squatters. Here's my plan. . . ."

As he began talking, Grant nodded his head.

Seventeen

Frank counted the number of workmen busy working on three new buildings being put up in the town. Twelve of them. They lived in tents pitched behind the new additions. The men were all fairly large in build, and all looked as if they'd been around the block a time or two. In fact, he didn't think he'd ever seen a tougher-looking group of men who weren't wearing any guns, and they looked like they could handle themselves if push came to shove.

Frank walked over to the workmen and located the foreman, taking him to one side and talking with him. After a few moments, Frank and the foreman shook hands and the foreman went back to work. Frank walked over to Wallace's General Store and had a chat with Joe. After a moment, Joe smiled and nodded his head in agreement. After Frank had mounted up and headed back to his homestead, Joe walked to the store's gun rack and counted the rifles. Just enough. He grinned and waited for the workmen to show up. If the Diamond and GP hands showed up in town to make trouble, they would certainly be in for a surprise.

Frank didn't know if Rogers and Grant would even think of attacking the town, but it never hurt to be ready for anything. Frank could not think of anything else he could do.

At his homestead, Frank fed Dog, and then fixed a pot of coffee and sat outside on a bench, watching the day gently fade into night. If Mark Rogers was in bad shape, that meant that his son, Mark Junior, would be stepping into the leadership role. Frank didn't know if that was good or bad. But he reckoned he'd soon find out.

It was a quiet night, and a cloudy one. The air was heavy and smelled like rain. That would be all right, for the ground needed a good soaking. It would help the crops. Frank smiled as he struck a match on his pants leg and put the flame to the cigarette he'd built. He was a little surprised to find he was thinking like a farmer. Well, it wouldn't be a bad life, he supposed. His thoughts abruptly switched to Lydia Carmondy, and that made him uncomfortable. He forced the woman out of his head and sent her back to her brother. Frank did not want any romantic entanglements at this stage of his life. Every time he got seriously involved with a lady, it seemed as though he drew a losing hand. He was better off alone.

He sipped his coffee and leaked smoke from his nostrils as his thoughts went back some years to the last time he'd seriously considered sharing his life with a woman. Her name was Angela and she was just on the right side of twenty years old. Her ma and pa owned a general store in Las Cruces, New Mexico Territory, and she worked there helping with the customers. She hadn't been what most men would call a "looker," but she had a strong, honest face and a laugh that would warm Frank's heart whenever he heard it.

He'd gone in to buy supplies one day after deciding to stay in a rented cabin for a few weeks to let the snow in the mountain passes melt down enough for him to ride through them on his endless journey.

Angela was waiting on an Indian couple, and was laughing and teasing their young son as she slipped him a piece of peppermint candy without charge. Frank found himself smiling for the first time in over a month at her infectious laughter and easy manner with people.

When she came over to the counter to add up his purchases, he asked her where the best food could be found in the town. She'd smiled and, with a blush creeping up onto her cheeks, said, "Well now, mister, that'd be my house of course, especially on Sunday afternoons when I fry up a couple of chickens for my parents."

Frank had laughed and replied, "That sounds awfully tempting, but I need a place I can go to and eat."

She'd stared at him seriously for a moment, taken a deep breath, and said, "Supper's at seven, and if you're late, don't expect there to be much left because it doesn't last long."

Frank tipped his hat and left without thinking to ask directions to Angela's house or even to get her name. Both of these tasks he accomplished before Sunday rolled around, and he showed up at ten minutes to seven, dressed in his best Sunday-go-to-meeting finery.

Angela's parents had been as charming and as welcoming to a stranger as she had been, and the evening was one of the most enjoyable Frank could remember.

So too were the picnics and rides in the countryside that he and Angela began to have on almost a daily basis. Weeks passed, the snow began to melt, and still Frank stayed in Las Cruces. He began to inquire of the local banker about ranches in the area that might be up for sale, and he even went so far as to begin to attend church on a regular basis with Angela and her parents.

He'd asked her to marry him, and they'd gone to see the preacher to set a date for the ceremony, when Angela began to cough and came down with a high fever. The doctor said later it was pneumonia, and that she had about a fifty-fifty chance of surviving it.

Frank sat by her bedside for six days, sponging her forehead with cool water and giving her bottle after bottle of any patent medicine he could find in the town, hoping to find something that would cure her.

On the morning of the seventh day, Angela opened

her bloodshot, teary eyes, grabbed Frank's hand, and whispered she loved him as she squeezed it with all her might. Seconds later, her grip relaxed and she left him forever.

Frank brushed away the tears that had formed as he remembered Angela and drained the last of his coffee, flipping his butt out into the yard in a shower of sparks.

Frank suddenly came alert at the sounds of a rider approaching out of the darkness of early dusk, his hand dropping to his Peacemaker.

"It's Dan Jones, Frank," the rider called.

"Light and sit, Dan," Frank said, returning the shout.

"No time, Frank," Dan said as he reined his horse in and leaned cross-armed on the saddle horn. I brung news though. Nellie Frazier died a few hours ago. She just up and died. Heart quit on her, I reckon."

"I'm sorry, Dan."

"Me too. I gonna go tell Claude and Mavis. Nellie and Mavis was good friends. See you, Frank."

"What's going to happen to their kids?"

"Tom and Colleen Johnson are going to take them in and raise them. They're good folks and they love kids."

"All right. Be careful out tonight, Dan," Frank warned. "Riding alone out here near the ranches is dangerous."

"I will."

Long after Dan had vanished into the night, Frank sat on the bench and smoked and drank coffee. He made up his mind to do something that he probably should have done weeks back. And he'd do it first thing in the morning.

"As long as the packhorse is stabled, Dog will stay in the stall," Frank told John Platt. "You take good care of them, John. I'll be back as soon as possible."

"You don't worry about them, Frank," the liveryman assured him. "They'll be just fine. You look after yourself in the county seat. And don't believe a damn word that crooked sheriff says."

"I've got to see for myself, John. I've got to hear the words coming from his mouth."

"What you'll hear is a pack of lies. Be careful."

"See you in a few days."

Frank rode into the county seat two days later. Someone had seen him on the trail and ridden into town to tell the sheriff, for there were four deputies waiting for him, lined up on the boardwalk in front of the sheriff's office. Frank ignored them and reined up at the livery, stabling his horse. He walked over to the hotel and got a room and washed up a bit. Then he found a small café and had some breakfast and several cups of coffee. He was working on his third cup of coffee, and had just rolled a smoke, when a tall man with a handlebar mustache strolled in, accompanied by two deputies. The man sat down, uninvited, at Frank's table. The deputies stood behind the man with their legs spread and their hands on their hips as if they were expecting trouble. The tall man opened his coat and showed Frank his badge.

"I'm Sheriff Ned Breedlaw."

"I'm Frank Morgan."

"I know. Why are you in my town?"

"I came to see you."

The sheriff blinked at that. "To see me?"

"That's what I said."

"What about?"

"The lawlessness in a little community about two days' ride from here. It's located in a series of valleys. You familiar with the settlement?"

"I am."

"People are being burned out of their homes over there. Kids being shot. Men killed and women assaulted and raped. You know all that and yet you haven't seen fit to do a damn thing about it. Why?"

"I don't like your tone of voice, Morgan."

"I don't give a good goddamn what you like or dislike, Sheriff. I asked you a question. Answer it."

"I ought to arrest you, Morgan!"

"On what charge?"

"I could think of something."

"You want a bloodbath in this café, Sheriff?" Frank asked softly, leaning back in his chair and letting his right hand rest on his right thigh next to his holster. "Try to arrest me on some trumped-up charge."

"I said I *ought* to arrest you, Morgan," the sheriff explained, relenting. "I didn't say I was."

Frank relaxed and put his elbows on the table and leaned close. "Let me tell you something, Sheriff. Mark Rogers is a sick man. Word is he's losing his sanity. His son has taken over the ranch and the war to drive the farmers out, teaming up with Grant Perkins and his hired guns. There is about to be a bloodbath in the valleys, Sheriff, and I'm asking for your help."

"This is a big county, Morgan," the sheriff said, having the good grace to blush at Frank's implication he wasn't doing his job. "It's a good two-day ride over to the valleys. I don't have the deputies to spare. I've got two deputies out chasing rustlers now, and two more about to go out chasing down some damn renegade Indians who jumped the reservation and are raising hell. If you got problems over in your neck of the woods, you folks handle it."

"And you don't know anything about it?"

"I didn't say that. Sure, I heard about it. I heard you've killed a couple of hired gunslicks and you'll probably kill several more. I heard you whupped Mark Rogers in a fair, stand-up fistfight. I'd like to have seen that. Mark and Grant have been the big he-wolves in this country for a long time. But times are changing and so am I. I got to if I want to keep on being sheriff. And I like bein' sheriff."

"What are you telling me, Sheriff?"

"I think you can figure it out, Morgan. Way I hear it, the settlement is growing. Some folks want to name it Valley View. If that happens you can elect a marshal, or the mayor can appoint one. You get my drift?"

Frank poured another cup of coffee and leaned back and rolled a cigarette before replying. "We handle it ourselves and you stay clear of it, right?"

"You said it, not me."

"We've got a dozen or so workmen over there now. Might as well get them to build up a jail while they're there," Frank said, almost to himself as he tried the idea on to see if it fit.

"That might be a good idea. And a marshal's office while they're at it."

"You're awfully accommodating, Sheriff."

"Morgan." The sheriff leaned closer, lowering his voice. "You might say I can see the handwriting on the wall. The sodbusters is here to stay. Times are changin' fast. I don't want no federal judge sendin' troops in here, and since I'm still sheriff of the county, the marshal will be under my jurisdiction. As long as he keeps the lid on over there and doesn't make too much noise doing it, I won't have a problem with him. We on the same page now?"

"Same page, same book."

"Good."

Frank tossed the makin's on the table, and the sheriff rolled himself a smoke and signaled for the waitress to bring him a cup of coffee. " 'Sides, Morgan, I hear you're a wealthy man. Got stock in factories, mines, railroads, and such as that. I know that fightin' a man with bags of money is a losin' proposition. 'Specially a man who's got the grit and the guns to back it up, and you definitely got all three of them things."

Frank finished his coffee and sat for a moment, he and the sheriff not speaking, just staring at one another. Finally, Frank pushed back his chair and stood up. "Nice talking with you, Sheriff. I'll have to tell John Platt he was wrong about you."

The sheriff smiled. "That old horse thief! Hell, I been knowin' John for more years than I care to count. Well . . ." he drawled, "he wouldn't have been wrong a year or so back. But I'm smart enough to know a man's got to change with the times, and I smelled the wind and I'm changin'."

"See you around, Sheriff."

"See you, Morgan. Oh, by the way, the land office is just around the corner . . . in case you want to drop by there." There was a definite twinkle in the sheriff's eyes.

"I might do that, Sheriff. Thanks."

"Don't mention it," the sheriff said, and after a moment's hesitation, he grinned and added, "And I really mean don't mention it, especially around some ranchers we both know."

Frank walked out of the café and went straight to the land office. There, he filed on ten big lots in the soon-to-be-named town of Valley View: five on one side of the main street, five on the other. Then he located the doctor's office and went in.

"Have a seat," a man called. "I'll be with you in just a few minutes."

"No hurry, Doc," Frank called. "I'm just looking for a man."

"What man?"

"The young doctor who is going to set up practice in a town 'bout two days' ride from here."

"That would be me." A young man appeared in the doorway. "I'm Dr. Archer. I'm just looking after things here for a few minutes while Dr. Camper is out." He walked to Frank and held out his hand. "And you are? . . ."

Frank shook the hand and said, "Frank Morgan."

"Nice to meet you. Let me finish inventorying supplies in here and I'll be right with . . ." He didn't finish his statement. The young man stared at Frank for a moment, high color creeping up his face. "Frank Morgan?" he asked in a low voice.

"Yes. Is something the matter?"

"Ah . . . I . . . ah . . . have heard the name back East. Read several stories about a man named Frank Morgan. Most . . . ah . . . were not very flattering, I must tell you that."

Frank laughed. "Don't let that bother you, Doc. It sure as hell doesn't bother me."

"Then you are really the duelist Frank Morgan?"

Frank smiled at the word *duelist,* and shook his head at the things some writers wrote. "I reckon so, Doc."

"Well . . . I . . . ah . . . nice to meet you, Mr. Morgan."

Frank smiled again at the young doctor's discomfort. "Relax, Doc. I'm not going to start shooting."

A smile slowly formed on Dr. Archer's lips. "That's good to know, Mr. Morgan. So, how may I help you?"

"I'm in town for a few days on business. I live near the community where you plan on setting up your practice. I was wondering when you might be heading that way."

"In a couple of days. Why do you ask?"

"Do you enjoy riding, Doc?"

"Yes, as a matter of fact I do."

"Want to ride over there with me?"

"Why . . . yes, that would be nice. I could better see the country and I would enjoy the company. It's kind of you to invite me."

"Do you have a horse?"

"Actually, no, I don't."

"You object if I pick one out for you?"

"Not at all, sir."

"I'll go do that now and get you outfitted. I'll bring the horse around in a couple of hours. You can sit the saddle and get to know each other."

"I'm looking forward to it, sir. I'll take that time to visit the bank and get a draft to pay you."

"My treat, Doc. Don't worry about it."

"Are you certain, sir?"

"I can afford it, Doc. Believe me, I can. Have you made arrangements to ship your equipment over?"

"That's all taken care of."

The men shook hands and Frank went to the livery, introducing himself and explaining to the liveryman what he wanted.

"I got just what you're lookin' for, Mr. Morgan. I got a chestnut that was gentle-broke but still full of spirit. Come on, you can see for yourself."

Frank checked out the horse and agreed that it was a fine animal. He bought the horse, then purchased a rig. Saddled up, he took the chestnut out for a ride. Satisfied that the horse would suit the young doctor, he rode back to Dr. Camper's office. Dr. Camper had returned, and looked at Frank through wary eyes.

"You really are Frank Morgan," Camper said. "I'll be damned. I thought you'd be a much older man. Dr. Archer stepped out to buy himself some trail clothes. Come on in and have some coffee. He'll be back in a few minutes. That will give me time to give you an examination."

"Do what?"

Dr. Camper laughed. "I want to see if you've been shot as many times as people say. Take off your shirt and sit over there."

Frank began unbuttoning his shirt. "Might as well, I reckon. Have at it, Doc. Tell me if I'm going to live another day or two."

As Dr. Camper began to poke and prod the many scars on Frank's body, Frank noticed a small stack of magazines next to the examining table. He picked one up off the top and saw it was a dime novel, written by Erastus Beadle, and had a picture of Deadwood Dick on the cover blazing away at some desperados in the background.

Just under the title was smaller print saying that inside

was the real, true, unabridged tale of how the infamous gun-fighter Frank Morgan shot down five Mexican *bandidos* in Del Rio, Texas.

Frank grinned. He didn't remember ever shooting down five Mexicans in Del Rio, *bandidos* or otherwise, but that probably didn't make any difference to the men who wrote in these penny dreadfuls.

Dr. Camper noticed Frank looked at the novel and pointed. "Those books belong to Dr. Archer," he said with a wry grin. "I'm afraid he's got rather a romantic idea about life out here in the West, and a rather distorted view of the people who live out here."

Frank shrugged and pitched the book back onto the stack. "Well, he'll find out the truth sooner or later, that for the most part, people are the same all over—some good, some bad, and some in between."

"Why, Mr. Morgan," the doc said, laughing, "I had no idea the infamous gunslick Frank Morgan was a philosopher."

Frank arched an eyebrow. "You face as many men over the barrel of a gun as I have, Doc, and you get to be a pretty good judge of human character, or the lack thereof."

Eighteen

Frank and Dr. Archer pulled out at dawn, after only a single cup of coffee. "We'll stop up ahead after a few miles and I'll make breakfast and coffee," Frank said. "We'll both have us a good appetite by then."

Archer yawned hugely. "You Western folks certainly are early risers."

"We don't believe in burning daylight, Doc."

"You certainly don't," the doctor replied drily.

About two hours later, by a tiny creek, Frank made coffee first and then began preparing a trail breakfast. He sliced up a half pound of bacon, fried some potatoes, and laid out bread he'd bought in town the day before.

"I am ravenous," the doctor declared after sipping his coffee. "I don't recall being this hungry in years."

"It's the trail, Doc. Good clean, cool air smelled from the back of a good horse will do it every time."

"What is that you're cooking with those potatoes?"

"Onions, Doc. With a little bit of red pepper. Makes them nice and spicy."

"They smell wonderful."

The doctor ate half the bacon and fried potatoes, then took a hunk of bread and sopped out the skillet with it. Then he poured another cup of coffee and while the coffee was cooling, he stuffed his pipe and lit up.

"What a wonderful meal," Doc Archer said. "It's the best I've had since . . . why, I don't remember when."

"That saddle sittin' all right?" Frank asked the Easterner.

"Quite comfortable actually. Very different from what I'm used to."

"You're used to ridin' on those pincushion saddles. Never could understand how you folks sat those things for long distances. Damned uncomfortable if you ask me."

"It's all what one gets used to, I suppose."

The men finished the coffee, and Frank cleaned up the tin plates and made sure the fire was out. They were back in the saddle, and had covered half the distance to the settlement before Frank called a halt and they made camp for the night.

"No telegraph in the settlement, Frank?" Archer asked after supper and over some of Frank's strong coffee.

"Not yet. I'm told the wires will be strung before fall . . . if everything goes according to plan."

"The settlement has to be an official town, I suppose."

"Something like that, I think. Valley View is the name it's going to go by, so I'm told."

"That's a nice name. Has a nice sound to it."

"I reckon."

"Frank . . . please forgive my lack of tact, but I have to ask you something."

"Go ahead."

"Have you really been in shoot-outs with a thousand men and killed them all?"

Frank chuckled for a few seconds. He leaned closer to the fire, refilled his coffee cup, then leaned back against his saddle. "No, Doc. I haven't been in a thousand shoot-outs. But looking back," he added ruefully, "it sometimes feels like it."

"How did you ever get into such a dreadful life?"

"Dreadful, Doc? Well . . . I suppose it is, or would seem like it to many people. Back when I was just a kid, 'bout fourteen or so, I was pushed into a gunfight. I lucked out and killed the man before he could kill me. Then, after the War of Northern Aggression was over . . ."

Dr. Archer smiled at Frank's name for the Civil War.

". . . the man's brothers came looking for me. I killed them. After that"—he shrugged his shoulders—"trouble seemed to look me up and I handled it. The term gunfighter stuck to me."

"And you're a rich man, or so I'm told."

"That was not of my doing, Doc. My ex-wife was a mon-eyed woman. She left me a lot of stocks and bonds and so forth. I really don't know how much I'm worth. I try to do good with the money."

"So I've heard. A modern-day Robin Hood."

Frank smiled at that. "That might be stretching things somewhat. If I recall the story, Robin Hood stole from the rich and gave to the poor." He shook his head. "I don't usu-ally go around stealin' from nobody, not even the rich. I just try to spend my money where it'll do the most good for the most people."

"Oh, I don't know. I have heard some good things about you, Frank," Doc Archer said.

"That would be a very short list, Doc," Frank said, re-membering the story about him in the book in the doctor's office and how he'd been portrayed as a mad-dog killer.

"Perhaps, perhaps not. Do you believe in the Hereafter?"

"Sure."

"That's when the list will be read, Frank. It matters not what people here on earth believe."

"You're probably right, Doc. Well, I'm going to sleep. Night."

"Good night, Frank."

Frank threw his coffee in the fire and rolled over, fluff-ing up his saddle blanket on the saddle he was using as a pillow, and fell almost immediately asleep.

The doctor, not quite through with his coffee yet, sat star-ing into the fire as he slowly sipped the potent brew, trying to reconcile what he'd read about this famous figure of the West with what he'd seen so far.

While in medical school back East, in Philadelphia, not Boston as the reverend and his sister thought, Archer had been fascinated with all the lurid tales of the Wild West, as it was called back there. He'd read everything he could get his hands on about the West and the characters who lived there.

Before long, he'd decided that was where he wanted to set up his practice when he graduated. He began to haunt the mortuaries and morgues in the city, entreating the men who ran the establishments to let him see all the gunshot and knifing victims, sure that that would be the majority of his practice in the Wild West.

He chuckled to himself. So far he'd been out here almost six months, and the only gunshot he'd seen was one where a rancher blew his little toe off when he was bucked off his horse and his pistol had gone off accidentally.

Hell, he thought, so far he'd been more of a dentist than a doctor. He'd had no idea how bad people's teeth could become if they weren't taken care of, and cowboys, it seemed, took damn poor care of their oral hygiene.

His eyes flickered over to Frank Morgan lying a few feet away from him. Well, if the stories he'd been reading for the past six years were true, going to practice medicine in any town where Morgan lived would surely entail his treating any number of gunshot wounds.

They had just reached Van and Virginia Calen's homestead, on the west end of the valley road, when Van ran out of the cabin and waved at the pair, yelling at them to stop.

"What's the matter, Van?" Frank asked.

"The Watsons got hit night before last, Frank. Their house and barn burned to the ground."

"Anyone hurt?"

"Hugh took a bullet in the shoulder. Passed right through. He's hurtin' some, but he's up and around. Jessica and the kids are all right."

"Thank the Lord for that."

"That's what I say too, Frank. Who's your friend?"

"This is Dr. Archer." Frank introduced the men.

"Your stuff come in a few days ago, Doc. Joe's got it stored at the general store. Glad to see you made it. It looks like you're gonna be busy here."

"Certainly looks like it. Where is Mr. Watson now?"

"Just up the road at the Joneses'."

"We'll stop and I'll have a look at him," the doc said, thinking he'd been right the night before. Here he wasn't even to the town yet and he was already being faced with treating a gunshot wound.

"Anybody taking responsibility for the attack, Van?"

"The men was ridin' horses with both the GP and the Diamond brand, Frank."

"It's really started now." Frank sighed. "Well, I knew it was coming. We'll be pushing on. You and Virginia take care."

"Will do, Frank."

When Frank and Doc Archer rode into the Joneses' yard, Reverend Carmondy's buggy was there. "The local preacher," Frank said. "He's from back East. Boston."

"Oh?"

"Yeah," Frank said. "He and his sister figured you probably trained there in medical school."

Doc Archer shook his head. "No, I trained at the University of Pennsylvania, though I do know some people from Boston. We probably have some mutual acquaintances back there."

The doctor was introduced all around, and Lydia's eyes sparkled when they exchanged pleasantries. Dr. Archer was a handsome man, and would be quite a catch for any woman, especially one as ambitious and as well bred as Lydia.

Doc Archer cleaned up Hugh's wound and put on a fresh bandage. "The bullet hit nothing major," he said. "You're fortunate in that respect. You'll be good as new in no time, assuming infection doesn't set in." He got to his feet, and added to Hugh's wife, who was standing nearby, "You need to change the bandages at least once a day, and be sure to boil the new ones before you put them on the wound."

She nodded as Hugh spoke. "I'm going to rebuild," he said. "I'm going to stay. No low-down snake of a rancher is going to run me and my family out."

"I'll help you rebuild your house and barn, Hugh," Frank said.

Doc Archer smiled when he heard Frank say that. He thought: *The list is much longer than you think, Frank.*

"You men step outside," Dan said. "There is something you need to know, Frank."

"You can speak in front of us," Hugh's wife said. "We agreed a long time ago there would be no secrets between us, Dan."

Dan nodded his head, and then he cut his eyes at Frank. "A man rode into town right after you left for the county seat, Frank. He's a hired gun. Says his name is Scott Dice."

Frank slowly nodded his head. He was silent for a moment. "Scott Dice," he finally said, his voice low.

"You know this man?" Dan asked.

"I know him."

"Is he fast?" Hugh asked.

Frank smiled. "Fast? Scott Dice is the best."

Doc Archer, who was washing his hands in a basin in the corner, looked up at this statement by Frank. In the books he read, all the gunfighters were inveterate braggarts and never admitted any other gunman was any good with a gun.

"I always heard you were the best, Frank," Hugh said.

Frank laughed. "You know what the definition of the best gunfighter is, Hugh?" he asked.

Hugh shook his head.

"Someone who just hasn't met anyone faster . . . yet," Frank answered.

Nineteen

"If this Scott Dice is so good, why isn't his name as widely known as yours?" Dan asked.

"Because he's very secretive," Frank replied. "Someone hires him, he comes in, does the job, and is gone within hours. He works under a dozen names."

"But not this time obviously," Doc Archer said. "And why would that be?"

"Because he's going up against me. He wants it known he's the man who put me down."

"Can he do it?" Hugh asked.

Frank shrugged his shoulders. "He's got as good a chance of killing me as any man I've ever faced."

"You say that calmly enough, Frank," Archer said.

"No point in denying it. It's the truth."

"So what are you going to do?" Hugh asked.

Frank looked at the homesteader. "Ride into town and face him."

"Now?" Archer asked.

"Right now."

"You heard what happened out at the Watsons'?" John Platt asked, coming out to meet them as Frank and Doc Archer rode up to the livery.

"We stopped out there."

"Then you know who's in town?"

"Scott Dice."

"He's over at the saloon now."

"How's he looking?"

"Mean, Frank. He didn't make no bones 'bout who he was or what he was doin' in town. Come right out and said he was here to kill you."

"He's got it to do."

"Can you take him, boy?"

"I reckon we'll see. This is Dr. Archer, John."

"Pleasure, I'm sure," the liveryman said, shaking Archer's hand. "Did you see Hugh Watson? I heard he got shot by those bastards who tried to burn him an' his wife out the other night."

"I did," Doc Archer replied. "He's going to be all right."

"We got us a name for the town, Frank."

"I heard. How'd it come about?"

"Joe Wallace wrote the governor months ago. We all forgot about it—including Joe. Letter come in the day you left. It's now official. Valley View it is."

"Sounds good to me." Frank squatted down and petted Dog for a moment. Without speaking, he looked up over his shoulder at John Platt and raised his eyebrows.

John nodded, indicating he'd take care of Dog if Frank didn't survive his upcoming battle.

After speaking a few soft words to Dog that the others couldn't hear, Frank stood up, removed the hammer thong, and slipped his Peacemaker in and out of leather a couple of times. "I think I'll go over to the saloon and have me a beer. Cut the dust out of my throat."

"I'll go with you," John said.

"So will I," Doc Archer said.

"Both of you stay out of my way," Frank told them. "Things might get raw in a heartbeat."

When Frank walked into the saloon, every patron except one jumped to their feet and left in a hurry. The one remaining was seated at a table, his back to a wall. He did not look up as Frank entered. Frank walked to the bar and ordered a beer. Mug of beer in his left hand, Frank turned from the bar to looked at the man seated alone.

"Hello, Scott."

"Frank. Nice day, isn't it?"

"Real nice. Long time since I've seen you."

"Years, Frank. It was back in '68 or '69, I believe."

"El Paso, I think."

"Yes. Somewhere down along the border."

"What brings you to town, Scott?"

Dice smiled, a cold movement of the lips that didn't extend to the rest of his face or to his eyes. "Money. A lot of money."

"To kill me?"

"Yes," Dice replied.

"Somebody must want me dead awful bad."

"Somebody does, Frank."

Frank knew better than to ask who hired Scott. Scott followed the gunman's code closely. He would never tell.

"Even if you got lucky and killed me, Scott, that alone wouldn't make the homesteaders quit the land."

A flash of irritation crossed Dice's face. "I don't have to get lucky to kill you, Morgan."

"I'd say you're going to have to get very, very lucky to kill me, Scott. Because, speaking quite honestly, you're just not that good." Frank drawled out the last few words, slurring them with derision.

"Damn you!" Scott chuckled, smiling at Frank's ploy to get him riled up so he'd act without thinking.

Frank smiled when his trick didn't work. He shrugged slightly and took another sip of his beer, his eyes never leaving Scott's.

"Well, looks like it's time to strike up the band and have ourselves a little dance," Frank said, his voice level and cool.

As Scott got to his feet, the bartender slipped out the side door of the saloon.

Scott moved his shoulders a little, getting loose and ready as he stared back at Frank, neither man showing the slightest trace of fear.

Suddenly, Scott's hand closed around the butt of his .44.

Frank's draw was cat-quick, but even as fast as he was, Scott matched his speed. Frank's .45 and Scott's .44 roared simultaneously. Scott's bullet dug a painful slash on the top of Frank's left shoulder, spinning him half around. Frank's bullet ripped into Scott's chest with a wet, thunking sound, causing him to take a quick step back to stay on his feet. Scott grinned in a macabre fashion as blood began leaking from his mouth. He cocked his .44 and lifted the muzzle. Frank raised his pistol and drilled him again, this time in the belly. Scott moaned as he doubled over and took several steps backward, to lean against the wall. His pistol discharged and blew a hole in the table in front of him.

"You bastard," Scott said, choking on the blood in his mouth.

Frank said nothing. He felt the slow drip of blood leaking down from the top of his shoulder.

"Damn, you're good," Scott said, paying Frank the ultimate compliment he could offer. Again, Scott lifted his .44 and slowly cocked the weapon, using the palm of his left hand to ear back the hammer.

Frank put a third round into the man, about an inch from the first one in his chest. This time Scott went down to the floor, sliding down the wall to come to rest on his butt. His pistol clattered to the floor between his legs, the fingers of his right hand moving but unable to pick it up.

Frank walked over to the man and looked down at him. Scott's face was deathly pale, his lips bloody. "I guess . . . I just wasn't lucky enough this day, Drifter."

"I reckon not, Scott."

"But I got lead into you anyway."

"You hit me."

"Do me a favor, Drifter."

"Name it."

"Bury me proper?"

"You got it."

"One more thing . . . tell me I'm the best."

"You were until today."

"I guess that'll have to do. See you in hell, Drifter." Scott Dice closed his eyes for the final sleep.

The batwings flew open and Dr. Archer and John Platt rushed into the saloon. They'd been watching through the front windows and had seen the gunplay firsthand.

"My God!" Dr. Archer said, his voice filled with awe. "I must take pen in hand and put today's events to paper. This is a story the newspapers will be clamoring to print."

Frank let the hammer down on his .45, twirled it once, then slipped it into leather.

John Platt laughed at the sight and slapped his knee.

"One more obstacle gone on the way to peace in the valleys," Joe Wallace said from the batwings.

Frank walked to the bar and waited until the barman slipped back in the side door before he ordered coffee. He looked up as Reverend Carmondy stepped into the saloon. The preacher walked over to stand looking down at the bloody body of Scott Dice.

"Oh, Lord," Carmondy said, and cut his eyes heavenward as he clasped his hands together. "When will it end?"

"When Grant Perkins and Mark Rogers are dead," John Platt said simply, grinning at the thought.

"More killings?" the preacher asked, turning away from the body of the dead man.

Frank did not reply to that. He walked over and stared down at the body of Scott Dice, thinking: *That will be me someday. There lies my fate, sure as hell. But what can I do to change it? Move to a big city, like maybe Boston or New York City, change my name, wear a fancy suit and stiff collar and uncomfortable shoes? I couldn't live like that. I won't live like that. So that leaves me? . . .*

He shook his head, and turned away and met Reverend Carmondy's eyes. "I'll get some people to wrap him up in a blanket and carry him off. Get one of the carpenters to knock together a coffin. He asked me to give him a proper burial. I said I would."

"What were you thinking while you looked down at that poor man, Frank?" the preacher asked.

"Nothing of any importance."

Doc Archer set his black bag on a nearby table and motioned for Frank to join him.

Frank moved over to the table and took a seat while the doc opened his shirt and peered down at the wound on his left shoulder. He pursed his lips. "The bullet cauterized the wound, Frank, and the bleeding has already stopped. I'm going to put a small bandage on it to keep it clean, and you'll need to let me change it every day for at least a week," he said as he applied a soft cloth to the wound and taped it in place.

"Thanks, Doc," Frank said, and he got to his feet, fixed his shirt, and walked out of the saloon.

Frank looked up and down the street for a moment, then began pacing out his just-purchased lots. That done, he walked over to the workmen and spoke with the foreman.

"You sure about this, Mr. Morgan?" the foreman asked. "This is gonna cost you some good money."

"I'm sure," Frank told the man. "This is going to give you men steady work for a long time."

"Damn sure will," the foreman agreed. "All right, sir. I'll do a work order and get the material ordered."

More than one way to bring the big two ranchers to a cease-fire, Frank thought. *And I can damn sure afford it, so what the hell? Might as well do something worthwhile with my money.*

Frank walked back to the livery, a smile on his face.

* * *

He took a small bottle of whiskey from where he'd seen John Platt hide it, sat down in the hay next to Dog, and slowly scratched the dog's ears as he thought about his life and how close it'd come to be ended for him a short while ago.

He smiled at the thought of the lawyers and money managers in San Francisco and Denver when they read his will. They would be terribly disappointed to lose control of so much money, but all of it would go to good causes. He had a list of cities where the money would be used to open and fund orphanages, libraries, and in some cases small hospitals. But his favorite use of the money was in his instructions for the lawyers to search out men who'd served in the Confederacy and had fallen on hard times. Frank planned that at least a third of the money remaining at the time of his death would be used to make life a little easier for these veterans of the War of Aggression by the North. Lord knows, they hadn't had it easy in the war, but by God, if he had anything to do with it, their last remaining days would be a little bit better than they had been.

Dog moaned and moved his head under Frank's light touch, showing he'd missed his master the last few days. Frank reached into his shirt pocket and pulled out a piece of bacon he'd saved from breakfast. He held it up where Dog could see it until the cur's mouth drooled.

Finally, with a short laugh, Frank pitched the bacon high and watched as Dog jumped and caught it in midair.

Twenty

"He did *what*?" Grant Perkins almost screamed the words.

"He's building a damn town," Mark Junior told the rancher. "I heard he's sent letters to his attorneys asking them to invite people to settle in the town of Valley View."

"What the hell is a Valley View?" Grant asked, sitting down and pouring himself a drink of whiskey.

"That's the name of the settlement now. It's official too."

"Since when?"

"Ever since the territorial governor signed some damn paper making it legal."

Grant sat and sipped his whiskey and stared at the younger man. "That means they'll soon have a marshal and mayor and judge, and maybe even a town council and all that crap."

"I guess so."

Grant cussed, loud and with much feeling.

"I say we attack the town," young Mark said. "Tonight. Burn the damn place to the ground."

Grant shook his head. "No. That's completely out of the question."

"Why?"

"It's a town now. A regular town. You pull something like that, and the governor will ask for troops to be sent in. That, or federal marshals. We don't want that."

"No, we sure as hell don't." Mark looked puzzled for a moment. "Then . . . what do we do?"

Grant slowly shook his head. "I don't know. Give me time to think on it some. Time. I need time to think. How's your pa?"

"Out of his head. He's crazy. This time he ain't comin' out of it. We got him locked in his room. He rants and raves and slobbers and hollers. I guess we're gonna have to chain him up like some wild animal and haul him off to an asylum somewheres."

The young man spoke of his father's condition with about as much emotion as asking for someone at the dinner table to pass him the mashed potatoes.

"You don't seen too broke up about it, boy," Grant said, his distaste for the young man showing on his face.

"I ain't broke up about it at all, Grant. And neither is Peaches or Mike. Livin' with Pa was like livin' in the house with a grizzly bear."

He hesitated and looked around for a moment. "Grant, your house is awful quiet today. Where is everybody? Where is Mrs. Perkins?"

"I sent Darleen out to California to visit her sister. Tried to get Lucy to go with her, but she refused to go. You know what a hardhead she can be, don't you, boy?"

"Yes, sir. I do. I reckon that's why she and Peaches get along so well. They're so much alike."

"I don't know where Lucy has gone off to. She and your sister are probably together, gettin' into trouble. Victor's probably laid up somewheres drunk. He isn't worth killin'."

"Do we hire more gunhands, Grant?"

"No. I thought when Scott Dice got here we'd finally be rid of Frank Morgan. That didn't work out worth a damn."

"Town buried him the other day."

"Yeah. I know."

"Grant, I know you and Daddy are worth a lot of money—I finally got to open the books—but all these gunslicks on the payroll is expensive. And there ain't no work gettin' done."

"You ain't tellin' me nothin' I don't already know, boy."

"Our foreman just quit yesterday."

"So did mine," the older man admitted. "Said he was pulling out and wouldn't be back."

"Grant?"

"Yes, boy?"

"I'm scared. We could lose everything we got if this . . . mess don't turn around in our favor."

"No, boy," the older rancher corrected the young man. "We won't lose everything. But we will lose a lot of land and access to some water and have to cut back the size of our herds."

Mark met the eyes of Grant Perkins. "I don't intend for that to ever happen, Grant. I'm not gonna *let* it happen."

"Don't do nothin' stupid, boy."

"We can't just sit here and allow it all to disappear, Grant. Pa wouldn't have allowed that, and since he's . . . well, out of it, then I guess it's all up to me, right?"

"It's up to us, boy."

"Well . . . what do we do?"

Grant sighed and stood up. He reached for his gun belt, hanging from a peg on the wall. "Let's take a ride out to the river and think about this situation. We'll come up with something."

"We better," Mark said, a grim note behind his words.

"I've been appointed Mayor of Valley View," Joe Wallace said. "And I have full authority to name a marshal."

"Don't look at me," Frank said, setting down his coffee cup.

The men were in the Sunburst Café. With them at the table were John Platt and the blacksmith, Earl Martin. Those two men, so far, made up the entire town council.

They'd been appointed after a meeting the day before of all the farmers in the area.

"You've toted a badge before," John said. "And I happen to know that you were once appointed to be a federal marshal. Right?"

"I can see where this is going," Frank grumbled.

"And I got this here message from Sheriff Breedlaw." Joe pulled out a piece of paper. "Come in on the stage yesterday. You been named a deputy sheriff." He held up the paper for Frank to see. "Says so right here."

Frank took the paper and read it carefully. Sheriff Breedlaw had indeed named him a county deputy sheriff. He grunted. Breedlaw had set him up, for a fact. And probably Joe and John Platt were in on it as well. "You boys sure must have given this a lot of thought," Frank said, looking first at Joe, then at John with a scowl on his face.

The men looked at each other and smiled, John saying happily, "You might say that. But not only can you enforce the law here in town, you can work out in the county too."

"How wonderful," Frank replied.

The men grinned at him like cats in a canary cage.

Sheriff Breedlaw sent this over too," John added, taking a badge out of his pocket and laying it on the table and pushing it toward Frank. "Pin it on, Frank."

"Somebody has to swear me in."

"Consider yourself sworn in," Joe said, adding, "Marshal and Deputy Sheriff Morgan."

Frank sighed and picked up the badge. John signaled toward the kitchen, and Charlie Jordan and his wife, Becky, came marching out, Charlie carrying a large cake. He set it down on the table. "Congratulations, Marshal Morgan," the café owner said.

Frank pinned on the badge. "I reckon I'd better see about getting a jail built."

"On one of those ten lots you bought?" Joe asked with a smile.

Frank picked up the cake knife and grinned. "Why not? It'll probably be the only jail in the territory where the marshal owns it."

"I'll get the saucers," Becky said.

After everyone had a hunk of cake and another cup of coffee, it was time for the lunch crowd to come in, and Frank and the mayor and town council left. Frank stood on the boardwalk for a moment, waiting for the foreman to show up. He had definite ideas about a jail . . . since he was paying for it.

The small town of Valley View and the area around it grew by 150 people in a month's time.

"It's gonna be a regular city," John Platt said.

The liveryman and Frank were sitting on a bench and talking outside the stable on a warm summer's morning. The sounds of hammering and sawing filled the air, mixed with the sounds of huge wagons bringing in construction materials and store fixtures and smaller wagons bringing in families to operate the businesses and farm the land.

Frank pointed to several mounted men passing through the town. "That's the third bunch of gunslicks I've seen leaving over the past few days."

"You reckon the war is over?" John asked.

"No." Frank's reply was flat. "The Diamond and the GP haven't given up. Not by a long shot. They've got too much to lose to throw in the towel. The fire isn't out yet. It's just smoldering."

"What do you think they're gonna do?"

"I don't have any idea, John. But we've seen about ten or twelve gunhands pull out. That still leaves thirty or forty men on the payrolls, drawing fighting wages."

"The pretenders are leaving, the hard cases staying," the liveryman said softly.

"Yes."

John pointed to a line of heavily loaded wagons rolling through town. "More wire for the Diamond and GP. They're stringin' miles of the damned stuff."

"Barbed wire is the boundary line of the future," Frank said. "Never thought I'd see it happen, but there it is."

"Hell, Frank, they can't wire out the flow of water. That's impossible," John argued.

"No. But they can dam it up."

John slowly turned his head to stare at Frank. "The river makes a split some north of your place, both branches narrowing down, then comes together again south of town."

"I know."

"If they built a dam just after the split, they could divert water onto both ranges."

"That's right. And the homesteaders would be left high and dry—literally—during the dry months, when they need the water."

"You reckon? . . ."

"I think so, John."

"Well, you're the law, stop them."

"Nobody's done anything yet. Besides, that would take a court order and that might have to come from a federal judge. I don't know anything about the finer points of law." Frank stood up.

"Where are you goin'?"

"To take a ride. I'm going to snoop some."

"Let me know what you find."

"Will do," Frank replied, saddling Stormy. He swung into the saddle and headed north, toward the river's fork. An hour and a half later, his suspicions were confirmed. The Diamond and GP hands were building an earthen dam, reinforced with logs.

"And so far as I know, there isn't a thing I can do about it . . . at least for the present." He turned Stormy's head for the ride back to town. "But I can sure write some letters to find out what I can do."

Twenty-one

Frank wrote letters to officials of the territory—including the governor—as well as to his own attorneys, in California and Colorado. But he knew that it would be weeks before he heard from anybody.

"The territorial governor is a rancher," John Platt told him. "You better not count on any help from him."

"I'm not," Frank replied. "But if somebody with the power to do something doesn't act quickly, this war could flare up again. And you know as well as I do who's going to start it and how."

"Paul Adams," John said without hesitation. "He'll blow the dam."

"That's right, and then the GP and the Diamond will start digging canals to divert the flow. A dam might be illegal, but canals aren't."

"Wonder why Grant didn't think of that in the first place."

"Too much work and time involved in something that complicated. He'd have to bring mules and earth-scrapers in, and people with enough sense to use them."

"You seen this done?"

"Yes. There's a lot of work in doing it. And when it's done, it's permanent."

"I hope he don't think of it."

"You and me, John."

Frank walked over to the newly constructed shell of the marshal's office, standing for a moment outside the building. Stone was being hauled in to build the cell area. When completed, the jail would be as secure as man could make it.

Frank looked up and down the main street. Valley View was fast becoming a real town. Some of the new stores were already open and doing a brisk business. The church/school was completed and painted. Men were working from can to can't stringing wire for the telegraph. A telegrapher had been hired.

"Amazing how a little village can spring into a real town practically overnight," Frank muttered.

"It just takes the will of the people," Doc Archer said, walking up to Frank. "All working together."

"I reckon so, Doc."

"Are you going to stay on here and make Valley View your permanent home, Frank? After the trouble is settled, I mean."

Frank smiled. "Doubtful, Doc. I'll drift on in a few months."

"And do what, Frank?"

Frank lifted his big hands in a gesture of "who knows?" "Just drift, Doc, like I been doin' for longer than I care to think about."

"And play Robin Hood somewhere else?"

Frank laughed at that. "You're giving me too much credit, Doc. You said it yourself: It's the people who made this town. It was started months before I arrived."

"Perhaps, Frank. But you were the catalyst."

Frank did not reply to that. He wasn't sure what catalyst meant. "Are you going to stick around, Doc?"

"Probably. I like the country and I like the people."

"You won't get rich practicing here."

"I never looked to get rich, Frank."

"You been paid in chickens and eggs yet?" Frank asked with a smile.

"As a matter of fact, I have." Both men looked up the street at the sound of a yell. "My word," the doctor said. "Who are those two ladies?"

"That would have to be Peaches Rogers and Lucy Perkins."

"Peaches?"

"That's all I ever heard her called."

"They are both quite, ah, buxom young ladies."

"I reckon I'd have to agree with you, Doc."

Peaches and Lucy rode closer, and Doc Archer's eyes bugged out a bit. "Ah . . . Frank, it appears from all the jiggling, those ladies aren't wearing any undergarments. At least not from the waist up."

"Sure looks that way, Doc. Quite a sight to behold, isn't it?"

"It's embarrassing!"

The workmen had stopped their hammering and sawing to stand and stare in awe.

"My stars and garters," one workman exclaimed. "Them bonnie lassies ain't got nothing on under them shirts."

Several of the town's ladies had stepped out of a dress shop to stare at the ranchers' daughters. One of them clucked her tongue and said, "That is positively disgraceful."

"It certainly is," her friend agreed.

"Ah, shut up!" Peaches hollered at the women. "You dried-up old biddy."

"Well!" the woman said, stamping her foot. "Marshal!" she hollered at Frank. "I insist you do something about those hussies!"

"Hussies!" Lucy yelled. "Who are you callin' a hussy, you old bag?"

"They haven't broken any laws, Mrs. Hunsacker," Frank called.

"There should be a law against *them!*" Mrs. Hunsacker hollered.

Peaches told the women where to shove their remarks.

The two women's hands flew to their mouths in shock at the profane—and probably quite uncomfortable—suggestion.

"Whoa!" Frank said.

"My heavens!" Doc Archer said.

"What's the matter with you two?" Lucy hollered at Frank and the doctor. "You both look like you just ate a green persimmon."

"Yeah," Peaches said. "Both of you are all puckered up worser than them two old bags."

"Now that will do, ladies," Frank told the two young women, stepping out into the street.

"Or you'll do what?" Lucy yelled. "Arrest us? On what charge?"

"Disturbing the peace," Frank said, walking over to the young women. "Perhaps creating a public nuisance."

"You wouldn't dare!" Peaches hollered.

"You want to try me?" Frank asked softly.

"Is that man bothering you ladies?" Bobby Doolin asked, stepping out of the hotel.

"Shut up, Doolin," Frank said. "This is none of your affair. Keep your mouth out of it."

"He sure is bothering us," Lucy yelled. "He's a big damn pain in the butt, that's what he is."

"Damn sure is," Peaches said.

"What don't you pick on somebody your own size, Morgan?" Doolin asked, walking to the edge of the boardwalk to stand and smile at Frank.

"You've decided this is the day you brace me, Doolin?"

"Looks like it."

"You're a damn fool."

Bobby Doolin did not take any outward offense at Frank's words. He continued to smile and stare at Frank.

Lucy and Peaches walked their horses out of the way and swung down from the saddle. They stepped up on the boardwalk to watch the impending action between the two gunfighters, both of the young ladies jiggling as they walked.

The workmen's eyes were busy, shifting from Frank and

Bobby to Lucy and Peaches. It was a difficult choice for the men to make.

"You settle the marshal's hash this day, mister," Lucy said, "and you can have anything you want."

Bobby cut his eyes just for an instant. "Anything?" he asked.

"You're lookin' at it," Peaches answered.

"Disgusting!" Mrs. Hunsacker squalled.

"Whoors!" her equally large companion said. "That's all they are. Both of them."

Peaches made an obscene hand gesture to the women.

"Oh, my word!" Mrs. Hunsacker hollered. "Did you see that, Edna?"

"Do something, Marshal!" Edna yelled. "I demand you do something with those vile women."

"Yeah, Marshal," Bobby sneered. "Do something." Bobby stepped off the boardwalk into the street.

"Any time you're ready, Doolin."

"I think I'll make you sweat a little before I kill you, Drifter."

Frank smiled at that. "Or give yourself a little more time to work up some courage."

Doolin lost his smile. "You flatter yourself, Drifter."

"I don't think so. I just spoke the truth, that's all."

A large crowd had gathered, lining the boardwalks on both sides of the street. Doc Archer and Richard and Lydia Carmondy were among the onlookers. Lydia had her little hanky at the ready.

"I'll send you to hell, Drifter!" Doolin spat the words at him. "No man calls me a coward and lives."

"Then stop talking and make your play, Doolin. Before you cause me to fall asleep right here in the street."

Doolin regained his smile and after a quick glance at Lucy and Peaches, said, "You pretty ladies ready to see Morgan fall?"

"Yeah, kill the bastard!" the young women yelled.

Frank stood in the street. Silent. Waiting. It was something he'd done a hundred times in his long and gun-smoke-filled past. He was as ready as he could be.

"Arrest that man for ignoring the law, Marshal!" a newly arrived woman yelled. She had been in Valley View for less than a week. "And those two women as well."

"Shut up, Ginny," her husband told her. "This is gonna be a killin', not an arrest."

"Don't tell me to shut up, Henry," she snapped right back. "Or you can make the davenport your bed tonight."

Someone in the crowd laughed at that.

Frank paid no attention to the comments coming from the crowd. He took a step toward Doolin. Doolin took a couple of steps toward him. Frank judged the distance at about forty feet. A comfortable shooting range.

The crowd fell silent. Somewhere in the town a dog barked, a rooster crowed, a cat yowled.

Neither man standing in the street paid any attention to the sounds around them. Their focus was on each other. Neither man blinked; their eyes were locked on each other. Each one waited for the other to make a move.

Bobby Doolin's right hand twitched, and Frank's Peacemaker seemed to leap into his hand at the same time Doolin's six-gun roared flame and smoke.

A woman standing on the boardwalk watching the gunfight screamed in fright and shock as Doolin's slug buried itself in the wood next to her head.

Bobby Doolin slowly sank to his knees as bright crimson began staining the front of his white shirt. He lifted his six-gun, earing back the hammer as he did so.

Frank shot him again, and a second splash of crimson appeared on his shirt.

"You son of a bitch!" Bobby Doolin said, then fell over on his face in the dirt.

Twenty-two

Doolin's pistol dropped from suddenly weakened fingers. He made no attempt to pick it up. He remained on his knees, in the dirt of the street, with his head hanging down, watching the blood that pumped from his chest pool underneath him. Frank slowly walked toward the man, stopping a few feet from the hard-hit gunfighter.

"You're supposed to be dead, Morgan," Doolin said, his voice surprisingly strong for a man with two .45-caliber slugs in his chest.

"I decided to stick around for a while longer, Bobby."

"I can't believe I missed you."

"It happens."

"I don't ever miss."

"You did this time."

"I reckon so."

"The doctor is standing right over yonder on the boardwalk, Doolin. You want me to call him over?"

"What the hell for? I'm lung-shot."

"Just thought I'd ask. How about the preacher then? He's a good man."

"I ain't exactly the prayin' type, Morgan." A pink froth was forming on Doolin's lips, confirming the man's belief he was lung-shot.

"Want me to take a look at your wounds, Doolin?"

"Hell, no!"

"Well, here comes the doctor. You tell him that."

Doc Archer knelt down beside the men. "Will you let me unbutton your shirt?" he asked Doolin.

"Leave me alone, sawbones."

"As you wish. But I might be able to save your life."

"Don't piss on my leg and tell me it's rainin', Doc."

"I beg your pardon?"

"I'm hit in both lungs. And I know it. I'm havin' trouble breathin' and I'm not long for this world. Leave me alone."

"The Lord will not desert you," Reverend Carmondy said, walking up. "Have no fear of that."

Doolin lifted pain-filled eyes to look at the preacher. "Who in the hell are you?"

"Reverend Carmondy. I serve the Lord."

"You don't reckon you could serve me a glass of whiskey, could you?" Doolin asked, his lips curling in a half smile.

"Most certainly not!" Richard replied indignantly. "Strong drink is not what you need right now."

"Says who?" Doolin asked. Then he coughed out a mouthful of scarlet blood and fell over on his side, his eyes closed.

"Has the man expired?" Richard asked, taking a step back as if the condition might be contagious.

"Not yet," Doc Archer said, checking Doolin's pulse. "But it won't be long. He's unconscious."

"You want him carried over to your office?" Frank asked.

"Might as well," the doctor said, standing up and brushing the dirt from the street off of his dark trousers, "though he was right about one thing. There isn't much I can do for him now." He glanced around and added, "Somebody can go tell the new undertaker he's got a customer. What's the undertaker's name? This place is growing so rapidly I can't keep up."

"Wilbur Morris," Frank told him. "I'll send . . . no, wait. Here he comes now."

"He's a barber too, isn't he?" Archer asked.

"Yes. And he's having a proper bathhouse built behind his place."

Doolin was toted off to the doctor's small patient room, and Frank walked over to the Sunburst Café for coffee. Men and women congratulated him as he pushed through the crowd. Frank smiled and nodded his head in acknowledgment of the compliments.

Sitting down at a table, Frank suddenly felt weary. He wasn't sad about killing Bobby Doolin. The man had killed a lot of perfectly innocent men for money. That wasn't it. Frank was just tired—tired, well, mentally, he guessed was the right word for it.

The newly hired waitress set a mug of coffee in front of him, and Frank thanked her. He dumped in some sugar and stirred it, watching as the door opened and John Platt entered. The liveryman got a mug of coffee and sat down at the table with Frank.

"Might not have seemed like it from where you was standin', Frank—probably didn't—but you was a blink of an eye faster than Doolin."

Frank slowly nodded his head. "What I was, was lucky, John. Real lucky," he said, thinking that he'd always been lucky when it came to killing people. It was living with them that caused him trouble.

"Lucy and Peaches took off out of town."

"Good. I don't feel like putting up with the foul-mouthed antics of those two."

"They are a pair, ain't they?" John grinned at Frank. "But they do jiggle nice."

"You better not say that in front of your wife," Frank said, returning the grin.

"Don't worry. I don't want a fryin' pan upside my head."

"What's the latest word on Mark Rogers? Have you heard anything more about him?"

"Just that he was tied up like a wild animal and hauled

off to the insane asylum. Feller I talked to said he was a babblin' idiot. Foamin' at the mouth crazy."

"You don't seen very surprised about it."

"I'm not. I always knowed somethin' was wrong with him. I've seen the man go out of his head over nothin' at all. But I can't imagine what's gonna happen to the Diamond with Mark Junior at the reins. Nothin' good, I can tell you that."

"Won't Junior listen to Grant on this matter?"

"Maybe. For a time. But Junior is a lot like his dad in that he's thickheaded. Mark was never wrong about anything, and Junior is just like him. And he's got a bad temper. He's dangerous, Frank. Like a rattler."

"I'll keep that in mind."

John looked out the window and smiled. "It's gonna be a real nice town, Frank. Thanks to you."

"I played only a small part, John. The people did most of it."

"If you say so, Frank. You give any thought to sticking around and making this your home?"

"Very little, John. I like to keep on the move. Makes life more interesting."

"Don't you ever get lonely?"

"Sometimes. I don't dwell on that."

"As long as there's a trail, you're gonna find it and follow it?"

"I guess that sums it up."

Both men fell silent and watched as a rider came galloping into town, reining up in front of what would soon be the marshal's office and jumping out of the saddle.

"I think he's looking for me," Frank said, pushing back his chair and reaching for his hat.

"Sit still. He's headin' this way on the run."

"You know him?"

"One of them new homesteaders. I don't know his name."

The man jerked open the door to the café and stepped

in. He was all wild-eyed and red-faced. "Marshal! You gotta come quick."

"Settle down," Frank cautioned. "What's happened?"

"Somebody blowed up the dam. Killed a couple of Diamond hands."

"Good," John grunted.

"When did this happen?"

"'Bout a couple of hours ago, I guess. I don't rightly know. But that ain't all. Bunch of cowboys attacked the Mosby homestead. . . ."

"Wait a minute." Frank stopped the man. "Where is the Mosby place? That's a new one on me."

"The Mosbys bought the homestead from the Spencer family. They pulled out last week."

Frank looked at John. "Spencer?"

"Don't ask me. Folks is buyin' and sellin' homesteads faster than I can keep up with it."

"Spencer filed on a section that butted up against the mountains," a man drinking coffee at the counter said. "The land's all right, but he didn't stay on it long. It was idle for some time. Mosby was just provin' it up."

Frank blinked a couple of times. "Who are you?"

The man smiled. "Dick Edwards. I just bought the Landry place over east of here. Landry told me all about the settlers in the valleys and the two big ranchers . . . and about you, Marshal Morgan."

"I met Landry once," John said. "He was a rawhider."

"He sure was that," Edwards said. "Place was held together with rawhide and rope. But I been workin' from can to can't gettin' it back in shape. Took me a break today and brung the wife in town to do some shoppin'."

"Here comes the doc," Charlie Jordan called from the counter.

Doc Archer pushed open the door and started over to Frank's table. "Coffee, please, Charlie."

"Comin' right up, Doc."

"Doolin just died," the doctor said, shaking his head. "He regained consciousness long enough to ask me to tell you he'd see you in hell."

Frank smiled. It was just like Doolin, who'd always been known for his warped sense of humor.

"I notified Wilbur Morris," the doc continued. "He's going to handle everything. What about Doolin's horse and personal belongings?"

"Did he had enough money to pay for the funeral?" Frank asked.

"Oh, yes."

"I'll take care of the rest of his things. I want to check in his saddlebags for the addresses of some family he might have."

"What about the dam and Mosby?" the man who brought the news hollered, impatient at being ignored while Frank talked to Dr. Archer about Doolin.

"Was Mosby hurt?" Frank asked.

"Hurt? Hell, no, he wasn't hurt. He was kilt!"

Twenty-three

The bodies of the slain Diamond hands had been removed from the site. Frank found only a couple of dark stains on the dirt to show where they'd fallen and bled out. He eased Stormy to the bank of the river and sat there watching it, thinking of all the trouble it was going to cause in the town. The river was flowing freely once again. The dam had been destroyed by a massive charge of dynamite. Large boulders and even some trees had been uprooted and strewn about by the force of the blast.

Frank sighed and headed over to the Mosby homestead. The house and barn had been burned to the ground. There was no sign of Mosby or any members of his family. Frank had no idea who might have hauled off the body of the homesteader or where the body might have been taken.

Stymied as to what to do next, Frank rode back to town, stopping at his house to feed Dog. It was full dark when he swung down from the saddle at the livery. John stepped out of his office to greet him.

"What'd you find out there, Frank?" John asked.

"Nothing, John," Frank told him. "No bodies, no nothing. Lots of tracks, leading in all directions."

"Figures."

"Anyone from the Diamond been in to file a complaint?"

"Nope. You didn't expect them to, did you?"

"Not really. I wouldn't if I were walking in their boots. I'd want the law to stay far away."

"I think Mark Junior has taken the bull by the horns, Frank," John said, "An' now there's no tellin' who's gonna get gored."

"You think Grant was unaware this was going to happen?"

"I'd bet on it. Grant's not the fire-breather Big Mark was. Given half a chance, I think he'll pull back and take his losses."

"You think it'd be worth my time riding out and having a talk with the man?"

"Sure wouldn't hurt none. Joe was tellin' me just today a bank is lookin' to come in here."

Frank had to smile at that.

John picked up the smile in the lantern light. "That was your doin', wasn't it, Frank?"

"I might have had my attorneys write a letter or two."

"I thought as much when Joe told me about the bank."

"You mind if I bed down here tonight, John? I just don't feel like riding back to my place."

"Help yourself. You know where the bunk and the coffeepot is. See you in the morning."

"I'll head out to the GP early. Maybe I'll get there in time for breakfast."

"See you."

"One more thing, John. You seen Steve Harlon around lately?"

"I ain't seen hide nor hair of him in days."

"It wouldn't be like Harlon to pull out of a fight. Something's going on, and I'd better find out what it is. I don't like surprises. Good night, John."

Frank rode up to the main gate to the GP ranch house just after dawn the next day. He did not have a long wait before riders came out to meet him.

"You got a lot of damn nerve, Morgan! Comin' out here

where you ain't been invited an' you ain't wanted," Bob Campbell told him.

"The El Paso Kid," Frank replied with a friendly grin on his face, as if he were greeting an old friend. "You're a long way from home, Kid."

"I come and go as I please, Morgan. I don't need no nanny to look after me."

Frank looked at the other riders, his expression remaining pleasant and open, like he was just out riding and had stopped to chew the fat. "Jack King. I'm surprised you're still alive, Jack."

Jack grunted at him.

"Jess Stone," Frank said to the third man. "How have you been lately, Jess?"

"Just like a grade of cotton, Drifter. Fair to middlin'."

"What do you want, Morgan?" Bob asked.

"To speak to your boss."

"Maybe he don't want to talk to you."

"Then let Grant tell me that."

The three gunslingers exchanged glances. After a few seconds, Jess said, "You wait right here, Morgan. I'll see." He turned his horse and rode back to the main house.

Jack King and Bob Campbell sat their horses and stared at Frank, neither man speaking. Their expressions were grim, their jaws set.

Frank smiled and said, "Nice day, isn't it, boys?"

"It was till you showed up," Bob replied.

"Now, Bob," Frank said, "that isn't a very neighborly thing to say."

"I ain't feelin' neighborly, Morgan."

"Too bad. Are you ill, Bob?"

"No, I ain't ill, Morgan! I just don't like you."

"Now, now, Bob. Calm down. What did I ever do to you?"

"You whupped Dick Fuller, for one thing. He was a friend of mine. We rode a lot of trails together."

"*Was* a friend of yours? What happened to him?"

"You cut his spirit, Morgan. After that whuppin' you give him, all the sand seemed to drain out of him."

"Well, now, Bob, it seems to me that Dick was a tad on the cocky side. He got all up in my face that night. He was asking for a come-down. Don't you agree?"

"Not one as bad as you give him. He was stove up for a damn month after that fight."

"I'd be lying if I said I was sorry to hear that."

"He's workin' for thirty a month and found down in Kansas. He ain't packed a six-gun in years."

"I probably saved his life then, Bob. Dick was no gun-hand, and it seems to me a man ought to know his limitations."

Jack King smiled at that. "I got to agree with Morgan on that, Bob. Dick couldn't hit the side of a barn with a pistol. It was only a matter of time till somebody blowed him outta his boots."

"He was still a friend of mine. And I ain't got no use for you, Morgan. None a-tall."

"I'll probably lose a lot of sleep worrying about that, Bob."

"Hell with you, Morgan!"

"Whatever," Frank said, his eyes shifting to look over Bob's shoulders toward the distant ranch house. "Here comes Jess with a couple more men. This might get interesting now."

"That's the boss with him," Jack said after twisting in the saddle for a look-see.

Jess and the other hand, a man Frank didn't know, hung back while Grant rode up to the closed gate and sat in his saddle, glaring at Frank. "What the hell do you want, Morgan?"

"To talk to you, Grant. Am I in time for breakfast?"

Grant blinked at that. "By God, Morgan, you got your share of nerve. I can't take that away from you."

"The ride out here made me hungry, that's all."

Grant smiled and reached down, unlatching the gate.
"Well, hell, come on in. I ain't never turned nobody away
hungry."

Frank never had any doubt about that. It just wasn't the
Western way, and for all of his faults, Grant was a man of
the West.

After beefsteak and eggs and fried potatoes and biscuits,
the men took coffee into the study and sat down. Both
rolled cigarettes. Grant looked over at Frank and smiled.

"I think I'd rather put boots on your feet than feed you
for any length of time, Morgan. You've got a right good
appetite."

"That was a fine meal, Grant. I thank you."

"Thank the cook."

"You mean Lucy didn't prepare that?" Frank asked with
a smile.

"You have to be joking!" Grant said with a snort and a de-
risive grin. "That girl wouldn't know a fryin' pan from a
coffeepot." He screwed the butt into a corner of his mouth,
put a flame to it, and said, "Enough jabber. Let's get down to
it, Morgan. Spell it out for me. What do you want?"

"I want this war to end."

"Tell the sodbusters to clear out of the valley and it will."

"You know they're not going to do that."

"Then the fight goes on."

"You don't sound too happy about it."

The rancher sighed heavily. "Truth is, I'm not."

"How many hands you have working for you, Grant?"

"Not countin' the gunhands, 'bout twenty or so. More
come roundup time. Why?"

"Have each one of them file on a section of land. Then
buy it from them. Same with your kids. You've already
proved up hundreds, maybe thousands of acres on your
own. It's yours . . . legally. Add twenty or twenty-five sections to that, and you're not going to lose very much land
at all."

Grant thought about that for a moment, then slowly nodded his head. "Yeah. Sounds simple, don't it?"

"It is simple, Grant. And bloodless." Frank stared at Grant through a haze of cigarette smoke hanging in the room. "And the beauty of it is it's not much more expensive than payin' for all these gunhands to sit around waitin' to kill somebody."

"There's one hitch to that, Morgan. If I let these gunhands go, Mark Junior will hire them. And that's a fact you ain't takin' into consideration." He looked at Frank. "And it is a fact."

"You let me worry about Junior."

Grant sat staring out of the window and smoking and thinking for a few moments, and then he stubbed out his cigarette and looked over at Frank. "Town's growin', ain't it?"

"By leaps and bounds, Grant. Got a telegraph ready to go, and probably a bank is coming in."

"We need a bank close by. I'm glad to hear that." Again, he sighed. "Hell, I'll be glad to see the war over. I ain't a young buck anymore. I'm not full of piss and vinegar like I was years back."

"Plus you've got cattle wandering all over hell and back since you been neglecting them to fight this war with the homesteaders."

"You mighty right about that. Roundup time's come and gone. Time for my regular hands to get back to work."

"Then end your part in it. Most of the guns you've hired will move on. Some will hire on with the Diamond, but not all of them. Junior can't continue this fight on his own. It'll be too expensive for him to try and foot the bill for it all by himself."

"He'll damn sure try, Morgan. I'm really beginnin' to believe Junior's got some of his father's madness in him."

"Maybe. You might be right. But your part in all this is over?"

"You have my hand on it, Morgan." Grant rose from his chair and extended his hand.

Frank stood up and took the peace offering. Half the battle had been won.

Frank rode over to the Diamond spread, hoping to talk to Mark Junior. He was met at the main gate by Steve Harlon and Pete Dancer.

"I was asking about you, Steve. Hadn't seen you around lately. Thought you might have pulled out."

"I'm staying in the main house here, Morgan. Mark was kind enough to offer me a room. Much nicer than the bunkhouse."

Pete Dancer rolled his eyes at that, and Frank smiled at the expression on the man's face.

"Is Mark here?" Frank asked.

"He isn't receiving visitors at this time," Steve replied.

Again, Pete rolled his eyes at Steve's reply.

"Well, that's too bad, Steve. When do you suppose he might be receiving visitors?"

"You? Never."

"You will tell him I stopped by?"

"He knows you're here, Morgan. Peaches wanted to shoot you."

"I'm certainly glad you stopped her."

"I'm reserving that pleasure for myself, Morgan," Steve said with a nasty grin.

"You want to do it now?"

"In the very near future, Morgan. Soon."

"How do you figure you can do what Doolin couldn't? You going to back-shoot me, Steve?"

"You're pushing me, Morgan. That's not a wise thing to do."

"When I decide to push you, I assure you, you'll know it."

"Go on back to town, Morgan," Dancer said. "You

ain't gonna get to see Mark this day . . . or any day, for that matter."

"You always rode for the brand, Pete. But you're riding for the wrong brand this time."

"Maybe so, Morgan. But I took the man's money."

"Is it enough money to die over?"

Steve shrugged. "No one lives forever."

Before Frank could reply, Steve added, "You've overstayed your welcome, Morgan. Ride on."

"And you're talking for Mark?"

"I'm talking for Mark."

Frank turned Stormy's head and put his back to the two gunslingers. He headed back to town. He stopped at the Calen homestead on the way back and brought them up to date.

"The GP is really out of it?" Van asked.

"We shook hands on it. Out here, that's as good as a signed contract," Frank said.

"But Mark Junior is still going to pursue the fight?" Virginia asked.

"Looks like it. But he can't last alone. I'm hoping he'll soon realize that and fire his gunhands."

"You think he will?"

Frank shrugged his reply.

Virginia poured the men coffee and then sat down at the table with them. "I got some pie I baked yesterday, Frank. You want some?"

"No, thanks. I had breakfast at the GP."

Van looked up in surprise. "You actually sat down at a table with Grant Perkins?"

"Yes. Had a nice chat with him."

"Well, I'll be damned. I guess the GP is really out of this trouble."

"I think so."

"Was his daughter, Lucy, there?" Virginia asked.

"She might have been in the house. She wasn't at the breakfast table."

"How about the boy, Victor?" Van inquired.

"I didn't see him. I don't think he'll be any threat. He's a drunk."

"But Lucy might be, if anything were to happen to the father," Virginia said.

"That's a possibility," Frank agreed.

"Have you told Paul Adams about your meeting with Grant?"

"No. I stopped here on the way back to town. You're the only people I've spoken with."

"Is it all right to tell the others?" Van asked.

"Sure."

Virginia reached across the table to touch her husband's hand. "It's hard to believe there will finally be some peace in these valleys."

"Thank the Lord," Van said.

Virginia smiled. "And Frank Morgan."

That simple statement highly embarrassed Frank. He mumbled his good-byes, grabbed up his hat, and headed for the door.

"Thanks for the coffee, Mrs. Calen," Frank said as he climbed up on Stormy.

"Sure you don't want some of that pie?" she asked.

Frank grinned as he pulled Stormy's head around. "If I keep eatin' your pie, I'm gonna have to get a bigger horse," he called over his shoulder.

Twenty-four

Frank sat on a bench in front of his almost finished marshal's office and watched as a dozen gunslingers rode out of the valley. Most of them were men he didn't know. What bothered him was that none of the known gunfighters were leaving. That meant they had probably signed on with the Diamond spread.

"So the war is half over," Frank muttered just as John Platt walked up and sat down.

"The bad boys are still around," the liveryman said. "Junior ain't gonna give up."

"He's a damn fool, John."

"You'll get no argument from me on that."

"I guess that's the end of the gunfighters leaving," Frank said, looking up the road.

"Not a one from the Diamond pulled out."

"No. And I guess Junior hired a bunch from the GP. Damn him for a fool!"

"Wire's up!" a man yelled from the edge of town. "They're gettin' ready to send test signals."

"Finally connected with the outside world," John said. "That's both a good thing and a bad thing, I reckon."

Frank pointed to a building under construction across the street. "The new bank building. Going to be a nice place."

John grinned and said, "You going to take a hand in gettin' us a newspaper in here, Frank?"

Frank shook his head. "No. I don't really know anybody

who'd be interested in doing that. But I heard Doc Archer and Joe Wallace talking this morning at the café. They know somebody. Now that the wire is up and they can get news in here, I don't think it'll be long before some printer comes along and sets up shop."

"I do like to read the newspaper," John said wistfully.

"The stage is bringing in papers every week, John."

"And I read ever' damn word in all of them. When I can get my hands on 'em. Usually by the time I get hold of 'em, all the words has damn near been read off 'em."

Frank laughed and stood up. "I'm going to take a walk, John. Want to come along?"

"Nope. I got a shipment of feed comin' in any time. It's overdue now. I'll see you later."

Frank started his stroll at the west end of the town, and began walking up the south side. The town was growing daily. This was not going to be some fly-by-night settlement. Valley View was here to stay . . . although not necessarily by that name. New towns had a habit of changing names after a few years.

They also had a habit of getting rid of gunfighters-turned-marshals after the town had settled down. It seemed once they got all citified and highfalutin, they forgot about the men who'd put their lives on the line to make it happen. It was as if they were embarrassed that they'd ever needed anyone as low-class as a gunfighter to help them become civilized. And if he stayed around, Frank knew the same thing would happen here . . . to him. But he had no plans of sticking around long enough to be asked to leave.

Frank smiled and touched the brim of his hat as he met several ladies out for a morning of shopping and gossiping.

"Such a handsome man," Frank heard one of the ladies whisper.

"Too bad he's a cold-blooded killer," another said.

"Hush," the third said. "He might hear you."

Frank walked on. He did not take offense at the remarks

of the women. He'd heard it all before—and much worse—from good citizens. Many times, in fact.

Joe Wallace hailed him from across the street. "Wait up, Frank!" the mayor yelled, then jogged across the wide street to join Frank on the boardwalk.

"Joe, slow down," Frank said with a smile. "What's the rush?"

"Got news, Frank. We have another new business coming in."

"Oh?"

"Carpenters working on the building right down there at the end of the block." He pointed to the west end of the town. The town had now grown to two full blocks.

"I know, Joe. I gave the people the lot to build on."

"I might have known you'd be one step ahead of me. Doc Archer is really excited to have our own apothecary shop. Now all we need is a newspaper."

"All in good time, Joe."

"I know, I know, Frank. I'm getting impatient. Can't help it."

Frank laughed and patted the man on the shoulder. "This town will be busting at the seams before long, Joe. You'll be making so much money you and your wife will go to Paris, France, to celebrate."

"Oh, no, we won't," the merchant quickly corrected. "All I have to do is look at the waves on a lake and I get sick. You'll not get me on an ocean."

"Joe!" his wife called from across the street. "Supply wagons are here."

"See you, Frank."

"Take it easy, Joe."

Frank could understand why the merchant was excited. His store business had increased dramatically in only a couple of months.

Frank stopped and watched a trio of GP hands ride into town. They waved and smiled at Frank.

What a change in attitude, he thought. Before his talk with Grant Perkins, the man's hands wouldn't've given him the time of day, much less a cordial howdy.

He returned the greeting. "You boys tried out the new café yet?"

"Not yet, Marshal. Food good?" one of the hands answered.

"Best in the territory."

"We'll give it a whirl. Thanks for the tip."

"Glad to oblige. You boys have a good time."

The GP hands tipped their hats and rode on, reining up in front of the saloon. Frank's smile faded as he watched several Diamond hands ride in from the other end of Main Street. Frank had been told by several longtime residents of the area that while the cowboys who rode for the Diamond brand were not gunhands per se, they were a randy bunch, used to getting their own way at any cost. According to the townspeople he'd talked to, the Diamond men had been that way even before the current troubles started.

The Diamond hands dismounted and entered the saloon. Frank stepped off the boardwalk and walked across the street. Time to earn his pay and make sure they didn't cause any trouble while they were in town, he figured as he unconsciously reached down and loosened the hammer thong on his right-hand Colt.

Doc Archer approached him, intercepting Frank before he could enter the saloon. "Frank," the doctor greeted him. "You look troubled. Is something the matter?"

"Maybe. Diamond and GP men just came together in the saloon."

"And you think there will be trouble?"

"Possibly. You better stay out here."

"I might better serve the public if I go in with you, don't you think?"

"You might change your mind if the lead starts flying."

"Let me worry about that."

"Suit yourself." Frank walked to the batwings and stepped inside, Doc Archer right behind him.

In the couple of minutes the hands had been inside the saloon, they had already taken up defensive positions, spread out and facing each other from opposite ends of the bar.

Frank stepped to one side, out of the direct line of fire, pulling Doc Archer with him. The GP hands had noticed Frank, but the Diamond hands had their backs to the front of the saloon and did not see him enter.

"You're all a bunch of yeller bastards," a Diamond hand said, laying his feelings on the line to the GP hands, sticking his hand out in front of him and pointing his finger at the other men.

"Back off, Dale," one of the GP hands warned. "'Fore you step into somethin' you can't pull away from."

"Maybe I don't want to pull away from it, Shorty," the Diamond hand said right back. "'Specially if that somethin' you're talkin' 'bout is somethin' as low as snake crap like you."

"I don't take that kind of mouth from no one," Shorty said, stepping away from the bar.

"That's it!" Frank said sharply. "There'll be no gunplay in this town as long as I'm marshal unless it's me doin' the shootin'. Now, back off and settle down, both of you."

"Or you'll do what?" Dale challenged, turning to face Frank with his right hand hanging down next to the butt of his pistol.

"You really want to fight me, cowboy?" Frank asked, his voice low.

"I might," Dale replied. "I damn sure ain't a-feared of you."

"No one said you were. I'm the law in this town and this part of the county, and I'll telling you to cool down, both of you."

"And I'm tellin' you to go right straight to hell, Morgan!"

"Dale," one of his pards cautioned, moving close to him and putting a hand on his shoulder. "Take it easy."

"Shut up, Nicky," Dale told him, shaking his hand off. "And stay out of this. This is between me and Morgan here."

Frank took a step toward the angry Diamond hand.

Shorty held up both his hands. "I'm out of this, Marshal. We didn't come in here lookin' for trouble."

"I know you didn't," Frank said, taking another step toward Dale. "Dale, cool down, man. Have yourself a drink and everything will be jam and honey."

Dale told Frank where he could stick his suggestion.

"You're backing me into a corner, Dale," Frank warned him. "Don't say anything more." Frank took another step toward the Diamond hand.

"You go to hell, Morgan."

"Dale," Nicky said, "Morgan's givin' you a break. Back off."

"Shut up!" Dale shouted as Frank took another step toward the man. "This ain't none of your affair." Dale's right hand clenched and unclenched as it hovered over the butt of his six-gun. "I'm gonna kill you, Morgan."

"I don't think so, Dale."

"I do! Draw!"

Twenty-five

Just as Dale's hand touched the butt of his pistol, Frank gave him a hard right fist to the side of the jaw, snapping his head around and sending teeth and blood flying. Dale's boots sailed out from under him and he landed on his butt on the floor. Frank reached down and jerked Dale's six-gun from leather, laying it on the bar.

Dale rolled over, moaning, and crawled to his hands and knees, his head hanging down dripping blood onto the dusty boards of the saloon. Frank bent over, grabbed him, and jerked him to his feet, twisting one arm up behind his back. Dale howled in pain.

"Now, by God, you'll do what I tell you," Frank growled in his ear. "Or I'll twist your arm off and beat you to death with it."

"All right!" Dale hollered through split and swollen lips. "All right. You're breaking my arm."

"Better that than him shootin' you," Nicky said, shaking his head in relief that his friend was still alive and breathing.

"You're going to jail, mister," Frank told Dale. "Now walk!"

Dale was escorted out of the saloon, across the street, and into the recently completed jail. Frank shoved him into a cell and slammed and locked the barred door.

Dale bounced off the far wall, slipped, and sprawled across the bunk bolted to the wall. "I'll kill you!" he hollered, trying to get to his feet as he sleeved blood off his mouth.

"Cool off," Frank told him.

"Let me outta here!" he screamed, rushing to the bars and trying to grab Frank through them.

"Maybe tomorrow, Dale," Frank said, moving back a couple of steps so the enraged cowboy couldn't reach him. "Depends on your attitude an' how reasonable you get by then."

Dale cussed him.

"Yeah, yeah," Frank said, walking out of the cell block and into the office. He closed the door behind him. He could hear only the muffled yelling of the Diamond hand.

Frank picked up the jail ledger and wrote Dale's name, the date, and the charges against him. He looked up as the front door opened. Nicky and the other Diamond hands walked in, Nicky carrying Dale's pistol.

"Figured you'd want this," Nicky said, laying the six-gun on the desk.

"Thanks. I'll keep it for your friend."

"When do you reckon he'll get out?"

"Tomorrow. It'll take him that long to cool down."

"You could have killed him."

"I figured I could take him without gunplay."

"He owes you his life," one of the other hands said, nodding his head and staring at Frank as if he couldn't believe the marshal didn't shoot Dale instead of going to the trouble of keeping him alive.

"He'd been drinkin' some before we left the ranch," Nicky said. "And he don't handle whiskey too good."

"He'll have plenty of time to sober up," Frank said.

"And he'll be madder than hell when he does," a Diamond hand said. "Maybe you better let us keep his six-gun, Marshal."

"Good idea. Take it back to the ranch with you."

"You got any objections to us havin' a few drinks and a meal 'fore we leave town?" Nicky asked.

"None at all. Providing you steer clear of the GP hands."

"We ain't got no quarrel with them," another Diamond hand said. "Personal, I wish to hell this fight would stop so we could all get back to work. We got cattle spread all over the damn place and a whole lot of calves that need brandin'."

"And them gunslingers on the payroll is a real pain in the ass," Nicky added. "They don't do nothin' 'ceptin' lay around and eat and drink the boss's whiskey. Most of 'em wouldn't know a brandin' iron from a teacup."

Frank had to smile at that. For a fact, most of the hired guns he'd met over the years were lazy as a pig in slop, and smelled about the same. "Enjoy yourselves in town, boys."

Frank got his hat and locked the front door to the jail behind him as he once again resumed his leisurely stroll around the growing town. He was hailed by the blacksmith, Earl Martin. "Got your first guest in the new jail, Marshal?" the man asked with a grin.

"Just for overnight, Earl. I'll cut him loose in the morning . . . after he pays a fine."

"Money for the town's treasury," the leather-aproned blacksmith replied with an even wider grin.

Frank smiled and waved and walked on.

"Morning, Marshal," Wilbur Morris, the undertaker/barber, greeted Frank as he strolled up to the man's place of business. "It certainly is a wonderful day, isn't it?"

"Yes, it is, Mr. Morris. Very nice."

"First haircut is free, Marshal. Anytime you need a trim."

"I'll remember that, Mr. Morris. Won't be long, I'm sure."

"Anytime, Marshal. Anytime at all."

Frank smiled and walked on.

Frank stopped in at the telegraph office, watching the telegrapher at work for a few minutes. No doubt about it:

Valley View was on the move. The key stopped its clicking, and the telegrapher looked up at Frank and nodded his
head in greeting.

"Staying busy?" Frank inquired.

"Yes, I am," the man replied. "Surprisingly so. I have a
telegram for a Mr. Mark Rogers, Junior. You know anyone
in town who can ride out to the ranch with it?"

"Some Diamond hands are in town now. I can give it to
one of them for you if you want."

"I'd appreciate that." He handed Frank a folded piece of
paper. "It's bad news, I'm afraid. A death in the family."

"Oh?"

The key began clicking and the telegrapher went back
to work. Frank walked out of the office and opened the
paper. The message was informing the Rogers family that
old Mark Rogers was dead. He had died in his sleep. Officials at the institution wanted to know what to do with
the body.

Frank walked over to the saloon and up to Nicky, the Diamond hand. "You better get this out to Junior." He handed
him the telegram.

Nicky read the brief message and nodded his head.
"They'll be a party at the ranch house tonight, Marshal."

"A party?"

"Yeah. Mark and Peaches hated their father. The youngest
kid, Mike, was the only one who could reason with Big
Mark."

"I never hear much about him. What kind of man is
he?"

"He's a good boy. Levelheaded. He's no hand with a
horse or a gun, but he's smart. Knows business."

"So if Mike took over the Diamond, you think the war
would end?"

"Oh, you bet it would. In a heartbeat." Nicky leaned
closer to Frank. "And Lucy Perkins has always been sort
of sweet on Mike. But Lucy's loud and brassy and Mike

is quiet. He's a thinker, likes to read books. I figure if Lucy would calm down a mite, her and him would get together."

"Any chance of that happening?"

"Stranger things have happened, I reckon. But Mike would have to take a belt to her rear end to calm her down."

Frank smiled. "That would be worth seeing."

Nicky nodded. "If she didn't shoot him."

Frank left the saloon and began walking back to his office. He paused when he saw Steve Harlon ride slowly into town, coming in from the east end. Something about the way the man sat in his saddle triggered an alarm in Frank's mind.

He's riding in for a showdown, Frank thought. *I don't know why he chose this day and time, but it's here.*

Steve reined up at the livery and handed the reins to the young man John had hired to help out. Frank stood on the boardwalk and rolled a cigarette, thumbing a match into flame and lighting up. He watched as Steve walked over to the café and stepped inside.

Frank slipped his Peacemaker in and out of leather a couple of times, making sure it wasn't hung up. With Steve he was taking no chances. None at all. Frank stepped off the boardwalk and into the street. He began walking toward the saloon.

Both Joe Wallace and Doc Archer had seen Frank work his .45 in and out of leather, and they both began walking toward him, the doctor coming from his office, the merchant from his store. They met Frank in the middle of the wide and dusty street.

"What's the matter, Frank?" Joe asked.

"It's time."

"Time?" Doc Archer questioned. "Time for what?"

"Time for me and Harlon to get this matter between us settled once and for all."

"How do you know that?" Joe asked. "Is this some pre-arranged thing?"

"No."

"But the man just rode into town. You two haven't exchanged a word. How could you know?"

"I just know. You boys keep out of the way." Frank started walking toward the saloon.

"We're going with you," the doctor said.

"Suit yourselves."

Frank pushed open the batwings and stepped inside, the doctor and the merchant right behind him. Harlon was standing at the bar, a pot of coffee and a cup in front of him. He looked up briefly as Frank entered and walked to the closest end of the bar.

"Morgan," Harlon said. "Share this pot of coffee with me?"

"Don't mind if I do, Steve."

"Barkeep," Harlon said, "a cup for the marshal, if you will."

A cup was placed in front of Frank, and the bartender, a new fellow in town that Frank did not know, quickly backed away. Harlon slid the coffeepot down the bar toward Frank and Frank filled his cup, then slid the pot back toward the gunslick.

"You want this sugar bowl, Frank?" Harlon asked.

"I'll take it without this time, Steve."

"As you wish."

"What's on your mind today, Steve?" Frank asked after taking a sip of the coffee and making a face. Unlike most bar coffee, it was just a little weak for Frank's taste.

"Killing you," Harlon said simply. He sipped his coffee, his eyes staring straight ahead over the rim and ignoring Frank.

"It took you a couple of months to make up your mind, Steve."

"I wanted you to worry a bit."

"I haven't worried about it at all, Steve."

Harlon smiled and finally turned his gaze to Frank. "Always calm and collected and ready, right, Morgan?"

"You could say that."

"I'm going to shoot you right in the middle of that fancy star you've got on your chest, Morgan. They can bury you with that piece of tin embedded in your heart."

"I don't think that's gonna happen."

"I'm better than you, Frank."

"We'll soon know, won't we?"

"Aren't you going to attempt to arrest me for threatening a peace officer?" Harlon asked with a smile as he placed the coffee cup on the bar and turned his body around to face Frank.

"No."

"Oh?"

"What would be the point?"

"I'm disappointed."

"Well, you can live with your disappointment, Steve. For a little while longer anyway."

Harlon laughed at that. "You really are a very arrogant man, Frank. Are you aware of that?"

Frank shrugged and raised his eyebrows as if the question surprised him. "I'm not aware of being arrogant."

"Well, perhaps not. Let's say supremely confident. Would you admit to that?"

"I suppose so."

Using his left hand and keeping his eyes fixed on Frank, Harlon reached across his body and lifted his coffee cup and took a sip. "You do find this coffee to your satisfaction, Frank?"

"It's a bit weak for me," Frank answered, setting his cup on the bar and turning to face the gunman. He leaned his left elbow on the bar and let his right hand hang at his side.

"I thought so. I found it the same. Pity."

"You can always have the barkeep fix another pot."

"No point, Frank." Harlon grinned insolently, a challenge

in his eyes. "You don't have time enough left to have another cup."

"One of us doesn't, that's for sure."

"Gentlemen, gentlemen," Doc Archer said. "I think—"

"I don't give a damn what you think, Doc," Harlon said, interrupting the doctor. "Stay out of matters that you don't understand and don't concern you."

"You, sir, are a very rude man," Doc Archer replied.

Harlon chuckled at that. "Your young friend has sand, Frank. I'll give him that."

"He's new to the West. From Philadelphia."

"Philadelphia!" Harlon replied. "Well, well. I went to college with a fellow from Boston. He was one of the most disagreeable people I ever had the misfortune to meet. Arrogant chap."

"*You* went to *college?*" Archer asked, his tone filled with incredulousness.

"Yes, Frank, your friend is from Philadelphia, all right. Same tone of superiority in his voice. Another insufferable bastard! Do you want me to shoot him, Frank?"

"I'd rather you didn't, Steve. We need him around here."

"Very well. But only as a favor to you." Steve slowly moved a step away from the bar and squared his shoulders, facing Frank dead on. "You ready, Frank?"

"I suppose so."

Faster than the blink of an eye, and without a change of expression, the men drew and fired. The roar of gunfire and the smell of gun smoke filled the room.

"My God," the barkeep said, ducking down and hiding behind the bar.

Twenty-six

Harlon leaned against the bar and smiled at Frank. He dropped his eyes and stared at the spreading red stain on the front of his white dress shirt. "I'll be damned," the hired gun said.

"We probably both will be," Frank replied.

"You beat me," Harlon said. He coughed, and blood dribbled from the corner of his mouth. "I can't believe it. You actually beat me."

"Not really, Steve. You just missed, that's all."

"I never miss."

"You did this time."

Harlon slowly raised his right hand and laid his six-gun on the polished bar, grabbing the edge of the bar to keep from falling down. "How in the hell could I miss, Frank? You're not fifteen feet away."

"You got anxious, I reckon."

"Damn!"

"Let me look at your wounds," Doc Archer said, stepping forward and raising his hand.

"Keep your hands off me, Doc," Harlon told him. "I don't like doctors and I especially don't like doctors from Philadelphia."

"I might be able to save your life," Archer insisted.

"Very doubtful, sawbones. Just keep away from me." Harlon looked back at Frank. His eyes were squinted against the pain, but Frank could still see the sadness in them. "There won't be any songs written and sung about me, will there, Frank?"

"Probably not."

"I'm faster than you, and yet you got all the glory. Somehow that doesn't seem fair."

"Glory, Steve? What glory?"

Blood was beginning to drip from Harlon's chin onto his shirt. "Books written about you, a stage play that's still being performed across the country, songs sung about your deeds. That's glory, Frank."

"And that's what you wanted, Steve?"

"I would have liked it, yes."

Harlon began coughing, and he lost his grip on the edge of the bar. He slowly sank to his knees. He did not have the strength to pull himself back up. With Harlon's gun out of reach of the dying man, Frank holstered his Peacemaker. Doc Archer started toward the downed man.

"Don't come near me, Doc," Harlon said between fits of coughing. "I'm dying. The bullet nicked my heart. Hurts every time it beats. I'm filling up with my own blood. I can feel it."

"You don't know that," Archer said.

Harlon laughed weakly. "Oh, I know it, Philadelphia. Take my word for it. I know it."

Frank motioned to the barkeep. "Make another pot of coffee. Make it stronger than you did this crap"—he pointed to the cooling pot of coffee—"and make it quick."

"Yes, sir. Right now, sir."

Harlon had stopped coughing and his breathing had evened out, though it had a rasping sound to it.

"I have some laudanum," Archer said.

"Drink it yourself," Harlon told him. "I'm not leaving this world all drugged up on painkiller."

"What do you want on your marker, Steve?" Frank asked.

Harlon's pain-clouded eyes cut to Frank and the gunman

smiled, his teeth gleaming redly in the low light of the saloon. "That I was killed by the best long before my time."

"You sure about that?"

"I'm sure."

"Then that's what will be on it."

The Diamond hands and the GP hands had gathered just inside the saloon, near the batwings. They stood together in silence and watched and listened.

"Got anyone I need to notify?"

"Not really. After my parents passed, I didn't see the use of going back to home territory." He grinned in a macabre fashion, his lips parting again in a bloody grimace that had no humor in it. "And then there was that warrant out for me back there. A little matter of a killing." Harlon began coughing hard and spitting up gobs of blood. "Bullet must have nicked a lung too. I don't think I care to hang around much longer to die naturally. Not like this."

"What do you mean?" Doc Archer asked.

"Not only are you an arrogant Philadelphia bastard, but you're hard of hearing too," Harlon said.

Doc Archer's face developed a deep flush. "I don't think I like you very much, Mr. Harlon."

"What I meant, Doc, is this." Harlon fumbled at his belt buckle and pulled out and cocked a small .41-caliber derringer.

As Frank's hand went to the butt of his pistol, Harlon grinned again and said in a raspy, hoarse voice, *"Adios, compadre."*

Frank relaxed his hand and nodded. "So long, Steve."

Harlon stuck the belly gun to his temple and pulled the trigger. The slug blew out the other side of his head as Harlon's body flopped back against the bar, dead with his eyes opened and bugged out.

"My God!" Archer exclaimed.

"Coffee's ready," the barkeep called.

Twenty-seven

Back in his office, Frank went through Steve Harlon's belongings. There were no letters, no address book, nothing that would tell how to notify any friends or family. It was as if Steve had never existed. *Well,* Frank thought, sipping at a cup of coffee, *maybe that's how Steve wanted it.*

Frank looked up as the door opened and Wilbur Morris walked in.

"What can I do for you, Wilbur?" Frank asked the undertaker.

"The dead man didn't have any money on him, Marshal."

Frank tapped Steve's wallet on the desk. "Plenty of money in here, Wilbur. Give him a good funeral."

"When was he born, Marshal?"

"I have no idea."

"How about his horse and rig and guns?"

"I plan to sell them and give the money to the town."

"Fine idea, Marshal," the man said brightly. "Fine idea. Well, I best get to work."

"You do that, Wilbur."

After the undertaker had gone, Frank poured another mug of coffee and took it back into the cell block. "Got some coffee for you, Dale," he told the Diamond hand. "Give a shout when you're hungry and I'll get you something to eat."

" 'Preciate it, Marshal. Sorry 'bout the way I talked back yonder in the saloon."

"You got ten dollars for your fine?"

"Shore."

"All right. Just as soon as the GP hands ride out, I'll cut you loose. How about that?"

"Sounds good to me. Say, you ain't got the makin's on you, have you? I seem to have lost mine."

Frank handed him a tobacco sack and papers. "Keep them, Dale. I have more in my desk."

Dale studied Frank's face for a moment. "You're all right, Marshal. You'll do to ride the river with. You'll have no more trouble out of me. You have my word."

"Sounds good to me, Dale. Enjoy your coffee and smoke. I'll be back to cut you loose in an hour or so."

Dale grinned. "I reckon I'll still be here. Say, Marshal, this jail ain't never been used, has it?"

"You're the first person to be locked up, Dale."

"That's kind of an honor, ain't it?"

"Well . . . I guess you could look at it that way."

"I ought to scratch my name in the rock, so's people will remember me."

"Go right ahead, Dale."

"Believe I'll do that."

Frank walked out of the cell block and through the office, out onto the boardwalk, smiling at Dale's remarks. Frank had never considered being put in jail much of an honor.

"Something amusing, Marshal?" Reverend Carmondy asked, walking up to Frank.

"Just something the prisoner said, Richard. How are you and Lydia today?"

"Both of us are well, thank you. Lydia is busy ordering books for the opening of school this fall."

"I'm sure she'll be a fine teacher."

"The Bible answers all things, right, Richard?"

"Certainly!"

"But sometimes a man sort of has to read between the lines, so to speak, right?"

"I don't know what you mean, Marshal."

"Well . . . I've read the Bible many times. Not the entire thing, mind you. But I enjoy just opening the Bible and reading."

"*You* have read God's word?"

"Many times, Richard. You believe that animals, such as dogs, cats, horses, go to heaven?"

Richard Carmondy looked at Frank for a long moment. "As a matter of fact, Frank, I do. Does that surprise you?"

"Not at all." Frank smiled and patted the preacher on the arm. "See you around, Richard." He walked away.

Richard stood and watched Frank walk away. Then he shook his head. "What a strange man. Simple in his style of life and wants, yet . . . so complex in other ways."

"Seen you talkin' to the preacher, Frank," John Platt said as Frank walked up to the livery. "Looked like it might have been serious."

"Oh, not really." He told John what they had discussed.

John nodded his head solemnly. "I believe that, Frank. I just know my good horses and dogs is waitin' for me inside the Pearly Gates. I think it would be a sorry damn place if they wasn't."

"So do I, John. So do I."

"Five more gunslicks rode out 'bout an hour ago. Did you see 'em?"

"No. Did you recognize any of them?"

"Not nary a one. But they was gunfighters. I'm sure of that. That don't leave too many still on the Diamond payroll."

"Did he have any kin or friends who might decide to come after you, Frank?"

"I don't think so. I didn't find any trace of family in his belongings, an' from what he said as he was dyin', I don't think he kept in touch with whatever family he may have had."

"You know, even takin' into consideration what kind of man he was, that's sad, Frank."

"I know. I felt the same way, John. But it's the life the Big Dealer handed us. So we live with it."

"You're not puttin' yourself in the same class as Steve Harlon, are you, Frank?"

"In a way, yes."

"That's balderdash! I ain't never heard of you hirin' out your gun."

"I've still got the brand of gunfighter on me, John. And no matter what I do, I'll always have it."

John shook his head in doubt. "People who know you put the man first, Frank."

Frank did not reply. He was watching a lone rider come in from the east end of town.

"Lucy Perkins," John said, following Frank's gaze. "All by herself too. Wonder where Peaches is."

"I don't know. But I need to speak to Lucy and cut that Diamond hand loose from jail. See you, John."

"You be careful, Frank. Lucy's got a mean streak in her."

Frank waved and walked across the street just as Lucy was reining up in front of the dress shop.

"Miss Perkins," Frank called, "may I speak with you for a moment?"

Lucy turned and looked at him. "Sure. Why not? What's on your mind, Marshal?"

and smiled at him. "You figure I can help you do that?"

"Yes, I do."

"I'd be real interested in learnin' how, Marshal."

"How about I buy you a cup of coffee?"

"Sounds good to me."

"I've got to turn a man out of jail first. I'll meet you at the café."

"I'll be there."

Five minutes later, Dale was riding out of town, heading back to the Diamond, and Frank was sitting at a table with Lucy Perkins.

"How can I help heal these valleys, Marshal?" Lucy asked.

"You like Mike Rogers, Lucy?"

The young woman smiled as a bright red blush started at her shoulders and worked its way up her neck to cover her cheeks. She really was a very pretty young lady. "You get around, don't you, Marshal?"

"I listen. I hear things."

She nodded her head as she sugared her coffee and added some milk from a small pitcher on the table. "Me and Mike been sort of likin' each other ever since we first learned to walk."

"What's been keeping you apart?"

"You sure you ain't that Cupid fellow in disguise, Marshal?"

Frank got a laugh out of that. "That is something I'm really sure of, Lucy."

Lucy smiled, and her eyes went vacant for a moment as she considered Frank's question. "Well, first it was Mike's pa kept us from really courtin'. He was always afraid if Mike and me got together, my father might try to interfere in the Diamond ranch's business."

somethin' wrong with Mike's dad's mind an' that if Mike an' me were to have kids, it might be inherited or some-thin'."

Frank looked at Lucy over the rim of his coffee cup as he drank. "You're old enough now to make up your own mind about who you want to court, Lucy," he said.

"That's right, Marshal, an' now that you mention it, I might just decide to mosey on over to the Diamond spread and see if Mike's still interested in us hooking up." She put her coffee cup down and stared at Frank. "But don't think that's gonna make any difference in this range war. Even if I could convince Mike it's the wrong thing to be doin', it won't make any difference at all."

"Why not?"

"'Cause Mark runs the Diamond, Marshal, not Mike. I think if Mike tried to interfere, Mark would turn hard against him."

"Violently, you mean?"

The young woman solemnly nodded her head. "You bet. Mark doesn't like Mike. Never has."

"Why?"

"Mike is smarter, by a whole bunch. Mark can't hardly even write his name. Mark has never read a book in his entire life. Mike reads all the time. He knows what's goin' on all over the nation. I mean, he's usually three, four months behind, 'cause of the delay in gettin' newspapers in here, but he knows what's goin' on, you can bet on that."

"You think Mark would physically hurt his brother if Mike tried to take over the Diamond?"

"In a heartbeat." She smiled. "Well, he'd try, at least."

Frank picked up on the smile immediately. "Mike's got a few secrets he's kept from his brother?"

is the answer to very much."

"He's right."

"Strange remark comin' from you, Frank Morgan."

Frank shrugged that off. "Mike is quick with a six-gun?"

"He ain't near'bouts as fast as you . . . hell, who is? But he's better than his brother, for sure. And he's a crack shot. He rides off miles from the house to keep in practice. Never wears a gun around the ranch house."

"I'd like to speak with Mike. You think you could arrange that?"

She thought about it for a moment, and then she nodded, her eyes happy. "Sure. I think I'm gonna take me a ride over to the Diamond spread in the mornin'. I'll tell 'em I've come to see Peaches, but I'll find a way to tell Mike you want to see him."

"Does Peaches know how you and Mike feel about each other?"

"Sure. She's sweet on a man owns a small ranch over near the county seat. They'll get hitched one of these days. Marshal, I know what people think and say about me and Peaches. But hardly any of it is true. I know we sometimes have bad mouths, but we're not bad girls. If my daddy ever even thought I was cuddlin' in a hayloft with a man, he'd beat me half to death. And Big Mark would have done the same with Peaches."

Frank smiled. "I thought that might have been the case."

The young woman blushed again. "Me and Peaches was just funnin' and eggin' that gunslick on. That Doolin fellow. If he had made a move towards me or Peaches, we'd a took off like a whirlwind."

Frank nodded his head. "You tell Mike I want to see him. All right?"

"I'll tell him tomorrow."

men worked on.

Esperanza said she didn't know, and so Frank stalked over to the sheriff's office and banged open the door. The

If . . .

married before, they hadn't needed a chaperone on their
many picnics and rides through the countryside.
He was just beginning to believe that he was settled in

Twenty-eight

Lucy rode into town about noon of the day after meeting with Frank. She rode in from the west, and that told Frank the young woman had indeed been out to the Diamond spread. She reined up in front of the marshal's office, where Frank was standing on the boardwalk.

"Mike'll be waitin' at Beaver Creek, Marshal. Where it splits off 'fore goin' underground for a time. You know the place?"

"I do. When?"

"Right now, Marshal. He left 'bout the same time I did."

"Thanks, Lucy. Did you and Mike set a date?" He asked that with a smile.

"We always talk 'bout gettin' hitched, Marshal, but we've never gotten right down to plannin' an actual time 'cause of our families. I'm hoping we might be able to tie the knot when this war is over."

"That might be sooner than you think."

"It can't be soon enough for me. I wish you luck with Mike."

"Thanks, Lucy."

She nodded her head and rode away, back toward GP range.

Frank motioned toward a young boy across the street, and the boy hotfooted it over to Frank.

"Run down to the livery and tell John to saddle my

"I'm gone!"

An hour and a half later, Frank swung down from the saddle and walked up to a young man standing under a lightning-blazed tree and stuck out his hand. "We finally get to meet, Mike."

Mike took the hand in a firm grip. "Marshal Morgan. I'm glad you asked Lucy to set up this meeting. I've wanted to meet you ever since you came into the valleys."

"You think we can help put an end to this fight, Mike?"

"We can try. What do you have in mind?"

"That's just it, Mike. I don't have a plan. I thought we'd talk some and maybe come up with something."

"I brought a coffeepot and some coffee."

"I'll get the water and start up a small fire."

"Sounds good to me."

Over steaming tin cups of hot, strong coffee, Frank and the younger man talked.

"With Pa dead and Mark in control, this war is never going to end," Mike said.

"How did your father's will read?" Frank asked.

"A third of the ranch to each of the children. But . . . the oldest son to be in charge. Pa knew I always preached getting along with the farmers. There's plenty of land for us all." He smiled, the humor reaching his eyes. "What Pa didn't know is that I been having people file on land and then buying it from them since I came of age. I own a lot of land that Pa thought—and Mark still thinks—is Diamond land."

"Wise of you," Frank complimented the young man. "How about the water rights?"

"Belongs to me. Near about all of it. And I'm a firm believer in building stock ponds."

"Drought comes, you'll sure need them. How about working capital for the spread?"

emergency funds. Mark doesn't know about that little hidey-hole."

"Would your sister back you up against Mark?"

"I think she would. Oh, hell, I know she would. She wants to get married and out of here, and I've told her I'll donate some of the land I own for her and her new man to make a start on. She's commented that Mark is acting as crazy as Pa did before he died."

"You've lost a few more gunslingers, I heard."

"I wish they'd all leave. But there is little chance of that."

"How many are left out there, Mike?"

"Eighteen, at last count."

"And most of them are very good at their work."

"That's one way of putting it."

Frank smiled at that. "I hear you're a pretty good hand with a six-gun yourself, Mike."

His eyes opened wide and a flush appeared on his cheeks. "My friend Lucy talks too much, Marshal."

"I think she's a good kid."

"Oh, she is. But both she and my sister, Peaches, are all mouth, nothing more. They enjoy shocking people." He grinned. "Especially some of those straitlaced old biddies in town."

"I witnessed that," Frank said.

"I heard," Mike said with a laugh. "You also scared the crap out of both those girls."

"They needed it."

"You'll get no argument from me about that." Mike finished his coffee. "All right, Marshal Morgan, I'll see if I can't come up with a plan to wrest the leadership of Diamond from my brother. But if my sister and I succeed in doing that, you know what's going to happen."

mond. He's got enough money to buy support from the gunslingers and he'll try to kill me." He sighed. "And if he fails, he'll hit the hoot-owl trail and still try to keep this range war going."

Frank poured another cup of coffee and leaned back against an old weather-beaten log. "That might happen. Unless he pulls something that I can arrest him on and hold him long enough for you to take control of the Diamond and talk some sense into him."

"That might just work," Mike said doubtfully. "But when Mark rides off Diamond range he's got half a dozen hired guns with him. Trying to arrest him would turn bloody in a heartbeat."

Frank nodded his head in understanding. "How about your regular cowhands?"

"They'll back me. To a man."

Frank rolled a smoke and thumbnailed a match into flame. "Quietly pass the word to them to stick close to you and Peaches."

"I already have," the young man said softly.

Frank went back to his ranch, and fed Dog and gave Stormy a good brushing and some oats to eat. After he'd fixed himself something to eat, he walked out into the fields and talked to the men who were sharecropping his land. He took a bucket of fresh, cold well water with him, and they took a break from tilling the fields and had a long talk with Frank.

Once he found they were still happy with their business relationship and needed nothing, he went back to the house and busied himself with doing some light repairs around the place. Dog followed him around as he mended fences

would be to settle down and raise a family in, which caused him to think about his estranged son and to even contemplate sending him a telegram and seeing if they couldn't reconcile their differences.

When he thought it through, though, he shook his head and looked down at Dog sitting patiently next to him. "No, I guess that wouldn't do, would it, Dog?"

The cur looked up at him and yawned before snapping a fly out of the air with a quick click of his jaws.

A week passed without a single incident of violence in the town or in the series of valleys. The farmers' crops were looking good, and the growing season, while relatively short, promised to yield a bumper crop. The several dozen carpenters who had been busy from spring to late summer in Valley View were now mostly gone.

Only one crew remained in town, doing finishing work. Valley View now boasted a full two-and-a-half-block-long main street, with buildings on both sides of the wide street. The new hotel was finished, two stories high. Some of the more expensive rooms featured a bath and other more personal facilities.

"Never heard of such a thing," John Platt remarked. "Don't seem a bit sanitary to me."

"It's progress, John," Frank told him.

"It's nasty, you ask me."

A new saloon was in operation. There were clothing stores for men and women, a leather and saddle store with shoe and boot repair. The apothecary shop featured the latest in medicines, mixed and prepared right there before your eyes, if you wanted to watch. Most people didn't. Dr. Archer had a small clinic added to his office, for the more seriously ill, where they could be kept overnight in a series of small bunk beds lined up on either side of the room.

been built, which would also be used as a place for stage plays.

"Maybe they'll bring in that play about you, Frank," John Platt said with a grin.

"The day they do is the day I leave," Frank replied.

Professor Fred Klugston, teacher of piano and other musical instruments, opened a studio just off Main Street. Alice Klugston, his wife, painted and sculpted and was, Frank heard, renowned in artistic circles. Alice opened a small gallery on Main Street, which featured her paintings of the mountains and scenes in the connecting valleys.

"I hear tell she wants you to sit for a painting, Frank," Joe Wallace told Frank.

"She'll wait a long time before that happens," Frank replied.

Valley View also had a band, made up of local people. They had several trumpets, a trombone, a tuba, and included a drummer and a cymbal crasher. Uniforms had been ordered for the band.

Several of the farmers' wives got together and opened a bakery, featuring all sorts of pies and cakes and fresh-baked bread, along with jellies and preserves and fresh-brewed coffee. The place was an immediate hit with the townspeople.

And Frank had not heard a word from Mike Rogers, nor had he seen any more gunfighters leave the area.

Things were going too well to suit Frank; he knew only too well about the lull before a storm. He'd been personally involved in many blowups over the years.

"What's the matter, Marshal?" Mayor Joe Wallace asked, walking up to Frank on a bright, sunny morning. "You look plumb grim."

"Things are going really well, Joe. Too well maybe. I'm just waiting for the other boot to drop."

ing. Maybe you're looking on the dark side for no reason."

"Maybe. I hope so. But I doubt it."

Joe smiled and patted Frank on the shoulder. "Relax, Marshal. Everything is going to be just fine."

"Joe," Frank replied, softening his reply with a smile, "you're a born politician."

Joe took the reply well. He laughed and said, "Maybe so, Frank. Maybe so." He waved his hand at the busy street. "But you can't deny progress now, can you?"

"I reckon not."

"But you'll still stand around looking glum, worrying over nothing while you wait for the lid to blow off?"

Before Frank could reply, both men turned to look as a fast-moving buckboard came rattling up the street, coming in from the west side of the valley.

"What the hell?" Joe questioned. "That driver is going too fast. There are women and kids out this morning."

"Who is that?" Frank asked.

"I don't know his name. I've seen him around a few times. I think he rides for the Diamond spread."

"Get Doc Archer!" the driver yelled. "Got a man shot here."

Frank stepped out into the street and ran alongside the racing horses for a dozen steps until he could grab their halters and halt the wagon. "What's going on?" he asked, moving to the rear of the buckboard and peering over the sideboard.

"It's Mike Rogers, Marshal," the drive said in a breathless voice. "He's been shot."

"Over here!" Doc Archer shouted from the boardwalk in front of his office as he motioned toward the wagon.

"Who shot him?" Frank asked.

"His brother, Mark!" The driver jerked the horses' heads

helped pick Mike's limp body out of the buckboard and carry it into Dr. Archer's office.

"You mentioned something about the lid blowing off, Joe?" he said, looking back over his shoulder. "Well, it just blew."

"I wonder why Mark would want to shoot his brother," the mayor said.

Frank had a pretty good idea, but he wasn't about to say until he'd found out exactly what had happened out at the Diamond spread.

Twenty-nine

Peaches came fogging it up in a cloud of just as Mike was being carried into Doc Archer's clinic. She jumped off her pony and onto the boardwalk. Frank grabbed her and held her back.

"Hold on, Peaches. He's still alive. Talk to me. Tell me what happened."

"I wasn't home. But a couple of the hands were. Jeff and Hootie said Mark and Mike had been arguing for about an hour. Mark was wearing a gun, Mike wasn't. Mike came staggering out of the house, holding his side. Mark came running out after him, yelling and cussing, saying he was going to finish the job. Jeff and Hootie got between the brothers and Mark backed away. Jeff got the wagon ready and Hootie rode out to get me. That's all I know."

"Where is Mark now?"

"Still out at the ranch, I guess."

"Will Mike file charges against his brother?"

"You bet he will."

"As soon as the doctor will let me talk to him, I'll get rolling on that and ride out to get Mark."

"You better go in ready to shoot, Marshal. Mark won't come in easy. You can bet on it."

"I'll worry about that, Peaches. You go on in and be with your brother for a time."

Frank walked over to the livery and saddled Stormy. He checked his rifle, a .44-40, before mounting up.

"You ought to put together a posse. It's crazy going out after Mark alone. He's surrounded by gunslingers."

"I doubt that Mark will still be at the ranch, John. He may be like his father, a little nutty, but he's not stupid. He's probably headed for the high country, hoping this thing will blow over."

"Has Mike filed charges against his brother?"

"Not yet. I'm waiting to talk to him."

"While you're waiting for that, I'll put together some men to ride with you."

"If you think that's best."

"I think it is," Mayor Joe Wallace said, walking up in time to catch the last bit of conversation. "And I've already got half a dozen lined up to go."

"Seven," John said. "I'm in."

"All right," Frank agreed. "Let me see if Mike can tell me anything. You boys get saddled up."

The bullet from his brother's gun had struck Mike in his left flank and passed clear through.

"I don't believe it hit anything vital," Doc Archer said, "or he would never have survived the ride in here in the back of a wagon. He's going to be all right. What he needs now is rest."

"Did he say anything, Doc?" Frank asked.

"He said his brother shot him. Said they were arguing about ending the valley war and cutting down the herd a bit. Mike said all of a sudden, with no warning except for some cursing, his brother pulled out his pistol and shot him. Then he laughed about it. Mike said he feels sure his brother has lost his mind."

"He sleeping now?"

"Yes. I gave him a dose of laudanum so he would get some rest. That's the best medicine for him now."

Harlon was quick, mean, and deadly. If he had any feeling for human life at all, Frank had never met anyone who
now.

"Where do you think you're going?" Frank asked.

"With you."

"The hell you are."

"The hell I'm not! You can't keep me from going back home, Marshal. I'd damn sure like to see you try."

Frank smiled at the young woman. The last thing he wanted was to tangle with Peaches. "Suit yourself, Peaches. Let's ride."

"I got me a fresh horse. Jeff and Hootie got fresh mounts from the livery. Anytime you're ready, Marshal. I want to get home. I got some orders to give to the Diamond hands."

Five more locals had joined the posse, all of the men heavily armed and ready for trouble if it came to that. To a man they wanted the valley wars over with.

Harvey Pitts, a lawyer who had recently moved into Valley View, stepped off the boardwalk to confront Frank and the posse. "I'm riding with you men," the lawyer said. "I want to make certain this doesn't turn into a lynch mob."

"There'll be no lynching, Harvey," Frank told the attorney. "I doubt we'll even see Mark Rogers. I'll make a bet he's headed for the mountains and timber."

"I'm riding with you," Harvey insisted.

"Get mounted then. And be quick about it."

"I'm going too," Reverend Carmondy said, riding up on a borrowed horse. "Someone might need some spiritual guidance."

"Yeah," Lucy Perkins said, joining the group. "You can pray over the bastards once we hang them." Like Peaches, Lucy had a pistol on her hip and fire in her eyes.

"Where'd you come from?" Peaches asked her friend.

"I come into town to shop. I just left the doctor's office. I

woman. "If we find Mark, I'll arrest him, not hang him."

Lawyer Pitts looked at Frank for a silent moment. "Yes, I believe you mean that, Marshal. Despite your rather nasty reputation, I believe you."

"Wonderful," Frank said sarcastically. "Let's ride!"

Just as Frank had predicted, Mark Rogers and his hired gunslingers were not at the ranch. A hand met the posse in the front yard.

"They took off right after you left, Miss Peaches. They headed straight north, for the mountains."

Peaches stepped down from the saddle. "All right, Jim. Get the boys together. Until Mike is back on his feet, I'll be running this spread. And effective right now, there are gonna be some changes made."

"Yes, ma'am!"

"Lucy." Peaches turned to her friend. "Will you stay with me for a time? We'll ride back into town later on this afternoon and see about Mike."

"Sure, I will." Lucy hopped down from the saddle, and the two young women walked in the ranch house.

"They've got a good three-to-four-hour jump on us, boys," Frank told the posse. "I think—"

"The rotten bastard cleaned out the safe," Peaches yelled from the porch, her hands on her hips and her eyes blazing.

"Relax," Frank told her. "Mike told me he knows where your dad kept some working capital. And you can get the boys to rounding up some cattle right now to sell . . . before your brother rustles them."

"And you can bet he'd do it too," Peaches called. "Great idea, Marshal. "Hootie!" she hollered. "Tell the cook to get the chuck wagon ready, then get the boys, we're startin' a roundup!"

ous Dan finished reloading his shotgun and snapped the barrels shut.

Frank's first bullet hit Dangerous Dan in the middle of

men can head on back home."

"You sure, Frank?" Mayor Wallace asked.

"I'm sure. Personally, I don't think we'll see Mark for some time. He's running scared and won't be back until emotions cool down. If he or any of his hired guns—and they're all outlaws now, in the eyes of the law anyway—show up on Diamond range, some of the regular hands will shoot them dead, and Mark knows that."

"You bet we will," the grizzled old cook said, walking toward the barn to hitch up a team. "Or hang the sorry bastards."

"Here now!" Lawyer Pitts said. "There'll be none of that."

"Who the hell are you?" the cook questioned.

"I am an attorney at law, sir," Pitts answered in a very indignant tone.

"Yeah? Well, that don't spell buffalo crap to me. My advice to you is this: You best carry your gimpy ass back to town and leave the lawin' to those who know how to do it."

Pitts puffed up like a balloon. "Well!"

The cook gave him a very vulgar hand gesture and walked on.

Frank thanked the posse and motioned to John and Earl. The three men waved good-bye to their friends and lifted their reins. The three of them rode off toward the north.

"Lawyer Pitts and Preacher Carmondy is followin' us," John said, glancing over his shoulder after they'd been riding for a couple of hours.

"I can't force them to turn back," Frank replied. "If they catch a bullet, it's their own fault."

"Don't neither of them have a bedroll or any supplies," Earl said, looking back at the two men.

"Then it's going to be a cold, hungry night for them," Frank remarked.

It didn't take long for the preacher and the lawyer to realize they had made a mistake. Several hours before the sun began to dip into the western horizon, Reverend Carmondy called out. Frank rode back to the lawyer and the preacher.

"I think we'll head back to town," Richard said.

"Good idea," Frank told him.

"Ah . . ." Lawyer Pitts said, avoiding Frank's steady gaze. "There is a small matter, however."

"You don't know the way back," Frank finished for him.

"Ah . . . well . . . in a word, yes."

Frank shook his head in disgust. "Head straight southeast. You'll come to the main road. There is no way in hell you can miss it."

Richard pointed. "That way?" he asked.

Frank sighed. "No, Richard. That's southwest. But . . . that will take you to the road too. You'll just be miles west of Valley View."

"The bunch split up," John called from a ridge after the preacher and lawyer had left. "Looks like they paired up and then scattered in all directions."

"I thought they would," Frank called back. "Come on back."

John and Earl returned and Frank said, "There is no point in us going on a wild-goose chase. We'd be chasing the wind. Let's head on back to town. Mark will show up one of these days."

"And his hired guns?" Earl asked.

"As long as Mark has the money to pay them, they'll stay. They'll all show up eventually. Then we'll deal with them. I'll wire the sheriffs in adjoining counties and tell them what's happening." He lifted the reins. "Come on, we'll be back in time for supper."

As he walked past the nicest restaurant in town, he glanced in the window and saw Frank Morgan and Sweet Sue sitting at a table, all cozy-like, having a meal and

to one side, with any luck you'd still down the man before he could do the same to you.

Frank shook his head and smirked. Funny how real life

not get a bet from me on that, John," he said. "Now if you want to wager whether we have to send out a hunting party to bring 'em in or not . . ."

"Only if I get to bet on them gettin' plumb lost," John answered.

his head. "I swear, I ain't never seen nothin' like that."

"What happens now?" Paul Adams questioned.

Frank tossed the butt of his cigarette into a mud puddle.

Thirty

Mike was awake and alert when Frank and the remaining members of the posse got back to town.

"The doc tells me you're going to be just fine, Mike," Frank said from the bedside.

"I'll be up and looking for that worthless brother of mine before you know it, Marshal."

"Let me take care of your brother, Mike. You just get well and get back to running the Diamond."

Mike smiled wearily. "I'll bet you Peaches can run it just as good as I can."

Frank told him what Peaches was doing . . . as much as he'd heard before pulling out with the posse earlier that day.

"Good for her. The doc says I can go home in three or four days. But I'll have to stay close to a bed for about a week."

"You rest, Mike. I'll stop by tomorrow. Lucy and Peaches will be coming into town later on this evening."

"See you, Marshal."

Frank rode back to his house and fed Dog, then played with the big cur for a time.

"Did you miss me, ol' fellow?" Dog barked loud and enthusiastically. Frank laughed and said, "I guess you did. I haven't had much time to spend with you lately. But all that is going to change very soon, I'm thinking. Another

"All right, all right. Calm down a little bit." Dog loved the trail, loved to stay on the move, seeing new country. "South it is. Now where south shall it be?" Frank poured a cup of coffee and sat down in a rocker. "How about Oklahoma Territory? We'll check out this strip of territory called No-Man's-Land. That sound good to you?"

Dog jumped up and down and barked.

"All right," Frank said with a laugh. "Sounds good to me too."

Frank drank his coffee and smoked a cigarette, then called it a night and went to bed, Dog sleeping on a rug beside his bed.

Frank rode into town just as dawn was cracking open the dark skies. At the Sunburst Café, Charlie and Becky had the biscuits baked and the coffee ready to pour when Frank walked in and took a seat.

"Everything quiet last night?" Frank asked.

"Quiet as a church here in town," Charlie replied. "You think Mark Rogers has left the country?"

"No. He's still around. I figure as soon as he learns his brother is all right, he'll make a move."

"Then when that's handled, the war will really be over, won't it?" Becky asked.

"Should be," Frank replied, sugaring his coffee. He buttered a biscuit with fresh-churned butter and took a bite. Delicious. The Jordans were really good cooks.

Frank would have been content to just sit and eat buttered biscuits for breakfast. But before he could fill up on biscuits, Charlie set a plate of ham and eggs before him.

"Enjoy, Marshal," Charlie said, filling up Frank's coffee cup.

was a letter from his attorney in Denver. A new gold strike had been hit in the mountains (the mine owned by one of the companies Frank owned stock in) and Frank was now considerably wealthier. The lawyer said the money was now on deposit at a bank in Denver. Frank put the letter in his pocket and smiled. The fifty a month he was being paid for his marshal's work was going into the local bank. It would stay there until he found someone who needed it more than he did; Frank would never touch it. He sure as hell didn't need it.

The other two letters addressed to him were from the legal firms handling his stock in railroads, shipping, and factories. He quickly scanned both letters. They told him how much he had earned thus far this year, and how much he currently had on deposit. It was quite an impressive sum. More money in various banks. It was a sum of money that was almost unbelievable to Frank.

More money than he could spend in several lifetimes . . . even if he went hog-wild crazy trying to spend it all.

What did he personally need that his money could buy? The answer was nothing. He had a couple of suits, some shirts. A fine pair of boots. Some jeans. He had his Peacemaker, and a short-barreled Peacemaker as a spare. He had a fine .44-40 rifle. He had a good saddle, a great horse. And Dog. He needed nothing more.

He rolled a cigarette and leaned back in his swivel desk chair. No, he needed only the time to roam, to drift, to be himself until that day when the bullet with his name on it caught up with him. When that day finally arrived, and Frank was sure it would, his attorneys knew what to do with his accumulated wealth.

The door opened, breaking into Frank's reverie. John Platt walked in with a solemn face on.

horse with me and told me if he didn't come back for him, I could have the horse and rig. Just pay for his funeral. Said he'd be waiting for you over at the new saloon."

Frank grunted at the news and stood up.

"You don't seem surprised at his ridin' in, Frank."

"I'm not. Pete's too good a man to take orders from an asshole like Mark Rogers."

"That don't explain his comin' in to brace you."

Frank smiled. "It does to me, John."

"I'll never understand gunfighters," the liveryman said.

"How could you?" Frank questioned. "We don't really understand ourselves."

Frank walked over to the saloon, pulled open the batwings, and pushed open the front door. The saloon was not due to open for several hours, but Pete had unofficially opened it . . . by threatening the old swamper. The gunslinger was propped up at the bar, drinking coffee.

"Come in and have a cup, Morgan," Pete said at the sound of the batwings and door opening. He didn't bother to look and see who it was . . . he knew.

"Believe I will, Pete," Frank replied, picking up a cup and walking behind the bar to the coffeepot. The swamper had headed out the back door with Frank's approach.

"You queered a good deal for us, Frank," Pete said.

"Oh? Now how did I do that?" Frank asked.

"Sidin' with the sodbusters and convincin' the GP to call off their fight."

"It's called progress, Pete. There's land enough for everybody."

Pee grunted his reply to that and sipped his coffee. After a moment he said, "You know why I come into town, Frank."

"This doesn't have to be, Pete. The war is over. Ride on out of here. I won't try to stop you."

Pete smiled at that. "You're pretty good, Morgan. I like to get everything covered after I make up my mind to do something."

"That's a wise move."

"Our day is just about over, Morgan. I figure men like us should go out the way we've lived."

"I don't plan on going out any time soon, Pete."

"Yeah . . . well . . . you probably won't."

"You go into this fight with that attitude and you won't make it, Pete. So why go into it?"

"Got to, Morgan."

"No, Pete. You don't have to do this. And I don't want to do it."

"What the hell's the matter with you, Morgan?" Pete sat down his cup and looked at Frank.

"Nothing. I'm just talking to a man I've known for years."

"We're not friends, Morgan."

"But we've never really been enemies."

"Well . . . I reckon that's true." Pete drew a long breath and exhaled slowly. "I reckon I could just ride out and we could call this a draw, couldn't we, Morgan?"

"We sure could, Pete. Why don't we just call it even and both of us walk away?"

Pete chuckled softly. "I come in here ready to die and damned if you ain't talked me out of it. You ever think of becomin' a preacher, Morgan?"

Frank laughed and walked down to stand close to Pete Dancer. "No, Pete. I've never given that any thought at all."

"You ever thought of hangin' up your gun?"

"Plenty of times."

"You know anyone who's ever done it?"

"Several. Dave Moore did just a few months ago. He's farming out in the valley now."

and the short of it, Mr. Morgan."

Frank did not immediately reply to that. He watched as several hired guns began walking across the street.

"You see him, give him my best."

"I will. Pete? I'm told Oregon is good farm country and there's plenty of land to be had for a man who isn't afraid of work."

"I growed up on a farm, Morgan. I damn sure ain't afraid of work. And I know somethin' 'bout farmin."

"Might think about that, Pete."

"Yeah . . ." Pete scratched his chin. "Yeah, I will. You really think a man like me could give it all up?"

"Yes, I do."

"You haven't."

"You had any plays performed, songs sung, and books and news articles written about you, Pete?" Frank asked, a twinge of regret in his voice, which Pete picked up.

The gun handler cut his eyes to Frank. "No. Thank the Good Lord. But I see what you mean. I read some of the books about you. Don't take this the wrong way, but I laughed all the way through them."

"They're awful, for a fact."

"Farmin', huh? Well, it's a thought."

"Do it, Pete. Show us both you can do it."

Pete nodded his head, then smiled. "By the Lord, I think I will, Frank. Yes, I will." He looked again at Frank, his eyes narrowing just a bit. "You ain't asked question one 'bout Mark Rogers or the men with him."

"I'm not worried about them, Pete."

"I left them 'fore we reached the mountains. Mark is crazy as his pa. Maybe worse. That's a bad bunch with him, Frank. Some of them has sworn to kill you."

"I know."

"I don't know what they're plannin'. I left 'fore Mark could lay out any scheme."

with me 'fore I pull out?"

"I'd be proud to do that, Pete."

The two top guns shook hands, and Pete Dancer walked out of the saloon and into the cool morning. Frank stood for a moment at the bar. The old swamper stuck his head around a corner.

"No shootin'?"

"Nope. We talked it out."

"Talked? Well, I'll be damned. Ain't that somethin'?"

John Platt walked in a few minutes later, accompanied by Doc Archer and Joe Wallace.

"Dancer come got his horse," John said. "He was smilin'. What the hell did you two talk about?"

"Life and death and choices a man had while on this earth, John," Frank replied.

"Don't tell me he's givin' up gunslingin'."

"He's going to try."

"Headin' west when he left my place," the liveryman said. "He goin' to California?"

Frank hesitated for just a few seconds. Might as well give Pete another small chance in this game of life and death. "Yeah, John. Southern California. He owns a business out there. Dry goods, I think."

"Do tell. Well, I wish him luck."

"So do I, John. So do I."

"He say anything 'bout Mark?"

"Just that he was crazy."

"Well, hell, we all knowed that."

"We'll deal with Mark when we see him, I reckon." Frank looked at Doc Archer and smiled. "How's Mike?"

"In good shape. He can go home in a couple of days."

"We're gonna have us a right nice town here," the mayor said. "Yes, sir. A right nice town."

his chin, "an' seen' as how the saloon's already open, how about us breakin' open a bottle of the good stuff and havin' us a drink on it?"

Frank laughed and pushed his coffee cup across the bar away from him. "Damned if that ain't a great idea, John."

Thirty-one

Several weeks passed very uneventfully. Mike Rogers went back to his ranch and after a few days in bed, began doing light office work. Mike and Lucy Perkins announced their engagement, as did Peaches and her gentlemen friend who ran a ranch over near the county seat. It was to be a double wedding, held in Valley View, with the services conducted by Reverend Richard Carmondy.

The crops were all in for that growing season, and it was a bumper crop for the homesteaders in the valleys.

School had started in Valley View, and the schoolhouse was filled with kids . . . some of whom had never before attended a regular school . . . having been schooled at home by their parents, if they had any schooling at all, and many had not.

In one short summer, the size and population of Valley View had grown phenomenally. The governor of the territory was making plans to visit the town.

"When the governor's plans are firm," Frank told the mayor and town council, "I'll pull out. You boys better be thinking about a new marshal."

"What are you talking about, Frank?" Joe Wallace asked. "We want you to stay."

"I'm a known gunfighter, Joe," Frank replied. "It wouldn't look good for someone like me to be wearing a star in your town."

"That's nonsense!" John Platt said bluntly. "We don't want nobody else, Frank."

"I'll be moving on," Frank told the gathering. "Start looking for a new marshal. Believe me, it's for the best. Otherwise you'll end up with a bunch of reputation-hunters coming around here tryin' to make a name for themselves by killing me."

"But you settled the troubles of not only this town, but of the entire valley," Joe said. "We want you to stay."

"I'll be moving on," Frank said, a finality in his voice. The men present knew to argue further would be futile.

"How can we ever repay you?" another council member asked.

"Your friendship is plenty payment enough," Frank told the men. "I'll never forget this town—or the many friends and neighbors I've met here. Believe it."

Frank made arrangements to give his farm—lock, stock, and barrel, so to speak—to a young couple who had just moved into the valley. They had lost everything to a fire on the trail. To say they were stunned at the generosity of Frank Morgan would be an understatement.

"I don't know what to say," the young farmer said.

"Then don't say anything," Frank told him.

Many of the gunslingers that had ridden off with Mark Rogers had been spotted as far south as Kansas, riding alone or in pairs. One had been arrested for stealing, and he had told a sheriff that most of the gang had broken up, each going his separate way. Mark had refused to share with them the money he had taken from his late father's safe, and then had killed one of the gang for no reason, according to the gunhand. He had no idea where Mark Rogers was, but he hoped he was dead. Adding: "The rotten son of a bitch!"

Frank shared that telegram with Mike, and Mike could only shake his head. "I guess we'll never see my brother again."

"He's crazy, Mike," Frank told him. "Don't let your guard down just yet. There is no telling what he's liable to do."

"I guess you're right, Marshal. Say, me and Lucy will be getting married this fall. I guess you heard."

"I did. I'm happy for you both."

"Will you be here for the wedding?"

"Probably not, Mike. I plan to pull out in a few days. I just wanted to stop by and give you my congratulations and best wishes . . . and to say good-bye."

"Good luck to you, Marshal Morgan. I won't forget you."

"Give my best to Lucy and to your sister."

"I will. I wish you were staying. But you're welcome here anytime, Marshal. I mean that."

"I know you do. See you around, Mike."

On a cool, crisp early fall morning, just before dawn, Frank Morgan rode out of the town, drifting south. He did not look back at the town of Valley View. The town he'd helped build.

He couldn't help feeling some pride in his soul when he passed farm after farm along the way, farms that wouldn't've been there except for him. "See that, Dog?" he said to the cur trotting alongside Stormy as they passed yet another farm with a man and his wife out working in the fields. "Your master did that. Aren't you proud of me?"

Dog glanced up, his tongue hanging out as he panted a bit from the heat. There was a question in his eyes, as if to say, "Master? What are you talking about? It's plain to see who the boss is around here."

Frank glanced down at him, and had to laugh. Yep. He was sure that was what Dog was thinking.

The man in the field stopped his work and leaned on the handle of his hoe. He took off his hat and sleeved sweat off his brow. And then he nudged his wife and waved at Frank. "Howdy, Marshal. Like to come in and have a piece of pie and some coffee?" he yelled.

Frank thought about it for just a moment, and then he chuckled. Why the hell not? Who knows how long it'd be before he was again treated to homemade pie?

"Sure, I'd be right obliged," he hollered back, and pulled Stormy's head around and headed up the trail toward the farmhouse in the distance.

Just across the line in Colorado, Frank stepped down from the saddle in front of a country store three days later. Before he could turn around, a very cold voice told him not to. Frank knew that voice.

"Reggie?"

"Yeah, Drifter. Reggie. Now I'm going to kill you. Step away from your horse and then slow-like, turn and face me."

Frank walked away from Stormy and then slowly turned to face the gunslinger. "I heard you boys pulled out from Mark Rogers. The war's over. What's your beef with me now?"

"You're you, that's what."

"That's not much of a reason, Reggie."

"It's reason enough. You ready, Drifter?"

"I'd rather we talked this out, Reggie."

"You done turned yeller on me, Drifter?"

Frank smiled at that. "No, Reggie. I just don't want to have to kill you, that's all." He glanced around at the clear blue sky and the snowcapped mountain peaks in the distance. "It's a damn pretty day, Reggie. Shame to spill blood on a day like this."

"Huh? Hell, Morgan. You're an old man. I seen gray in your hair. You're all used up." He leaned to the side and spat in the dirt at his feet. "Hell, a man talkin' 'bout how pretty the day is ain't no danger to anybody anymore, that's for sure."

"Then there isn't much point in standing here jawing, is there?"

"I reckon not."

Reggie pulled iron.

Frank put two bullets in the man's belly before Reggie could clear leather.

"Damn!" Reggie said, doubling over with his hands crossed over his stomach as he sank to his knees in the dirt. He dropped his six-gun. "I should have known better," Reggie gasped. "I should have just gone on with them others and let you be."

Frank said nothing. He stood there with the hammer eared back on his Peacemaker and waited for Reggie to topple over. He'd long since learned never to count a man out till he'd breathed his last breath.

"Oh, God!" Reggie moaned as the first wave of intense pain hit him hard. "I never had nothin' hurt me so bad." Reggie tried to get up, but succeeded only in falling over on his face. His gasping breaths raised small clouds of dust from the dirt around his nose.

A man and a woman stepped out of the country store to stand on the porch and stare.

"Help me," Reggie begged, sticking out a hand covered with blood and holding it out to them.

"Ain't nothin' neither of us can do, mister," the man said, glancing nervously at Frank. "We ain't doctors."

"Then both of you can go to hell!" Reggie told them as he grunted and groaned in agony.

"That's not a very nice thing to say," the woman admonished him, holding her nose high in the air and sniffing. "The Lord will frown on you for sayin' that."

Reggie did not reply. He was dead, facedown in the dirt and long past caring what the Lord would think of anything.

"Who are you, mister?" the man asked.

"Frank Morgan."

"Lord have mercy!" the woman said. "Frank Morgan right there in front of us, Otis."

"I see him," the man said. "What are you goin' to do with that man you shot, Mr. Morgan?"

"I'm not going to do anything with him. But you can have what's in his pockets and his horse, saddle, and guns if you bury him."

"I reckon that's more than a good swap. All right. We'll do that."

"You run this general store?"

"Shore do."

"I need supplies. I'll be looking around while you dig the hole."

"Sounds just fine to me," the man said. "Nell, you go fetch a shovel for me, will you?"

"You got any coffee ready to drink?" Frank asked.

"Shore do. It's on the stove. Help yourself." He hesitated, and glanced at his wife, Nell, as if she might contradict him. "No charge for the coffee."

"Thanks."

Frank picked up a few supplies, laid them on the counter, and then helped himself to a cup of coffee. While his coffee cooled, he opened a can of bully beef and fed Dog. He found a weeks-old newspaper and sat down to catch up on the news around the country.

Frank had just finished reading the paper when the front door opened and the man and woman walked in. "That feller you shot had a wad of cash on him, Mr. Morgan."

"Keep it."

"*All* of it?"

"Sure."

"But they's five hundred dollars here, Mr. Morgan."

"The dead man doesn't have any use for it, does he?"

"Well . . . no, sir, I reckon he don't. But don't you want part of it?"

"No. You fix me something to eat and let me bunk in your barn tonight and we'll call it even. How about it?"

The man and woman exchanged glances, the man replying, "Seems like you're gettin' the short end of this deal, Mr. Morgan. But if that's the way you want it . . ."

"That's the way I want it."

Frank was up and gone into the mist the next morning. Drifting south. He took no joy or satisfaction in the killing of Reggie. Reggie wanted a showdown, he got it. It was over and done. Frank put it out of his mind. That was something he had trained himself to do years back. He knew men who had killed other men and eventually went to pieces over it. Not Frank. Some trouble-hunter wanted trouble with The Drifter, he'd better have his will all written out. And when it was over, Frank would walk away and have a smoke and a cup of coffee. He'd never in his life killed anyone that didn't sorely need it, and he saw no percentage in worrying about it, so he didn't. It was as simple . . . and as complicated as that.

Frank continued his slow drift south, taking his time, seeing a stretch of country he hadn't seen in a long time.

At a still-active trading post in Colorado, Frank pulled up one cold, rainy morning and led his horses into the barn. "Hell with this, Dog," he said. "Let's hole up here until the weather clears. How about it?"

Dog barked his agreement and moved over to a corner before he commenced to shaking the water off his coat.

"Well, that settles it then," Frank said, stripping the saddle off Stormy and using double handfuls of sweet-smelling hay to rub both horses down. "You stay here, Dog. I'll check things out in the post."

It was not a bit unusual for men traveling alone to hold lengthy conversations with their animals. Historians do not record whether any of the animals ever replied to questions or comments by their owners, but Frank once knew a miner who'd had to walk for almost twenty miles back to town after taking out his rifle and shooting the mule that'd been his constant companion for almost twenty years. When Frank asked him why he'd shot the animal, the miner frowned and said, "The sumbitch was gettin' uppity on me. Kept disagreein' with me on jest 'bout everthing I had to say. Finally, one mornin' when I tole him it looked like it was gonna be a nice day, he snorted and gave me this look like I was crazy." The old man shook his head. "Well, there weren't nothin' to do but kill the bastard." He grinned. "That'll teach him to snort at me!" Frank had decided not to ask the man any more questions about his mule, and promised himself if Dog ever started answering him, he'd do his level best not to take offense at it.

Frank finished drying the horses and Dog off, and checked the brands on the half dozen or so other horses stabled in the barn. Doing this had saved his life on more than one occasion when it kept him from walking into an ambush. He did not recognize any of the brands or horses.

He walked over to the trading post and pushed open the door, stepping inside. Four men were seated at a table, sharing a bottle of whiskey. They looked up at Frank's entrance. Frank recognized one immediately: Jake Fabor, a gunslick from Arizona. He did not know the other three.

"Well, well," Jake said, a sarcastic edge to his voice. "If it ain't the living legend."

"What are you talkin' about?" one of the men at the table asked as he leaned over to spit a brown stream of tobacco juice onto the floor.

"Frank Morgan," Jake replied.

The men stared at Frank as he moved across the room and took a seat at a table as far away from the quartet as possible.

"You got to be jokin'," another of the men said.

"Nope. That's The Drifter hisself," Jake told him. "What the hell are you doin' in this part of the country, Morgan?"

"Passing through, Jake," Frank said, keeping his voice calm and level, but his eyes were hard as flint. "You have a problem with that?"

"I might."

"Coffee," Frank said to the man behind the rough bar. "Bring the pot and the sugar bowl."

"You gone sissy on us, Drifter?" Jake needled him. "Got to have some sweetener in your coffee. Maybe you better get the post owner's wife to make you a sugar tit 'fore you leave."

"I just might do that, Jake. But before I do that, I'll have him bring in a bucket of black paint."

"Huh? What you gonna paint?"

"I'm going to try to cover up that yellow streak that's running up and down your back."

The men seated with Jake got a laugh out of that. Jake flushed and pushed back his chair.

"Don't do anything you'll regret, Jake," Frank told him. "When you make a mistake with me, it could well be your last one."

"I ain't scared of you, Drifter."

"Sit down, Jake," one of his friends urged. "Don't be a fool. That's Frank Morgan, remember?"

"I know who it is!" Jake snapped the words. "But I ain't standin' for no man callin' me yeller. You take back what you said, Morgan. You hear me? You take it back."

Frank carefully stirred his coffee in silence.

"I'll kill you, Morgan!" Jake shouted the words and jumped to his feet. "You hear me? Stand and face me, you bastard."

Frank took a sip of coffee and said nothing.

Jake was so mad he was trembling. His hand was poised over the butt of his six-gun. "Stand up, Morgan!" he shouted.

"No, Jake," Frank said, finally breaking his silence. "You sit down. You really don't want to pull on me." Frank looked at the man through his cold pale eyes. "Do you, Jake?"

Jake hesitated, cursed under his breath, and sat down.

"Jake," Frank said, "you're not a coward. You just have a tendency to let your ass overload your mouth. And then you don't know how to get out of the crap you stepped in."

"That's sure the God's truth," one of the men seated at the table with Jake said.

Jake shook his head, grinned crookedly, and said nothing in rebuttal.

"You got anything cooked?" Frank asked the man behind the counter.

"Stew, fresh-baked bread, and apple pie."

"Start serving," Frank told him. "You're looking at a hungry man."

He glanced over at the other table and saw that there was no food on it, just whiskey. "And bring my friends plenty also," Frank added. "They look like they could use a bite to eat."

"We don't need no charity, Morgan," Jake said testily.

"It isn't charity, Jake," Frank replied evenly. "I'm just bein' neighborly is all."

"Oh, in that case . . ." Jake replied, smiling.

Thirty-two

Frank got a second big bowl of stew and half a loaf of bread for Dog, and took it out to the barn for the big cur. He forked hay for his horses and gave them both a bit of grain. While he was feeding the horses, Jake and his friends saddled up and mounted.

"You boys pulling out in this weather?" Frank asked.

"Got a job waitin' for us south of here," one of the men replied. "Sodbusters movin' in, cuttin' up the range. Some of the big spreads is payin' fightin' wages."

Frank shook his head. "You boys are fighting progress, you know that, don't you?"

"What do you mean, Morgan?"

"The law's on the side of the settlers," Frank explained. "And there's plenty of land for everybody."

"This is cattle country, Morgan. No place for farmers and their damn fences and plows. See you around. We're gone."

Frank watched them ride away in the downpour. He was not unhappy to see them leave. Frank had always felt Jake Fabor was not playing with a full deck of cards, and such men were dangerous. You never knew what they were gonna do, since they weren't constrained by logic. He had a strong hunch he'd be seeing Jake again.

Frank climbed up in the loft and smiled as he looked around. It was filled with fresh-cut hay and smelled wonderful. He would sleep warm and dry later on this night.

Frank waited until Dog was finished with his stew, and

then he took the wooden bowl he'd used to feed Dog back into the post.

"I wish we'd get another dog," the post owner's wife said when Frank handed her the bowl. "I like dogs. They're good company."

"When another one shows up, we'll feed it and keep it," the husband said. "Like I've told you time and again. But I ain't seen a dog out here in months. Them that do run off from a wagon train—if they're big enough to stay alive— sometimes hook up with a coyote pack."

Frank got another cup of coffee and walked over to a table near the window. He sat and watched the rain.

"You really Frank Morgan?" the man asked, cutting his eyes at Frank as he wiped down the rough-hewn board that served as a bar.

"I am."

"Read a book about you a couple of years ago. You really killed a thousand white men?"

Frank laughed and shook his head. "No. Those books tend to stretch the truth."

"You watch that damn Jake Fabor. I been knowin' him off and on for a long time." The man tapped the side of his hand. "He ain't all together up here. If you know what I mean."

"I know. I've known Jake for a long time too. I'm always careful about my back trail."

"He was accused of ambushin' and killin' a man last year. But no one could get enough proof on him for an arrest. But he done it. Everyone who knows him believes that. Want some more coffee?"

"I do. Good coffee."

"I'll tell my old woman. That'll please her. She's fixin' steak and potatoes for supper and she baked a cake too. She's a good cook. Aggravatin' as hell at times, but a good cook."

"I'll put in my supper order right now," Frank told the man. "I do like my steaks."

"You want me to cook one for your dog too?"

"Sure. He deserves it."

The store owner shook his head and his wife laughed. The laughter ceased when the front door was pushed open, letting in a blast of cold, wet air. Jake Fabor walked in.

"I told the others to go on," Jake said. "I'd catch up with them after I dealt with you, Morgan."

Frank slowly stood up. "You're making a mistake, Jake. You should have kept on going."

"I ain't no coward, Morgan."

"I believe I straightened all that out, Jake, when I bought you dinner. Why don't you just let it alone?"

Jake shook his head. "I want to see you beg me to let you live, Morgan. You do that, and I'll ride on out."

"You know that isn't going to happen, Jake. Why don't you sit down and have some coffee with me? We'll talk this out."

"I'll drink me a cup whilst I look at your dead body and laugh, Morgan."

"That isn't going to happen, Jake. Come on and sit down."

"Hell with you, Morgan. I come back to kill you."

The couple that ran the old trading post watched as Frank Morgan's face changed. His eyes turned flint hard and cold, his features seemed to tighten.

"Then do your damnedest, Jake," Frank said, letting his right leg straighten out with his right hand resting on his thigh. "I'm tired of trying to talk sense to you."

Jake dragged iron. The muzzle of his .44 just cleared leather when Frank's Peacemaker thundered. The bullet struck Jake in the chest and knocked him back. He stumbled out the open door, got his feet all tangled up on the porch, and fell off. He landed on his face in the sloppy mud and the cold rain and did not move.

"Whooo, boy!" the post owner said. "I seen some fast guns in my years out here, but you top the list, Frank Morgan. You are greased lightning with that .45."

"Is that man out yonder dead?" his wife asked.

"If he ain't," her husband replied, "he's shore doin' a bang-up job of pretendin'."

Frank stepped out onto the porch and looked down at Jake for a moment before walking down the steps, grabbing Jake by the arms, and dragging the man over to the barn. The trading post owner followed Frank.

"You want to bury him now?" the man asked.

"Might as well. He'll start puffing up and smelling if we don't."

"I'll fetch a couple of shovels."

The men dug a shallow grave in the rain-soaked earth and rolled Jake in, after wrapping the man in a blanket. His body made a small splash in the water pooling in the grave.

"You want to say some words over him?" Frank asked.

"I ain't a bit inclined to do so."

"That's it then." Frank patted down the mound some, and the men walked back to the barn. "I'm going to change into dry clothing and then have some hot coffee."

"I'll make fresh. Say, you reckon them friends of Jake will be back lookin' for him?"

"I doubt it. Truth be told, they're probably glad to be rid of him."

After a change into dry clothing, Frank walked back to the post for coffee and conversation.

"Where 'bouts you headin', Mr. Morgan?" the post owner asked as he placed a fresh pot and cup on the table.

"Thought I'd wander down into Oklahoma Territory."

"Stay out of No-Man's-Land. That place is wild and woolly. That's a real good place to avoid."

"So I've heard."

The post owner looked at Frank and smiled. "But you're goin' to check it out, ain't you?"

Frank returned the smile. "I thought I might."

Thirty-three

Frank built up the fire in the rusted stove in the old shack and put on water to boil. He had stabled his horses in the rickety shed out back and given them the last of the grain. It was damn cold out. He wasn't exactly sure where he was, but he thought he was in Colorado. He wasn't sure what the date was either, but he felt it was close to the end of November. If it wasn't, it damn sure ought to be, judging by the weather.

"We've got to find us a trading post somewhere, Dog," Frank said to the big cur. "We're running out of everything."

Dog looked at his master. Dog wasn't worried. He had killed a fat rabbit earlier that day and had a fine meal. Now he lay by a fire and was ready for a night's sleep. Dog yawned and closed his eyes. Life just didn't get much better than this.

Frank smiled at his four-legged companion. "We find us a more comfortable place to hole up for a time, you and me, boy, are going to have us a bath."

That opened Dog's eyes for a moment. He did not like baths. Dog stared at Frank for a time, then grumbled low in his throat and again closed his eyes.

"Got to find us a better place than this to ride out the winter," Frank said. "One good wind and this place will fall down. But I reckon it will have to do for tonight."

The morning dawned bright and sunny and cold. Frank

continued south. Two days later he came upon a trading post.

"You're 'bout seventy-five miles from the Strip, mister," the barman told him. "Was I you, I'd turn either west or east. Stay the hell out of that area. It ain't no fittin' place for a white man."

"I heard it was rough."

"Rough? Mister, they's three, four killin's ever'day down yonder. Outlaws and scum run that place."

"Well, I'm looking for an old friend of mine. I heard he might be somewhere in No-Man's-Land."

"You a lawman?"

"No. Just a man looking for an old friend."

"Best shy away from No-Man's-Land, partner. Don't no decent person live there."

Frank provisioned up and pushed on. As he drew closer to the northern boundary of No-Man's-Land, he began to see the remains of homesteads: half-burned cabins, fields that had at one time felt the bite of a plow, small gardens that had all gone to seed, and tiny grave sites. The homesteaders had built too close to outlaw territory, and had paid a terrible price for doing so.

Back at the trading post, the owner had told him that Kansas didn't want the strip of land and neither did Texas. He reckoned that someday Oklahoma would have to take it. But for now, it was strictly No-Man's-Land, a haven for the scum of the earth.

When he was about ten miles from the narrow strip of land, Frank was halted by a posse, some twenty strong. They had been heading east and had intersected Frank on his way south.

"You got a name?" the leader of the posse asked.

"Frank Morgan."

The man narrowed his eyes and frowned. "You tryin' to be funny, mister?"

"No. You asked my name. I told you."

"He's Frank Morgan," another man said, walking his horse up to the front of the posse. "I seen his picture lots of times."

"You bounty huntin'?" Frank was asked.

"No."

"Where are you headin'?"

Frank pointed toward the south. "Down thataway."

"That's No-Man's-Land, Morgan."

"I know it."

"No man in his right mind rides into that area alone," the posse leader said. "That strip of land is home to the vilest kind of criminal. Scum of the earth."

"So I've heard," Frank replied.

"And you're still heading in there?"

"Yes."

The posse leader placed both hands on his saddle horn and stared at Frank. "Mind if I ask why?"

"I'm the curious type," Frank answered.

"You go in yonder alone and you're goin' to be the *dead* type, Morgan. Do you know anything at all about that area?"

"Not a whole lot. But I intend to find out."

"Suit yourself."

"I plan on doing just that."

"There's a trading post right on the line, Morgan. 'Bout two hours' ride south. Man who runs it stays neutral. The outlaws let him stay in business because of that. Once you ride past that post, you're in No-Man's-Land. God help you." The leader of the posse lifted the reins and rode away, the posse following. As the men passed him, Frank received a lot of very curious glances.

Frank rode on, heading south. He really didn't know why he was heading into outlaw country. Like he had told the men of the posse, he was simply the curious type.

He topped a small rise and reined up, sitting his horse, looking down at several ramshackle buildings. The trading post. There were half a dozen horses tied at hitch rails in the front. There was a barn set off to the south side of the post. Frank could not tell if more horses were stabled there. He slowly rode down to the post, swung down from the saddle, and stood for a moment, looking around.

"You stay here," he told Dog. Dog immediately lay down between the hitch rail and the porch.

Frank pushed open the door and stepped into the post. He stood for a moment, looking around as he let his eyes adjust to low light of the gloomy interior.

Half a dozen men sat at tables, drinking and playing cards. Frank recognized one immediately. "Kincaid," he said. "I figured somebody would have hanged you by now."

Bob Kincaid glared at Frank. "Morgan," he finally said.

"You know that feller?" a man seated at the table asked.

"I know him. That's Frank Morgan."

"Frank Morgan!" another man seated across the room blurted out.

"You lawin', Morgan?" Bob asked.

"No."

"Bounty huntin'?"

"No. Just passin' through, Kincaid."

"You better bypass that strip of land south of here, Morgan. Lots of folks down there would just love to put lead in you. Including me."

"You want to try that now, Kincaid?"

The outlaw smiled, exposing stained and rotten teeth. "I'll git my chance one of these days, Morgan. I can wait."

Frank turned his back to the man and walked to the bar. "Coffee," he told the counterman. "In a clean cup," he added.

"Picky, ain't you?" the bearded bear of a man asked.

"You have a clean cup?" Frank asked.

"Yeah. I'll wash one special for you."

"You do that."

Frank sipped his coffee. It was surprisingly good.

"That suit your taste, Morgan?" the counterman asked.

"Matter of fact, it does. Do I know you?"

"I seen you in Kansas, right after the war. You gunned down a hothead name of Cledus Head."

"I remember. He pushed me into that fight."

"He did for a fact." The man moved away to the end of the bar and began polishing glasses with a rag that appeared to be dirtier than the glassware was.

Bob Kincaid stood up and walked to the bar, close to Frank. "You're a fool, Morgan. You got no business comin' into the strip and stickin' your damn nose into things that don't concern you."

"I'm just passing through, Bob," Frank replied. "As long as I'm left alone, I'll do the same for you and your kind."

"Hell with you!" Kincaid said, and walked out of the trading post. His friends pushed back their chairs and followed him.

"That man don't like you very much, Morgan," the counterman said. "You best heed his words."

"Nobody tells me where I can or can't go."

"The strip ain't like no other place in the country, Morgan. There ain't no law, no rules 'ceptin' what a man can back up with a gun. And you just one man, one gun. Alone, with no friends in yonder."

"That's certainly true."

"You enjoy stickin' your hand into a rattlesnake den?"

Frank did not reply.

"Ride on out of here, Morgan," the counterman urged. "I think you're a decent enough man, but that don't spell coyote crap in the strip."

"I need a few supplies," Frank said.

"You're really goin' into No-Man's-Land?"

"I am."

"You got any kin you want me to notify?"

"I'll send them a telegram when I come out."

"Morgan . . . dead men don't send telegrams."

For a sneak preview of
William W. Johnstone's next
Western novel—*Ambush of the Mountain Man*—
coming from Pinnacle Books in December 2003,
just turn the page . . .

One

Smoke Jensen and his friends, Cal, Pearlie, and Louis Longmont, turned their horses' heads south and rode out of the town of Noyes, Minnesota, for about two miles, until they came to the railroad station.

As they reined in their mounts in front of the stationmaster's office, Louis stretched and observed, "That was very nice of Cornelius Van Horne to arrange for us to ride all the way back to Big Rock on the train instead of on horseback."

"Yeah, it'll sure save some wear an' tear on my backside," Pearlie agreed as he stepped down out of his stirrups. "The way I feel now, if'n I never see another saddle as long as I live, it'll be all right with me," he added, rubbing his butt with both hands.

Smoke laughed. "Not only that, but Van Horne said we could ride in James Hill's own private car on our trip south."

"Hill?" Cal asked. "Ain't he the man Van Horne said bought up all the railroads in this part of the country?"

Smoke nodded. "That's right, Cal. Hill is the man who owns just about every inch of railroad track between here and home."

"Jimmy, then his own private car oughta be somethin' to see."

"I would imagine it will be rather lavish," Louis said as he got down off his horse.

"I don't know what lavish means," Pearlie said, "but I

hope it means it's stocked right well with food, 'cause I'm hungry enough to eat a bear."

After Smoke spoke to the stationmaster, and their horses and gear were stowed in the cattle car, the man showed them into James Hill's private car. As they entered, he told them to just pull the bell rope next to the door if they needed anything and a steward would take care of it.

Just before he left, he stopped in the door and looked around the car, shaking his head. "You boys must be powerful friends of Mr. Hill's," he said, " 'cause this is the first time I've ever seen him loan his car out to anyone."

"Thanks for all your help," Smoke said, shutting the door behind the man.

As the stationmaster stepped down out of the car, a man moved out of the shadows next to the train station building and stood there staring at the train.

When the stationmaster approached him, the man ducked his head and put a lucifer to the cigarette dangling from the corner of his mouth. He looked up, tipping smoke from his nostrils, and gave the stationmaster a lopsided grin. "Howdy," he said in a friendly tone of voice.

"Hello," the stationmaster answered. "If you're here to buy a ticket on this train, you need to see the man in the ticket booth inside the building."

"Thanks," the stranger answered. "I might just do that." He turned toward the building, hesitated, and then he looked back over his shoulder at the stationmaster.

"Uh, by the way, was that man I just saw getting on the train named Smoke Jensen?"

The stationmaster nodded absentmindedly, already thinking about the dozens of things he had to see to before the train could leave the station.

The stranger cut his eyes back at the train before he went into the station to buy a ticket, eyes that were filled with hate.

When he got to the ticket booth, he pulled a wad of cash from his vest pocket and placed it on the counter.

"Can I help you, sir?" the ticket man asked.

"Yeah. Can you tell me how far Smoke Jensen and his friends are going?"

The ticket salesman looked down at an open book in front of him and pursed his lips for a moment. "I believe they're ticketed all the way through to Big Rock, Colorado," he said, glancing back up at the man standing in front of his window.

"Then give me a ticket to the same place," the man said, pushing his money under the gated window.

"Yes, sir."

"And I need to know if I have time to send a wire before the train leaves."

The ticket man pulled a watch from his vest pocket and shook his head as he looked at it. "No, sir, I don't believe you do."

"Damn," he muttered.

"But I'd be happy to send one for you after the train leaves if you wish."

When the man nodded, looking relieved, the ticket man pushed a piece of paper and a pencil under the window gate. "Just write out who you want me to send it to and what you want to say, and I'll get it on over to the telegraph office just as soon as the train leaves the station."

"Uh," the man stammered, his face burning scarlet, "I can't write too good."

The ticket man pulled the paper back and smiled. "Then just tell me and I'll write it for you."

"It's to Angus MacDougal in Pueblo, Colorado." The man thought for a moment and then said, "Just say our friend is headed for home . . . should be there in ten days."

* * *

After Smoke closed the door and turned around, he saw Louis pouring himself a glass of brandy from Hill's private bar in the corner. Cal was lying back on the overstuffed sofa, feeling how soft the cushions were, and Pearlie was about to pull the bell rope.

Smoke smiled. "Pearlie, what are you doing?"

Pearlie glanced over at him. "I'm just ringing this here bell to see if the man who answers it can get us some food 'fore I faint from hunger."

Smoke shook his head, pointing to the corner of the car where a coffeepot was steaming on a potbellied stove. "Why don't you have a cup of coffee to fill your gut until the train leaves the station? Then we can see about getting some grub."

Louis looked up from where he stood at the bar. "And, Pearlie, there's a bowl of sugar and a pitcher of cream here on the bar to sweeten it up with."

Pearlie grinned and moved toward the potbellied stove. "Well, now," he said amiably. "I guess that'll do for a start."

"Coffee does sound good," Cal said, getting up from his perch on the couch. "But, Louis, you'd better dole that sugar out to Pearlie a little at a time if'n you want any left for the rest of us to use," he added as he followed Pearlie toward the stove.

Two hours later, the men had finished their meal and were sitting around a table in Hill's private car getting a poker lesson from Louis. Luckily for Cal and Pearlie, they were playing for pennies instead of dollars, because Louis and Smoke were both winning just about every hand.

Just as Louis was leaning over to rake in another pot, the train suddenly slowed, its steel wheels screeching as the engineer applied the brakes with full force.

"What the . . ." Louis began to say when Cal moved his

head to the side toward the nearby window, called out, "Looky there!" and pointed off to the side of the train.

A group of men could be seen suddenly appearing from a copse of trees near the track, all riding bent down low over their saddle horns, guns in their hands and bandanna masks over their faces.

"Well, I'll be hanged," Smoke said, his lips curling into a slight grin of anticipation. "It looks like the train is going to be robbed."

Louis unconsciously reached up and patted the wallet in his coat breast pocket, thick with the money Cornelius Van Home had paid them for helping with the surveying for his Canadian Pacific Railroad the past six months. "I'll be damned if any two-bit train robbers are going to take any of my money!" he exclaimed.

Smoke pulled a Colt pistol from his holster and flicked open the cylinder, checking to see that it was fully loaded. "No one's gonna take any money from any of us, Louis," he promised, the grin slowly fading from his face.

"I'll get our rifles from our gear in the next car," Pearlie said, referring to the sleeping car next door where they'd stored their valises and saddlebags.

"Bring some extra ammunition too," Smoke said, glancing out of the window. "It looks like there're fifteen or twenty riders out there we're gonna have to contend with."

He ducked down out of sight, motioning the others to do the same, as the train slowed and the group of riders drew abreast of the car they were in.

A gunshot rang out and the window next to Smoke's head shattered, sending slivers of glass cascading down onto his back.

The train continued its rapid deceleration. Probably because the robbers had dynamited or obstructed the tracks in some manner, Smoke thought as Pearlie came scuttling back into the car with his arms full of long guns. Smoke took the Henry repeating rifle from Pearlie, and watched as Louis took the ten-gauge sawed-off express gun and an extra box of shells from him.

"You're gonna have to get awfully close for that to do much damage," Smoke said.

Louis grinned. "I thought I'd wait until they came knocking on our door and then give them a rather loud greeting," he said in a light tone of voice.

Smoke nodded. "Good idea. I think I'll take Cal and Pearlie and slip out the far side of the car when the train stops. When the bandits get off their horses to make their way through the cars, it'll give us a chance to scatter their mounts."

Pearlie nodded, grinning. "And then they'll be trapped out here in the middle of nowhere with nothing to ride off on. Good idea, Smoke."

When the train finally ground to a complete stop, Louis turned a big easy chair around until it was facing the door, and took a seat, the express gun across his knees and his pistols on a small table next to the chair. He pulled a long black cigar out of his coat pocket and lit it, sending clouds of fragrant blue smoke into the air.

"Good hunting, gentlemen," he called as he eared back the twin hammers on the shotgun.

"You be careful, you hear?" Smoke said, tipping his head at his friend.

"It is not I who should be careful, pal," Louis replied, his voice turning hard. "It is those miscreants that are interrupting our trip."

As Smoke and the boys slipped out of the car and moved slowly down the line of cars toward the front of the train, Cal asked in a low voice, "Smoke, what's a miscreant?"

Smoke chuckled. "It's someone without a shred of decency in their character, Cal."

"Oh," Cal said.

As they neared the car just behind the engine that contained wood to be burned in the boiler, Smoke heard a harsh voice say, "Watch the hosses, Johnny. We'll get the passengers' money and be right back."

Smoke gave the robbers time to climb aboard the train before he sauntered out from between two cars and walked slowly toward the outlaws' horses, which were being tended by a large, fat man with a full beard and a ragged, sweat-stained hat set low on his head.

The outlaw's eyes widened and his hand moved toward his belt as he started to say, "Who the hell—"

Smoke drew his Colt in one lightning-fast motion and shot the man in the face, blowing him backward off his horse to land facedown in the dirt next to the track.

The other horses jumped and crow-hopped at the sound of the pistol shot, until Cal and Pearlie untied them from where they been hitched to the handrail on the railroad car and shooed them away by waving their arms and shouting.

Soon, only the dead outlaw was left next to the tracks, blood still oozing into a puddle under his head.

Smoke moved up to the engine and found the engineer lying on his side, holding his left arm, a bullet hole in his left shoulder.

Smoke knelt next to him. "Are you gonna be all right?"

The engineer nodded. "Yeah, but somebody needs to put some wood in the boiler or we're gonna lose all our steam."

Smoke glanced over his shoulder. "Cal, would you help this man and do what he says while Pearlie and I go after the robbers?"

"Aw, shucks, Smoke," Cal groused as he climbed up into the cab of the engine. "Pearlie gets to have all the fun."

"We just don't want you getting yourself shot again an' bleedin' all over Mr. Hill's fine car," Pearlie teased. "You bein' such a magnet for lead an' all."

"Now, Pearlie," Cal argued, his face turning red. "I ain't been shot in over three weeks now."

Smoke laughed. "That might be because we haven't been in any gunfights for three weeks, Cal."

Cal bent and helped the engineer to his feet as Pearlie and Smoke jumped down out of the engine and headed back along the tracks toward the passenger cars.

They eased up into the first one, and Smoke was surprised when a female passenger threw up her hands and screamed, "Oh, no, they've come back to rape and kill us!"

Smoke smiled and motioned for her to put her hands down. "No, ma'am. We're here after the robbers," he explained as he and Pearlie moved down the aisle between the seats.

They did this for three more cars before catching up to the robbers in the car just before Hill's private one that Louis was in.

Smoke motioned for Pearlie to kneel down in front of the door, and he stood over him as he jerked the door open.

The crowd of robbers in the aisle collecting passengers' money and jewels glanced back over their shoulders in time to see Smoke and Pearlie open fire, Smoke working the lever of the Henry so fast his shots seemed to be one long explosion.

Six outlaws went down before the others could return fire, and then it was wild and poorly aimed as they shouted and screamed and backed through the far door of the car.

The ones in the lead jerked the door to Hill's car open and rushed inside, to be met by the thundering explosion of twin ten-gauge barrels hurling buckshot at them.

Four more men went down, shredded and almost cut in half by the horrendous power of the express gun.

The seven men remaining alive dove off the train out of the connecting door to the cars, and began running as fast as they could back up the tracks to where they thought their horses were tired.

They slowed and looked around with puzzled expressions when they came to Johnny's dead body.

"Where the hell are the hosses?" one of the men hollered, whirling around and looking in all directions.

From thirty feet behind him, Smoke said, "They're gone, pond scum!"

The robbers turned and saw Smoke and Pearlie and Louis standing there, side by side, their hands full of iron.

"There's only three of them, boys, let's take 'em!" one of the men shouted.

"Uh-uh," came a voice from behind the outlaws. Cal stood there just outside the engine, his Colt in his hand. "There's four of us," he said, a wide grin of fierce anticipation on his face.

Nevertheless, the outlaws swung their pistols up and opened fire.

In less than fifteen seconds, it was all over and every gunman lay either dead or dying next to the train.

Smoke and Pearlie and Louis approached the group of bodies on the ground cautiously, kicking pistols and rifles out of reach of the wounded men.

Cal said softly, "Dagnabit!" as he glanced down at his thigh, noting a thin line of red where a bullet had creased his upper leg, burning rather than tearing a hole in his trousers.

He quickly turned to the side so his friends couldn't see the wound, calling, "I'm just gonna go on up and make sure the engineer is all right."

When the engineer looked at the blood staining Cal's pants leg, Cal shook his head. "Don't say nothin' 'bout this to my friends, all right?"

The wounded man just grinned, having heard what Pearlie and Smoke had said about Cal being a magnet for lead. "I promise not to say nothin', if you'll be so kind as to build me a cigarette while we wait for the steam to build."

THE LAST GUNFIGHTER SERIES BY
WILLIAM W. JOHNSTONE